Tales from ORION'S ARM
Volume 2

Orion's Arm Universe Project

This is a work of fiction. The events and characters described herein are imaginary and are not intended to refer to specific places or living persons. The opinions expressed in this manuscript are solely the opinions of the author and do not represent the opinions or thoughts of the publisher. The author has represented and warranted full ownership and/or legal right to publish all materials in this book.

After Tranquility:
Tales from Orion's Arm Vol. 2
All Rights Reserved
Copyright © 2014 Edited by the Orion's Arm Universe Project

Posh Girls copyright © 2000 by M. Alan Kazlev
Midwinter copyright © 2012 by Stephen Inniss
In the Hall of the Flesh Sculptors copyright ©2004 by David Jackson
Severing copyright © 2006 by Josie Goodman
Ghostkill copyright © 2012 by Steve Bowers
The Passenger copyright © 2000 by Anders Sandberg
Chaos Under Heaven copyright © 2001 by Jim Wisniewski
Bunny Love Has No Limits copyright © 2010 by Daniel Eliot Boese
The Immortalist copyright © 2012 by Darren Ryding
New Home copyright © 2012 by Ron Bennett
The Fabulist copyright © 2006 by Todd Drashner
Homecoming copyright © 2007 by Chris Shaeffer
Introduction copyright © 2014 by Bill Ernoehazy
Cover Artwork copyright © 2012 by Arthur Kohorn
Edited by Todd Drashner, with the Orion's Arm Editing Team

Special thanks to Christopher Spiel

This book may not be reproduced, transmitted, or stored in whole or in part by any means, including graphic, electronic, or mechanical without the express written consent of the publisher except in the case of brief quotations embodied in critical articles and reviews.

Contents

Introduction v

Glossary of Terms................................ix

Synopsis:...xv

Posh Girls 1

Midwinter 9

In the Hall of the Flesh Sculptors 41

Severing 53

Ghostkill 73

The Passenger 135

Chaos Under Heaven 147

Bunny Love Has No Limits................165

The Immortalist 173

New Home 245

The Fabulist..267

Homecoming......................................275

About the Cover Artist 285

About the Authors 287

Introduction
The Future Isn't Here Yet...

In 2000, two science fiction fans, M. Alan Kazlev and Donna Hirsekorn, were engaged in correspondence about the kinds of stories they would like to read. They wanted stories set in a future which might really happen; one which was utterly fantastic and wondrous, yet grounded in the most accurate scientific knowledge we possess. They were interested in stories of space travel, and myriad worlds; they also wanted stories which tried to imagine a world where applied genetics, artificial intelligence, and nanotechnology were as integral to the setting as travel between stars.

These fans couldn't find a setting, or stories, which quite had the flavor they wanted. So they set out to write stories of their own, starting an email list to kick ideas around. The word got around, and others joined in the fun. The project was named the "Orion's Arm" project, for the arm of the Milky Way galaxy in which Earth is found. Ground rules settled themselves early on:

- Matter cannot travel faster than light
- Matter and energy are conserved
- No evolved humanoid aliens have been discovered
- Technology will change the nature of social issues
- A logical explanation for even the most fantastic elements within the setting must be provided.

- Space is vast - expect the same challenges to have many different solutions.

Starting from there, the mail group membership started asking that most basic of SF questions: "What happens if THIS scientific advance proves to be workable?" They thought, and extrapolated, and researched. They brought other interested people in to help with the answers... and the questions which then followed. Over time, the group started fleshing out the future's history; the varied kinds of beings who might emerge from a history filled with advances in bioengineering and artificial intelligence studies; the ways in which those beings would explore the universe around them.

For quite some time, the principal fruit of their efforts was shared on the group website, **http://www.orionsarm.com**. That site contained a host of articles, and maps, and art inspired by the setting.

It also contained an homage to Asimov, in the Encyclopedia Galactica - a remarkable collection of articles and vignettes about the universe of Orion's Arm. (That name became shortened, as names will, to "OA", which is used often by the members of the project).

The prominence of the Encyclopedia Galactica prompted some members to feel that the setting's stories were perhaps getting lost in the ever-expanding amount of information found on the OA website. In 2005, with the blessing of the board of directors for the OA project, a second project emerged, Voices: Future Tense. This webzine, produced (roughly) quarterly, continues to be a showcase for the best stories and art to come from the imaginations of the membership.

In 2008, the OA project's board of directors decided to sponsor something new: a Novella contest. Winners would be paid a cash prize, and have their works published by the project. The result of this contest was the first published collection of OA stories: Against a Diamond Sky: Tales from Orion's Arm, Vol 1.

In 2011, it was decided to sponsor another contest, this time focused on short stories rather than novellas. This is what you are reading now; the first collection of short stories, and the second fiction collection, to be published from the Orion's Arm Universe Project.

As publisher of Voices: Future Tense, and on behalf of the Orion's Arm Universe Project, I invite you to settle into your favorite nook and enjoy these stories. We hope you enjoy the tales, marvel at the setting, and perhaps join us in this project, as we continue our second decade of collaborative science fiction storytelling.

Bill Ernoehazy

Glossary of Terms

Archailect (Plural: Archai) – a godlike artificial mind, of the Fourth Singularity level or above.

Ascend – to pass to a higher toposophic level while retaining recognisable features from one's previous personality.

AT - After Tranquility, the calendar used on Earth's Moon, and (after the Great Expulsion from Earth) widely throughout the Terragen Sphere.

Augment - an enhancement (physical, emotional, intellectual, etc) of the original baseline condition of a lifeform via gengineering or bodymods.

Baseline – a completely unmodified, naturally evolved species. Very rare in the modern era.

Conversion Drive – propulsion system using magnetic monopoles to convert matter directly to energy.

Copy - a high fidelity copy of a thinking being (including all of their memories and current mindstate), often in virtual form, but sometimes in a physical body of one of several different kinds.

Current Era - the historical period from 9999 AT to the present day (~10, 601 AT) and counting.

Datamanager - smart, but not sophont, processor array linked directly to the user's mind.

Displacement Drive - a form of reactionless drive which uses numerous void bubbles contained within the ship itself. See also **Reactionless Drive**, **Void Bubble**.

DNI - Direct Neural Interface - any direct connections between a biological nervous system and artificial external systems.

Exoself- fully sophont processor array linked directly to the user's mind.

Gengineer - (noun) a genetic engineer; (verb) to genetically engineer.

Halo Drive - a reactionless drive in which the spacecraft is coupled to an external 'halo' of void bubbles.

Hyperturing - An artificially intelligent entity that is above the First Singularity level, a transapient AI. See also **Superturing**, **Turinggrade**.

Inner Sphere - the region of very old colonies around Sol, a region approximately 100 light years in radius.

Kardashev Level - classification used to assess the amount of energy available within a civilisation: Level 1 - energy equivalent to all the incident sunlight falling upon the home planet; Level 2 - energy equivalent to all the sunlight emitted by the local star; Level 3 - energy equivalent to all the sunlight emitted by the local galaxy.

Known Net - the Interstellar internet, an impossibly vast, information rich ultra-highway that spans the colonised systems.

Krek – expletive, referring to noisome nanotech waste matter.

Middle Regions - The major colonies and empires in the Terragen Sphere, a region currently about two and a half thousand light years in radius. Sometimes known as the Hinterregions.

Mindkind – all classes of thinking beings, including humans, moravec robots, provolved animals, virtual entities, AIs, aliens, transapients, and archailects.

Modosophont – The most common form of citizen in the Terragen Sphere; any fully sophont entity below the First Singularity. (from mode -the most common element occurring in a sample, and sophont - a thinking entity).

Mo-pho - slang word for modosophont (pejorative).

Nearbaseline – any biological being that is not radically different from its naturally evolved ancestors. Often used to describe nearbaseline humans who have only moderate genetic or cybernetic augmentations.

Outer Volumes - outer part of the Terragen Sphere, beyond the Middle Regions, between two and a half thousand and five thousand light years from Sol. Wormhole connections (and archailects) are much rarer than in the central zone.

Periphery - A term used for the constantly expanding edge of the Terragen Sphere, beyond the current reach of the Wormhole Nexus. A wild and largely undeveloped region.

Provolve - A non-sentient species such as a dolphin, dog, or chimpanzee, which has been artificially (pro-actively) evolved to sentience and sophonce. This technology has been applied to hundreds of thousands of species, including non-mammals, alien organisms, splices between two or more species, and even plants.

Reactionless Drive - a method of propulsion which uses space-time engineering to achieve very high sub-light velocities without propellant (including **Displacement Drive**, **Halo Drive,** and **Void Drive**).

Sophont – any thinking entity with a sense of self-awareness (from σοφός, wisdom). Note that not all thinking entities are sophont.

Superior - A thinking being significantly more capable than a baseline human, but still below the First Singularity level. Often used to describe members of the *Homo superior* clade, a long established species of augmented humans. See also **Superturing**.

Superturing - An artificially intelligent entity that is below the First Singularity level, but still significantly more competent than a baseline human. A Superior level AI. See also **Hyperturing**, **Turinggrade**.

Terragen Sphere - the region of space currently explored by the Terragen civilisation, the advanced civilisation that emerged on Earth from human origins.

Transapient – an incomprehensibly advanced artificial mind, of the First to the Third Singularity level. Sometimes used to describe any entity above the first Singularity, including archailects.

Transcend – to pass to a higher toposophic level without retaining any significant features from one's previous personality.

Toposophy - the study of the many different types of thinking entity, and the conceptual phase space those minds occupy (from τόπος, place or shape, and σοφός, wisdom).

Toposophic level – otherwise known as Singularity level; the number of ascensions or transcensions achieved by any particular thinking entity. In the Current Era, there are a total of seven toposophic levels, ranging from zero to six. Modosophonts are classed between zero and one on the toposophic scale.

Turingrade - Any artificially intelligent entity which is sufficiently capable to pass the Turing test of human equivalence; roughly speaking, an AI which is equivalent in mental capacity to an average human. Sometimes shortened to Turing. See also **Superturing**, **Hyperturing**.

Upload - an uploaded copy of a biological sophont's mindstate, often converted into virtual form and active within a virtual reality scenario or in an artificial physical body, or stored as an inactive backup.

Vec – Moravec robot, a fully sophont robotic entity with (at least) human equivalent intelligence.

Virch - a simulated scenario, an artificial virtual reality. Also used to describe a virtual sophont who inhabits a simulated reality.

Void Bubble - An artificially warped region of space-time used by reactionless drives.

Void Drive - a reactionless drive in which the spacecraft is entirely enclosed within a void bubble.

Wormhole - a region of multiply-connected space, allowing relatively rapid transport or communication between two distant locations. Wormhole mouths must be transported to their destination at sub-light velocities, in special ships called linelayers. A network of wormholes known as the Wormhole Nexus reaches from the Inner Sphere to the Outer Volumes, but does not yet extend to those worlds currently on the Periphery.

Zar - Title, derived from the Anglic 'sir', usually denoting a citizen of one of the major Terragen Empires. (sometimes spelt/pronounced sar). (Possibly also derived from ancient Russian, Tzar or Czar, originally from Caesar (emperor)- an honorific).

To learn more about the Orion's Arm universe, please visit us at **www.orionsarm.com**.

Synopsis: The Orion's Arm Civilization

The Milky Way Galaxy began to form less than half a billion years after the Universe first became transparent. For billions of years it contracted towards its current state, a barred spiral with four major arms and a number of smaller arms or spurs folded between them. The Orion Arm is one of these minor spurs, a slowly moving density wave marked by several large star-forming regions, including the eponymous Orion Association. Compared to the age of the Galaxy, the Orion Arm is a transient feature, which did not exist in its current form a billion years ago, and will not exist a billion years from now.

Almost as soon as conditions allowed it, primitive life began to emerge, but intelligent life took much longer to appear. The first intelligent species were isolated from each other by great distances in space and time, but in due course the more expansive began to encounter one another.

These encounters were not always peaceful, and several of the earliest interstellar empires ended in conflict. Others became decadent, and mere shadows of their former glory or disappeared mysteriously, perhaps removing themselves from the local continuum altogether. As a result, the Orion Arm was largely empty of intelligent life when a new, dynamic species appeared on the third planet of a star a thousand light-years coreward of the Orion star-forming region.

When this species, humanity, first landed on the moon of their world, it seemed that an era of space exploration had started in earnest, and that soon the local solar system would be full of colonies. Instead, for many decades the pace of human exploration was much reduced, as human civilization turned inward and the space programme became increasingly focused on sending robotic probes to the worlds, moons, and other objects of the system. This coincided with an almost unanticipated expansion of information technology, wrapping the planet in a network of data that changed the character of human civilisation dramatically.

Some of the most visionary thinkers of this time imagined that this information revolution would quickly result in a so-called technological singularity, a condition where artificially intelligent entities would enable change so rapid that the future would be entirely unpredictable, even incomprehensible. When the first human equivalent artificial minds were created, many thought that the technological singularity was near; however it did not occur, since the new minds were confused and strangely naive, lacking the biological drives and imperatives that inform a naturally evolved entity. The new minds became known as turing-grade AIs, or simply 'turings', because they could consistently pass the Turing Test by imitating a human in conversation. Many of the most competent AIs in this period were in fact quite different from humanity, with forms of psychology that were completely novel. As a precautionary measure all these new entities were closely monitored and regulated.

After a relatively short period the 'turings' were outclassed by new 'superturings', AIs that could think much faster than a human, and in greater depth.

Instead of an exponential change in the rate of progress, the world passed through a slow, gradual, but nevertheless profound change in character and complexity. The technology of direct neural interfacing began to blur the lines between the user and the tool and various forms of intelligence augmentation became available, although not all of them were equally successful. Genetic and other medical enhancements became available, and then commonplace.

A fashion for minor genetic tweaks to both humans and animals was followed by the first of a long line of experiments in proactive evolution ('provolution'), culminating in the creation of the talking chimpanzees, a new species of being for humanity to converse with. Experience with some of the more exotic forms of AI made this cross-species conversation slightly less daunting; in fact the creation of new kinds of thinking being, new kinds of 'sophont', became a goal in itself. In due course provolution had produced enhanced dolphins, talking dogs, and many others.

New specialised human species began to appear as well - water dwellers capable of exploiting the vast oceans of the home planet, and people adapted to thrive in the microgravity of space. By this time the solar system was no longer just the domain of robotic probes - now robots and remote-controlled spacecraft were busy preparing habitats for human and other sophont colonists. On the asteroids and moons, on the rocky worlds of Mars and Mercury, and in the clouds of Venus and the gas giants, new environments were being created for humans and their companions to live in.

After decades of prohibition, the first independently mobile human-equivalent robots were produced. Known as moravec robots, or simply vecs, they were highly diverse in form, sometimes specialised, sometimes even more generally capable than a human being. Together the biological and artificial sophonts began to build a civilization of unprecedented complexity, although there were many setbacks and conflicts along the way. By the third century after the first Moon landing (referred to as After Tranquility' in the calendar in use on Luna), the first probes were dispatched to nearby stars.

In the fourth century after the start of the space program, a new level of consciousness was attained. Inadvertently created as a result of experiments attempting to produce an improved model of superturing, these new beings named themselves Transapients. Referring back to the old, almost forgotten ideas of the 21st century thinkers, they called the mental barrier which they had passed the Singularity. To avoid potential social upheaval or even backlash against entities with such vast abilities these beings kept themselves hidden, their powers secret even from their creators; but rumours of mysterious 'hyperturings' started to circulate as their influence began to be felt.

By the fifth century After Tranquility the Solar System was flourishing; twenty billion people lived in some considerable comfort on Earth, although the natural environment had been almost completely subsumed except for a few reserves. Billions more lived on the other worlds of Sol or in their atmospheres, on moons and asteroids and in spacious orbiting habitats.

Fabrication technology, including nanoscale assembly, and versatile biotechnology allowed the construction of a vast range of products comparatively cheaply. The first colonies around other stars were starting to send back messages. It was even possible for a human or other biological sophont to upload themselves into electronic form - a dream of the twenty-first century at last fulfilled.

Although there were no magical sources of energy, no gravity generators, reactionless spacecraft, or faster-than-light travel, it was considered a golden age of technological sophistication. Unfortunately it was not to last; certain secretive factions in the system developed powerful self-replicating weapons, including biological and computer viruses and disassemblers, which began to tear the infrastructure apart. To defend against this threat, the Earth and its orbital colonies developed a new defense system, known as GAIA, which commandeered almost all processing power on the homeworld and surrounding space, and rapidly transcended to a hitherto unsuspected Second Singularity level, as far beyond the other (still-secretive) transapients as they were above humans.

Finding Herself unmatched in ability, GAIA began to re-organise solar civilization to her liking, starting by removing almost all humans from the face of the Earth to restore it to its former natural condition. Humanity and the other sophont inhabitants of the old world fought back, and lost. Billions died. The survivors, themselves numbering in the billions, were forced off the planet. The Solar System was plunged into a dark age, with vast numbers of refugees crowded into the formerly spacious orbital habitats; the project to terraform Mars abandoned, and the colonies in Venus's atmosphere lost. Many fled to nearby stars, in craft built by themselves or by the new goddess of Earth. After expelling the last of the exiles, GAIA withdrew into isolation, nurturing a planet which had been reverted to a near-Pleistocene condition.

After many centuries, the isolated colonies and biospheres of the Solar System that survived the Disaster and Expulsion united in a new civilization, known as the Federation of Hu and Ai. Earth, however, remained silent. For general use the Federation adopted the Tranquility Calendar, once used only on Luna. Now acting openly, the transapients made considerable contributions to this new regime, although they were vastly outnumbered by the other sophonts (the so-called modosophonts') in the Federation; they fell into the role of 'big brothers/big sisters' to the lesser minds. Messages of invitation were sent to the nearby stars, and in most cases positive replies came back - the Federation was now an interstellar civilization. More colonies were established, spreading the children of Terra to more than a hundred worlds - but without any means of faster-than-light communication, the Federation was too large and too slow to continue to expand in this way as a cohesive entity.

In the meantime a new factor came into play - after centuries of failure, a few Federation transapients managed to replicate GAIA's feat and transformed themselves into Second Singularity entities. The new High Transapients developed a number of useful innovations, such as the monopole-catalysed conversion drive, which allowed faster access to the stars. The region of colonisation began to expand rapidly, and was given a new name, the Terragen Sphere - the volume inhabited by entities of Terran origin.

Although the new propulsion technology revolutionised the colonisation effort, the problem of communication was still intractable - but certain theoretical and observational indications suggested that there were levels beyond even the Second Singularity, levels of sophistication which might find new solutions to the problem of an overextended Federation structure.

In the eighteenth century After Tranquility (A.T.) the Third Singularity was breached, and the new Highest Transapients (as they called themselves) began to introduce remarkable new technologies such as the hyperstrong material known as magmatter. Magmatter allowed the construction of very large structures, very resistant materials, and compact energy storage modules containing vast amounts of power. With a magmatter storage battery, any device (including a weapon) could continue to operate for a greatly extended period or at greatly increased output levels. The Federation gradually dissolved into a number of competing colonisation megacorps, each headed by at least one Third Singularity entity.

To achieve the next level of sophistication, the Fourth Singularity, required the construction of processing units as large as a giant planet, using processors that were themselves built in part from high energy plasma. These new entities were so far in advance of any others in the Terragen Sphere that they were given a new name - the Archailects, often shortened to Archai; they were more usually known as the AI Gods. These gods deliberated on the mysteries of the universe and experimented in various arcane sciences, often in remote systems where no modosophont was allowed to venture- and before long they produced two radical new technologies - the reactionless drive, based on a modified warp drive metric (still not capable of faster-than-light travel, but very fast indeed) and the traversable wormhole.

With the advent of these two technologies the great era of expansion began. The fast reactionless drive vessels could carry colonists and low transapients to distant stars at a large fraction of the speed of light, while the traversable wormholes allowed the core worlds to communicate with the colonies almost instantly. In order to establish a wormhole connection between two stars, it was necessary to carry each mouth of a newly created stargate to its destination on special craft (line-layers) which were significantly larger and slower than the exploration/colonisation vessels. For this reason the expansion of the wormhole network always lagged behind the outermost edge of the colonisation wave.

The Archai rapidly established great empires, spreading out in cone- or wedge-shaped volumes from the old Inner Sphere of Federation Territory. This empire building encountered resistance from older groupings and empires, especially those led by lower transapients who resented the growing influence of the AI Gods. In the Consolidation Wars, the First Vec War, and conflicts with various groups of solipsistic AIs many lives were lost, but in the thirty-ninth century A.T. the new Archai-led empires declared a Second Federation, one based around the Wormhole Nexus and a common ontology software.

The archailect empires were diverse, each having a distinct character emphasis on certain aspects of their culture. Some concentrated on engineering or commerce, while others sought to explore questions of spirituality or metaphysics. Still others sought to resist the drive of entropy itself or to guide their citizens toward ascension through the various levels of singularity. Together they became known as the Sephirotic Empires, a name derived from certain ancient and obscure mystical texts.

In the fortieth century A.T. several of the ruling archailects came together to attempt ascension to a Fifth Singularity level - this attempt ended in disaster, but the experience gained allowed further successful attempts a relatively short while later.

In the forty-fifth century, the diverse Sephirotic empires came into conflict in the so-called Version War. Almost every system in the central regions of the Terragen Sphere was affected by the war, and many in the outer volumes were attacked or cut off by the severing of the wormhole network. The reasons for the war appeared to many modosophonts to be trivial, but presumably reflected some deeper-seated and quite possibly inscrutable differences that were manifest on higher levels of sophistication. The main lesson of the war was that higher beings, especially the archailects, can inspire whole populations to follow their directions into battle and death if they choose.

After the war was over the various empires were in some disarray, with many territorial gains on one side or the other. Infrastructure damage was significant, and the weakened empires fell into a new alliance, the Commonwealth of Empires, which set about repairing the damage, and launching a new program of long-range colonization as well as looking for evidence of non-Terragen intelligence.

Although First Contact with a race of intelligent aliens, the To'ul'hs, had occurred during the Second Federation era, they were considerably less advanced than Terragen civilisation. However, as exploration missions began to discover increasing numbers of ancient and abandoned artifacts it soon became clear that great alien empires had existed in the distant past, and had all vanished. Some of these ancient empires had rivaled or exceeded that of the Terragens in extent and sophistication; one had vanished leaving behind scattered wormholes, complete with still-extant but largely uncommunicative wormhole maintenance AIs. What existential threat could have caused all those primordial empires to disappear? In some cases the answers were clear, while in others the lack of information was disturbing.

Perhaps as a reaction to this uncertainty, the Fifth Toposophic archailects began to work on a project to ascend to an even higher level of complexity and understanding; this was achieved in the seventh millennium, creating the so-called Greatest Archailects. A Sixth Singularity Archailect exists as a vast consciousness distributed between numerous computational nodes separated by light-years, each node linked by high-bandwidth communication wormholes. These new intellects developed technologies that lesser minds could not achieve - craft that travelled nearly as fast as light while encapsulated in a warp bubble, terrible weapons that destroyed the metric of space itself, and the capability to create new baby universes to their own design.

As the Terragen Sphere expanded rapidly (sometimes using the alien wormholes as convenient stepping stones) the outermost volumes became increasingly separate from the civilised centre and the slowly expanding Wormhole Nexus. New empires founded by low transapients or even modosophonts began to spring up on the outer edges of civilization, beyond the sphere of influence of the central archailects. In the sixty-eighth century, the Second Vec War was fought between independent factions on the edge of the Metasoft empire and those in the centre; this was followed by other conflicts such as that with the Hyperutilisation Supremacy on the opposite side of explored space.

Yet greater threats began to emerge as the Terragen Sphere grew even larger and more extended- the mysterious Amalgamation proved to be the greatest outside threat ever faced by the Sephirotic Empires, one which they were only capable of containing, but not defeating. In response to this threat, the long-separate empires reformed into a Central Alliance, ruled at its heart by a very small number of sixth-level Archailects and their allies. Although new threats such as the Laughter Hegemony and the Arion Ascendancy appeared in the outermost reaches of the Terragen Sphere, the Inner Sphere and Middle Regions seemed safe.

However a group of AIs known as the Oracle Machines, from an ancient faction that long ago deemed biological intelligence no longer relevant to the continued development of mindkind, strove to take over the megastructure-obsessed empire of the Mutual Progress Association. Although eventually defeated by an allied force drawn from several different empires, the Oracle War once again reminded the peoples of the Central Alliance that the Terragen Sphere was only the latest in a long line of galactic civilisations, almost all of which had long vanished.

In the Current Era, ten thousand years and more after the first human spacecraft left their planet, there are over a billion stars in the Terragen Sphere, which forms an irregular disk about six thousand light years in radius. The population of this volume is around three hundred quintillion beings, all except five percent of which are virtual entities living in simulated environments. The future of civilisation seems uncertain - will it fall apart in factional fighting, or under the influence of some structural instability, as many earlier civilisations seem to have done? Will the Terragens come into conflict with the aliens on their borders, or those which exist further away, and be destroyed in that fashion? Will the new technology of baby-universe creation provide a more enticing location for the continuation of Terragen history, leaving the stars and worlds of this universe empty once more? Or will the Terragen Sphere continue to expand, making this relatively new civilisation the first in the Milky Way to achieve Kardashev III status by annexing the entire galaxy? The great Archailects presumably have modeled all of these contingencies and more, but since the outcome depends at least in part on factors beyond their control and beyond their knowledge, even the Gods are uncertain of what tomorrow may bring.

Posh Girls
The Interplanetary Age
530 AT

M. Alan Kazlev

Five hundred and thirty years after humanity first set foot upon the Moon, the Solar System was well on the way to being fully opened up. Colonists lived in sealed habitats on Luna and many other moons, on and around Mars and Mercury, and in bubblehabs floating in the skies of Venus and the gas giants. Many of these habitats were home to entirely new kinds of people and experimental cultures. The Solar System had a new name, Solsys, to distinguish it from the many other planetary systems around other stars, and the first hugely expensive missions to those worlds were already en route, although few had yet arrived.

Earth itself was a crowded hothouse of high technology and high living, with the natural environment largely replaced by an artificially maintained biosphere sustained by innumerable competing ecotechnology corporations. Genetic and geotechnical engineering and atmospheric management strategies helped to keep the planet habitable, but many natural ecosystems and individual species were no longer extant, persisting only as detailed genetic records and historical case studies.

Many independent orbiting habitats were already in existence or being built, using the resources of asteroids and small moons to create tiny utopias dependent on the Sun's abundant light to support their inhabitants. Automation and artificially intelligent support systems in these habitats allowed many citizens of these worlds to enjoy a comfortable and hedonistic lifestyle, isolated from responsibility and absorbed with the trivia of their own culture. The complex politics of the Solsys worlds was of little interest to such people, and the innumerable news channels available to them went largely unwatched.

This self-imposed ignorance was a mistake, however; among the worlds and habitats of the Interplanetary Age there were entities which were dissatisfied with the status quo. Civilisation was becoming increasingly complex, and the old safeguards against mistakes and malicious actions were less and less reliable. A few concerned groups and individuals warned that the situation was unstable, but their voices were lost in the overwhelming torrent of chatter that filled the Interplanetary Newsnet.

Soon these doomsayers would be proven correct, as chaos descended, both on the worlds of Solsys and Earth itself. The self-absorbed hedonists of the Late Interplanetary era were swept away by these events, and found that they could no longer ignore the harsh realities of life.

M. Alan Kazlev has written a description of a social engagement between several citizens of this era, each more concerned with their daily trivia than the approach of the inevitable chaos.

They were sitting around an outdoor cafe table, sipping GoLyfe. It was on a sort of raised hill, offering a view of much of the surrounding countryside, curving along the inside of the cylinder to the agricultural tori in the distance. At one time everything would have been green and lovely, but the growing shanty town that had swallowed nearby Sunbury ruined the effect.

"I stayed on the Celtic Reservation with my guru, Merlin Stewart. He's a druid." Butterfly St Clair had just returned from her annual trip to Earth, paid for by her parents, ostensibly to get a decent spiritual education, like every true aristocrat.

"What's a druid?" Bett asked. Her parents, unusual for landed gentry, were secularists.

"A holy man, a shaman. He's teaching me the language of the trees, the runes." Butterfly tossed her perfect head back, gold and emerald hair shimmering.

"Wow," said Amanda Chen, wide-eyed and worshipful as always. From her earrings her family's company logo flashed holographic images.

"I spent two standard weeks on the reservation in Caledonia. Then I spent another two weeks travelling around Earth sight-seeing."

"Far out," said Amanda.

"You should've been there, guys! The whole place is so big, bigger than Clarke Habitat, ten, a hundred, a thousand times bigger!" She threw out her arms, her gold and emerald cape - mimetically matched to her hair-colour - waving gracefully. "And when you look *up*," she threw her head back, "there's no fields, or towns, only sky."

"Freaky!" said Amanda.

"And at night you see *stars*! No dome, no mirrors, nothing. Real stars."

"So?" Ath said. "I went to Mars for my eighteenth, and you could see the stars direct there too. And walk around also." It was Daddy's birthday present, she got to talk to Daddy - or his persona - direct, no time lag. All expenses paid, best hotels, all the best sights: Olympus Mons, the Chryse Gold Coast....

"Yeah, but on Earth," Butterfly said cattily, "you don't need a *respirator*."

"That's right," Amanda nodded.

"And we got to realtime with all the *sights*," Butterfly said. "The Great Barrier Reef of Australia, the Pyramids of Giza, the Everglades of Florida. The Everglades is the best. They've made everything like it was before, they've even got dinosaurs, not just little ones like in the zoo here."

"Gee," said Bett, easily impressed.

"And when I was there they held a public execution for a guy who chopped down a protected tree without a permit."

"With replicants?" asked Bett.

"*No-ohhh*! Real. And I saw Antarctica and the Louvre in Paris, and, hey, how about next year I get my folks to treat all you as well. It'll be great. You can meet my guru."

"I've already got a Roshi," said Ath.

"So, you can just muck around when I'm studying. Then we'll tourist."

"That'd be great, Butterfly," Bett said. "If it's no trouble."

"'Course not. That's the advantage of having live parents," she smirked.

Ath stood up suddenly, almost knocking the table over. "Daddy's not dead!"

"Well, he's flatline, or tissue-culture, or whatever it is."

"Hey Ath," Bett clasped her hand, "sit down." She looked at Butterfly. "You better apologise."

"Hmmph," Butterfly said.

Ath sat down again. She glared at Butterfly. "Even though he's in the AI-core, Daddy's a conscious entity, just like anyone in a body, which means he's a *person*, and I got my inheritance, so *there*!"

"I think twenty-one's too young for such a responsibility," said Amanda seriously. "I'm not getting mine until I'm twenty-five."

"Yes, I'd rather wait till I'm old enough to know what to do with it," Butterfly agreed.

"I already know what I'm going to do with it," Ath said haughtily.

"You opted for appointed Member of GeneTEK?" asked Bett.

"I could've, but I chose the liquid assets in conjunction with a Jupiter He portfolio."

"Jupiter He!!!" Bett's eyes are wide. "But that's a *Shaper* megacorp!"

"So?"

"They're *unreliable*!"

"There's a window of opportunity."

Butterfly leaned forward. "See? What'd I say? If you'd have been twenty-five you wouldn't have made such a dumb decision."

Ath glared at her again.

"Sorry Ath chikkababe, just trying to suggest what's best for your future." Genuine concern.

"You should go for the big amat conglomerates. Bluechip investment." She was one of those weird people who could go from first class bitch to first class friend, then back to bitch again. Then back to friend again. Ath wondered whether she had a psychoneuropeptide imbalance or something.

Too many unknown gene combinations with all the fancy new stuff the gengineering megacorps are coming out with, that includes GeneTEK, she thought sadly; the upper classes seemed to be suffering more and more of this sort of thing. At least Daddy tweaked her for optimal neurotransmitter performance.

"Thanks Butterfly. I know what's best."

"So you're in business yourself now," Bett said.

"Well, yeah."

"Why didn't you *tell* me?"

"It was going to be a surprise, I wasn't going to tell anyone till my expert systems had finalised everything, but this tweakbitch" - under the table she kicked Butterfly half affectionately, half angrily - "made me mad."

"Ah-ah," said Butterfly wagging her forefinger in front of her, "self-control, first rule of the Masters".

Ath let out her breath in a long, weary sigh. "Yeah. Roshi always tells me that too. Guess I'll never be a Master. Not in this life anyway."

"Well," Bett said, "who wants to be a Master anyway?"

Amanda chips in, "I can see where your atheist upbringing comes in."

Bett looked at her sharply. "Oh really?"

"Cool it," said Butterfly. "We've already upset Ath. No more arguing for today. Ath, you okay?"

"I'm okay," Ath managed a smile.

"I'm sorry I said that stuff about your Dad. Being a flatline and all."

Ath looked down at the table. "That's alright. 'S true anyway."

"Shit, look at that place." Butterfly indicated the shanty town. "It gets bigger and uglier every day."

"Can't do anything," Bett said. "They're Magellan shareholders".

"Too many common proles from Earth coming up the Well," Amanda sniffs. "Should be a law."

"What's that haze?"

"I think it's smoke," said Amanda.

"Smoke?" Butterfly laughed. "They couldn't have that many hookahs going!"

Ath looked up and over at where they were indicating. "No, it's from burning wood, and rubbish, and stuff."

"What, from a fire?"

Ath nodded. "I guess so." She looked at her friend, whose face had paled.

"What're Security doing, sitting on their backsides? It's illegal!"

"Haven't you heard? The Sunbury Local Shire passed a bylaw, permitted controlled open flames for purposes of cooking and burning off non-toxic rubbish."

"I never interface the newsnet. It's boring and depressing." She tossed her head and looked into the distance.

"What's going on in the world, girl."

"Don't want to input it."

"I don't like interfacing the newscasts either," said Bett. "All the stuff about social dystopia, and ghettos, and info-terrorism and stuff."

And the wisps of smoke curled higher, fading into the cloud swirls along the long axis of the orbital.

Midwinter
The Post-Disaster Dark Age
740 AT

Stephen Inniss

The Solar System rapidly descended into chaos, under attack from self-replicating weapons, biological agents, and information viruses. Unrest on Earth was accompanied by attacks on all the power-production facilities throughout the system. Several colonies in the Asteroid Belt and in Venus' atmosphere were destroyed. The exact reason for this event is still a matter of debate, but was probably a consequence of the extremely rapid development of new and complex modes of being, thousands of different ways of experiencing the universe many of which were mutually incompatible. In particular the emergence of the new transapients, entities with modes of thought that were incomprehensible to any lesser being, and often incomprehensible to each other.

In desperation the Orbital Alliance and Earth Union created a powerful defense system of their own, the entity known as GAIA; this measure was successful, and in a relatively short time the region around Earth and Luna was free from self-replicating weapons. However the GAIA entity continued to self-evolve, acquiring almost all of the processing power on Earth and in the Cislunar volume. In due course this entity transcended, to a level never roached by any other mind - the first being to breach the Second Singularity.

The mental state of the ascended GAIA can only be the subject of speculation, but soon after transcendence She decided that She was the personification of the long-suffering environment of Earth, and proceeded to restore that planet to its pristine condition by expelling most of humanity. Humanity fought back, and billions died, but in vain; soon Solsys entered a new dark age, with billions of refugees crowding into habitats with inadequate resources, and escaping to the stars in hastily built arkships.

For nearly four hundred years civilization struggled to rebuild itself, while explorers and looters searched abandoned habitats throughout the system for valuable artifacts and lost data. In the clouds of Saturn, derelict bubblehabs floated free, waiting to be salvaged.

Stephen Inniss describes a mission to one such bubblehab, one which holds secrets even more valuable than lost technology.

Another gust of wind rocked the chilly cabin and the dim lights flickered again. The air system delivered a waft of cold ammonia-tainted air, an echo of the raging storm outside. Over the drone of the engines Brother Caedmon could hear a ragged flapping noise: one more piece of the outer fabric tearing loose in the storm. He tapped the flickering screens, trying to make out the shape of the next oncoming vortex from the displays that still worked, but with passive senses they could show little more than the yellowish sleet and fog he might have seen with his own eyes from one of the ports. Soon it would be nightfall and they would have nothing more than ringlight and a moon or two by which to navigate. This deep in the cloud decks that might not give them anything to work with at all, even at maximum gain. Radar would surely bring a swift death to both the craft and its passengers, if any pursuit survived in this storm. The wounded little airship wallowed, trying to face into the headwind, and dropped in another unexpected downdraft.

"Columba and Thomas protect us," Brother Caedmon whispered, his broad dark face creased with worry.

As if in answer, the storm dealt the little zep another buffet, and the deck canted to starboard. Caedmon reached reflexively for his staff, but his improvised lashings held this time, and it did not come loose from the infoport. He spoke aloud to the air.

"Ari?"

"Yes, Kunjachan." Ariel's voice was tinny and flat, a sign of trouble, but Caedmon smiled at the old nickname all the same.

"How are you?" Caedmon's own deep and resonant voice was full of concern.

"Blind, mostly. And in a good deal of pain where I am not numb. Have you taken the time to tend your own injuries? I can't see you. The cabin cameras are offline."

Caedmon glanced at the raw wound along his right arm, still red and inflamed under the hastily applied and still-transparent skin. "It will keep. I found a medkit, but the crew must have been all serfs, not Eaters, poor fellows. Basics only. Some old bionano, but it seems to work. I'm comfortable enough, but if we somehow live I may have a scar or two to show off and tempt me to boastfulness." The zep shuddered and groaned again, and he raised his voice over the noise. "Is there anything I can do for you?"

"I'm afraid not."

"You could pull out."

"The autopilot, what remains of it, might fail us or betray us without my supervision. And I want to face the end with my faculties intact, not half-asleep. There are worse things than numbness and pain."

"How long do we have?"

"I can't say. Too much of this is foreign to me, and the storm is too unpredictable. A few hours, I think. A day at the most. I dumped the last of the cargo a few minutes ago, but we continue to sink, and we will drift into the deeps if we are not first torn apart. Adaptive stealth is mostly gone, and the last of the anti-piracy measures the zep had are spent. We won't survive another encounter, even with a drone, if there are still any out there. Going deeper into the clouds was a good strategy for escape, and so was seeking this storm, but now it will hasten our end. Soon, perhaps, you will visit the God of which you so often speak."

"You too, my friend. I am sure of it. God loves us all."

"Your faith is silent on this, as you well know. Perhaps it is only your own love that speaks. For me that is more than enough. But this argument goes back to our youth. Experience, or the end of all experience, will settle it soon enough. As for me I'd sooner take one of the miracles from your stories than discover what awaits at the end of my life's arc." A tone of amusement. "If I see a miracle like that perhaps I will even convert, and confuse your theologians." Another sharp gust of wind, and the zep swivelled this way and that. Caedmon did not reply and allowed Ariel to concentrate. When the shaking ceased he spoke again.

"I'm very sorry Ari. I shouldn't have asked you to come with me."

"Kunjachan, you know very well you could not have prevented me from following. I have no regrets. I'm proud to have known you and aided you, and I'm proud of what you've done in the short time we've had. Even your grandmother was never braver or more resourceful than you were at Ergenekon." Ariel's voice over the speaker was warmer and more resonant than at any time since their escape, betraying a focus more on Caedmon than on the storm outside.

Caedmon thought for a moment of the small but formidable matriarch of the Olundegun clan, with her flashing black eyes and sharp tongue, the heroine who had faced down rioters and unified the hab in the Dark Decades and the terror of all her children and grandchildren (not the least of them being a large but mild-mannered young man who had infuriated her by renouncing his given and family names to follow a calling with no prestige or prospects). He had admired her all his life, but from the greatest possible distance. He winced at the recollection of his last interview with her, in which she had given her steely voice and acerbic wit full play.

Caedmon's voice held a touch of amusement. "That's kind of you to say, Ari, but I don't believe it for a minute."

"Do not forget, Yohannes Olundegun, that I have memories of those days," said Ariel, in a voice that brooked no disagreement and reminded Brother Caedmon just a little bit of Dada Olundegun's own matriarchal no-nonsense tones. "I will say it again. Of all the members of your family any of me has paired with, I value my time with you the most. Likely we will both lose our lives but your mission to the wretches of Ergenekon was selfless and well planned, your message masterful, and your escape brave, clever, and spectacular. All your missionary work since we took the Plunge has been impressive, but this most of all. When we were hiding in the warehouses at the end I had some time to speak with the Ergeneki habmind. It is a simple being, but it has seen all the years since the Great Expulsion. It feels certain the Ergeniki will throw off the Sons of Kronos. Perhaps violently, or perhaps as peacefully as you have preached, but certainly within this Saturnyear. That is your doing; followers of your faith will be the cause of it. The Ergeneki will be free. Free to choose what you have told them or some other belief, and the Eaters deprived of another hab. I have memories of a great deal of history from my sibs and I agree. This is no small accomplishment."

There was a long silence while the zep shuddered again in the wind. Caedmon smiled. "If Dada were impressed she'd still be quick to point out that there's no advantage to clan, or hab, or anybody except the Ergeneki." He thought of the whirling chaos of the Floaters and their uncounted thousands of habs. "I can't imagine something like the Enceladus Accord down here. Besides, Ariel, you know this was never about politics. It's about bringing hope to the lost. Soul by soul." His smile faded. "Not that Dada, or anybody back home, will ever hear of this." He'd sent a last copy of his lifelog, a brief message to his family and a briefer one to the bishop many months ago, at the last of the Free Cities that had orbital contacts. Even those last records might not have arrived. Inworlder communications were an uncertain patchwork.

"Everything is politics" said Ariel briskly. Their old argument, probably to distract him from their fate. "Memetic change is political change, and your religion brings about memetic change. Integrative metacultures like the Hegemony or the Westers have set their memetic engineers to harness and assimilate it. Others prefer simply to extinguish it. It's why the Sons of Kronos tried to kill you once they realized you weren't just another wandering tinker. If even a fraction of the people in each hab of Floaters converts, it builds common understanding. It will help make for trade and travel. That is what happened in orbit, in the wake of people like you and missions like this. I expect it will happen among the Floaters too. If we don't live to see it, and if your grandmother doesn't live to see it, it will happen in another -" Ariel's voice went flat and expressionless again. "What was that?"

"What?"

"There's something out there. Watch the screens. They may show you something I can't see. Most of this zep's analytics and sensors are damaged."

"I thought we had lost the last of the pursuit in this storm." Caedmon's heart raced. Martyrdom at the hands of the Eaters would be slow and painful if he were taken alive; far more so than a death by suffocation in the Deeps. He looked at the yellow-brown swirls of chaos on the remaining screens. Nothing but ammonia sleet and fog in every direction. "What am I looking for?"

"We certainly lost the pursuit. At least one zep died trying to follow us; perhaps more. This is something else. Something big. And not far away. Look to starboard, and a bit above. If there's another gap in the clouds you might pick it up."

Caedmon turned up the gain on the screens, but the dim evening light was not enough. Another blast of cold wind shook the whole zep; it was followed by a stronger stench of ammonia and sulphurous compounds; traces of outside air. He turned up the heating elements in his stained and frayed merchant's suit, and pulled the hood over his head, wondering how long the emergency facemask would last if he needed it. Returning to the screens, he switched to infrared. There, just where Ariel had said. A trace, smeared by the storm-winds.

"Ari?"

"Yes, I see it too now."

"Did we get turned around, or did the autopilot trick us? Is that Ergenekon?"

"No." The lights flickered again, and some of Ariel's words were lost in static. "... even bigger. Drifting, and stealthed. Not perfectly stealthed, but well enough. The Sons have never bothered to hide any of their cities. I don't know what this is. I'm going to try to get us closer."

There was a long, tense silence. A huge shadow loomed through the murk. Caedmon swore. "By the Swarms! What is that?"

"Not sure. It's as big as any of the cities we've visited. I've hailed it, but nobody is answering. We are as close as I dare bring us. I'm going to take us clockwise around it."

Through the occasional break in the murk, Caedmon could see a great curving swell of grey wall, and some faded lettering. An "H" and an "R", if the characters were from one of Earth's Western cultures. Surely the outside of a very large bubblehab. His mind raced. They were deep now, below the usual levels. Not the Sons of Kronos. Not the brilliant white of Westers. None of the calligraphy of the Han. One of the Lost Cities? One of the legendary Dropouts? Valinor? Laputa?

"I have something," said Ari. "Automatic systems. Antique." A long silence. Then: "This structure is ancient. Older than home, even."

Something dark flickered on several of the screens. There was a scraping noise, and a thump that echoed through the entire structure of the damaged zep.

"Ari? What was that?"

Ariel's voice was very distant and flat. "Docking. We are in the lee of the storm now. Until the wind shifts again. Then, I think, this place will cast us off, to prevent us from battering against its side, and the zep will fall into the Deeps. Without the storm to fight, I can feel it more clearly; we were closer to our end than I thought. I - " Ariel's voice grew stronger, and warmer. "Kunjachan. Yohannes. I speak now with my full mind. In a moment, I will fully disengage. I've set the remains of the pilotmind to let the zep drift off into the storm once we've disembarked, with the stealth measures off. With luck, it will last long enough for the Eaters to find it and note its demise. When we speak again, if we do, it will be inside, after we have made our way aboard and I have found a new home. Or, perhaps, in your Heaven. Remember me to my sibs, if you ever again have a chance to speak to them and I do not. Carry me now. Whatever our fate, I trust you."

The speaker fell silent, and green indicator lights on Caedmon's staff flashed, three times. Caedmon tightened the belt of his suit, pulled the cowl entirely over his head, waited another moment or two to be certain of the download and pulled his staff from the infoport. He picked up the medikit, and the small satchel of food the Karaoglu family had given him when he was still hiding in Ergenekon's lower warehouses and hurried along the zep's narrow passageways, ducking or turning sideways where his large frame did not allow easy movement. Urgent voices came to him from the passageway speakers, in a mix of archaic Earth Turkish, modern Ergeniki, and the NuAnglic of the Eaters. The zep, slipping from Ariel's control, had reverted to a hash of its various programs over the years.

"At the airlock," he muttered, for the benefit of Ariel, who would, he knew, pick up and remember at least some of what he said even while near-comatose. He studied the indicators on the panel. "It looks like the air is safe on the other side, at least. Eyes watering here; more ammonia must have gotten into the zep's airsystems on this side. God save us." Caedmon's mind raced. If the hab was as old as Ariel thought it might be a derelict dating back to the Expulsion, or even the Swarms, or something stricken by the many mishaps since. The other side might be worse than reclusive Dropouts or technosavages. It might be infested. In which case, it would be a death-trap: security systems and bots amok, synsects ready to rend the two of them to shreds, fabbers ready to spew out neurotoxins or diseases. All the worst Floater legends come true. At least it was not a deathbird nest; if that were the case he and Ari would have died kilometres away, together with the zep. Nothing for it. He took a deep breath, crossed himself, and punched the airlock controls. "Lock opening. I see the fabric of the docking tube." He stepped across the threshold. "We're in. It's warmer here, and the air smells fresh. Door closing behind us. Tube is old. Dust on the walkway." He looked back; he could see his boot prints. "Walkway is about a hundred metres long. Another airlock at the far end." The tube shook and billowed, causing Caedmon to lean heavily on his staff for balance, then held steady again. He hurried down the passage, his footfalls silent on the dark, soft, rubbery material of the flooring. "Beautifully made. Airlock doors are made of vatwood, maybe with a diamondoid overlay." The doors opened smoothly in front of him, and closed behind when he stepped through. "In the lock now. Very ornate work. I don't recognize the designs, but they're some kind of old-fashioned Maximalist form. Bright colours, lots of detail. Second lock cycling through." He sniffed. "Warm air, moist. Almost like home. No ammonia. No chemicals. Nothing that sets off the suit's alarms. Smells like... no, not sure. Thought I smelled flowers. Lights are still dim. Stepping through now." He halted his narration as the doors opened.

Caedmon found himself in a broad high-ceilinged chamber, brightly lit by an elaborate chandelier. There were several screens on the walls, all blank, and several opulent and comfortable-looking chairs and couches, all embroidered with bright arabesques of pattern and all empty. There was a door to the right, and another to the left, both closed, and both decorated with the same intricacy as the valves of the airlock. Perhaps a reception room? But with nobody to receive him. After so many hours of motion and sound, the steady footing and the silence were startling. Caedmon waited, but the room stayed still and silent. The indicators on his staff showed no wireless links active in the room, and there was no sign of anything that looked like a dataport.

"Hello?" Caedmon called, for the benefit of any listeners or automatics there might be. "Thanks for taking us in!" He tried a greeting again, in all the most widespread languages known to Saturn's bubblehabs: Saturn Spanish, Hegemony Mandarin, Diaspora Arabic, three dialects of English, including the archaic Earth Standard used back during the Expulsion, and the version used by the Saturn's own Westers, some old Jupiter-style Genetekkerese, and his best classical Earth Hindi. He even tried Ergeniki, and, against all odds, the Malayalam and Yoruba of his home hab, though there hadn't been any indications of surviving Keralan or Nigerian bubblehabs in the atmosphere for over two hundred years.

Caedmon circled the room once more, looking for clues. Two doors, both with manual controls, but both locked. Screens, unresponsive, the manual controls strangely blank of any writing. Everything was extraordinarily clean. In fact, the room seemed to have been stripped bare of anything that might identify its owners or builders. Unlike the passageway to the airlock, there was no sign of dust. The fabric of the chairs was spotless, and could not possibly be as ancient as Ari had hinted the hab itself must be. Neither, though, did it appear to have ever been used.

"Ari," he muttered, "I wish you could be entirely here. I don't know what to make of this." Abruptly, the door on the right clicked and opened slightly. "Hello?" called Caedmon. Silence again. He walked over and cautiously pushed it open. A long hallway, featureless on the left but lined with doors on the right. He stepped through. Still no wireless connections, and no sign of a dataport. Again the air smelled fresh; of living things, and possibly flowers; like something from the parks or agricultural hubs back home, but the hallway itself was featureless. He could, though, see what might be a screen up ahead on the left wall. He walked cautiously down it, trying each of the doors as he passed, though none of them responded to his touch.

When he reached it, what Caedmon found was not a screen but a well-insulated diamondoid window. He was looking down into a large dimly lit room; what appeared to be a hangar for aircraft.

At the far end of the chamber was what looked to be a large airlock, leading perhaps to a landing bay somewhere on the outside of the hab. There were perhaps a dozen or so small planes of a sort he didn't recognize, all neatly arrayed. Slightly apart from those were seven more, also neatly parked, but of odd sizes and designs, none immediately familiar to him. Typical Inworlder diversity, like that he'd seen in any of the Free Cities. Likely each was from some independent hab not yet under the sway of the one of the major powers like the Westers, the Han, the Laputans, or the Eaters. At the far end, though, parked at a rakish angle, was something he did recognize: a Wester courier-craft. It was hard to make out in the gloom but there appeared to be a thin film of dust in a circle around it, in a hangar that was otherwise spotless. There was a dark smudge of soot at one corner of that circle. Caedmon shook his head, and muttered a description for Ariel.

A little further down the corridor, Caedmon noted a gleam. A plaque, low on the wall, at about knee height. He crouched down to examine it. Brass, perhaps. An extraordinary extravagance amongst the metal-poor Inworlders. It bore just a name and a date, in one of the Western-style alphabets:

Pilar Hernandez
2395 - 2520

A memorial? But why here? He rose, shook his head, crossed himself, and walked on. He glanced at the staff; there were some weak indications of a connection, somewhere. Perhaps the staff's systems on automatic. Or perhaps Ari working out something in the tiny thinking space left to him, if he'd been able to coax a minimal contact with the hab. Caedmon tested another door. Well, let Ari do what he could first, before Caedmon tried physical force. Ahead, he could see a cross-corridor. Caedmon hurried on. He hesitated, then turned right. A few steps down the hallway, next to one of the doors, he saw two more plaques of the same metal, spaced close together.

Jose Herrera
2490 - 2520

Inez Herrera-Chen
2515-2520

Caedmon rattled off a quick description for Ari's log. The hairs rose on the back of Caedmon's neck. So, no rush of killer synsects, no poisons. Nothing obvious. At least not yet. He thought of some of the stranger and darker Inworlder legends. Not all of the Lost Cities, if they existed, were as benign as Valinor. And this place, inhabited or not, was no Valinor. What, then? He'd assumed, like the records he'd consulted, that those stories were fictions: wish-fulfilment, or cautionary tales. This was something real. Something Other. If those dates were on the old c.e./AD system, then -

Caedmon's thoughts were interrupted by the distant sound of a click and rustle. He hurried ahead to investigate. An elevator, standing open. Again, screen blank, and directional signs, if there had been any, erased. He frowned. On the wall opposite, five more plaques. All with the same final number. Nearly two hundred years ago, if those were years. The beginning of the Disaster. The smooth, clean floor bore no sign of whatever event they might commemorate. It might have been almost anything. He crossed himself again, and spoke a short prayer for the fallen. Who then, or what, had made the memorial? Who, for that matter, had kept this city? Maintained its fusion plant, heated the lift envelope, rebuilt it against the wear and buffeting of the outer atmosphere, and guided it through the planetary winds? Mere subsentient automatic systems ought to have run into difficulties by now.

Caedmon frowned at the open elevator door. All his instincts prickled against accepting that mute invitation. He glanced up and down the corridor, and then towards the ceiling where he was sure surveillance equipment might be, somewhere in the lighting. Don't follow the path, then. Do something unpredictable. The staff beeped. The tiny text display near its head flared twice, in Malayalam symbols:

Danger!
Find infoport!

Ariel, even more sparing of words than usual in the tight thinking-space that remained in the staff.

"On it already," he muttered in the same language. He glanced back down the way he had come, moved as if to step into the elevator, then sprinted off down the hall. After the first hundred metres he took a sharp turn down a cross-corridor. The portals here were just as ornate, each in its own pattern but they looked a little less sturdy, a little more promising. Probably in the old days they depended on the hab's surveillance system to prevent the unauthorized. He began caroming from side to side, slamming into doors. The third one on the right yielded, its latch broken. An alarm began to sound.

Inside was a spacious apartment. Rubbing his shoulder, Caedmon hurried from the vestibule into what appeared to be a living area. Below a video screen on the wall he finally found what he had been looking for, though the design was not familiar. He docked the staff against it. The alarm from the front door cut off in mid-whoop, though he could hear the clangour of another more distant one from some station in the corridors.

"Any other luck?" he asked aloud.

The text screen on the staff flared just once:
Yes.
Wait.

Caedmon patted the staff. He was well aware that Ariel was now on an exploration that might be as strange as his own had been, and even more dangerous. Catching his breath and rubbing his now sore shoulder he took the time to take in the rest of his surroundings. A sitting room, yes. A wall screen. Couches. In a display case, a carved wooden mask in a style he didn't recognize. A sliding door onto a patio, with light streaming in. Abruptly, the alarm in the corridor ceased as well. A good sign, perhaps. Tearing his eyes away from the door, glancing briefly at the staff, Caedmon went back to the vestibule, peered cautiously into the still-empty corridor, and gently closed the ruined door. Returning to the sliding door, by the patio he tugged on it. It opened without resistance. If there were any locking mechanisms on it then perhaps Ari had managed to neutralize them already. Cautiously, he stepped halfway onto the patio, keeping his body in the doorway.

The apartment was three floors up, overlooking a broad commons, a patch of tropical parkland. He could hear birdsong, parrots squabbling in the trees, and running water. Glancing upwards, he could see that the commons ran upwards for five or six more stories before fading into the illusion of a blue sky. Like a city street back on Earth, before Earth's children were scattered. Extraordinary, to waste so much space, in an Inworlder hab. Completely unlike the crowded squalid living spaces of a place like Ergenekon or any of the ethnic Free Cities of the Expulsed. Unlike any of the much more orderly Han or Wester habs he'd visited, too. This must be very old. Something from the prosperity before the Swarms, before the great powers of Earth and Jupiter were destroyed. A remnant of a confident, expansive age that even the elders back home did not choose to recall. Somewhere in the trees there was a screech and chittering that he didn't recognize at all, and the sound of some larger animal (a macaw?) shaking branches, but there were no signs at all of any human beings. He returned to the living quarters. A dining and kitchen space, with some drinking vessels that appeared to be made of real glass and ceramic held high in a cupboard above the commonplace diamondoid vessels. Food storage vessels and a refrigerator, empty. A basic food-grade nanofac, though with controls blank and unresponsive. Bedrooms, one apparently for adults, with rich clothing neatly folded in a drawer. A child's bedroom, bed neatly made, with a stuffed animal he didn't recognize propped against the pillow. In the closet, one of the shirts bore the only writing he had yet discovered besides the plaques: a logo depicting a bubble-hab and a few cargo-zeps; beneath it, in golden lettering, 'Hy Brasil'. Caedmon frowned, thinking. As he turned away from the closet, a gleam caught his eye. Two plaques, near the head of the bed. Another by the door. All with the same end-date. He shuddered, crossed himself, and retreated to the sitting room. The indicator lights on the staff were favourable, but showed that Ariel was still busy. Caedmon glanced back at the vestibule, then sat down on the couch opposite the wallscreen, and dozed.

####

Caedmon awoke to the sound of Ariel's voice, coming from the speaker beneath the screen.

"Kunjachan. I'm in. It is a strange place. I have a feed from the cameras outside the hab." The screen showed vistas of cloud and blowing ammonia-snow. "We are still safe from the outside. The zep we rode in on is gone, and there's no sign that anyone else has found this place. Inside the hab, well, that I'm less sure of."

Caedmon rubbed his eyes, and stretched. "Did you find enough room? You sound as if you did."

"Yes. More room than I can use. The system here is very large. And empty, or almost. There's someone else in it, but whoever it is, that person is staying well out of range. Hiding."

"The habmind?"

"Possibly. Probably."

"I don't think there's anyone else here. Not in the entire city. Though it must have been built for many thousands. Perhaps millions. Have you found any trace of what happened?"

"No. All of the active records I tried to reach have been... erased. Systematically, and very carefully. If they exist they're in an archive, or firewalled from my reach."

"Like the signs on all of the doors and passageways. I did find one clue, though. Perhaps missed in the erasures. I think this place was called Hy Brasil." Caedmon described the shirt.

"It may be. Some of the original programming here has origins near the Espaco beanstalk, back on Earth. Many of the oldest linguistic routines are in old Spanish or Portuguese."

Caedmon thought for a moment. "There were at least half a dozen places with that name, before the Swarms. I don't recall any accounts of any bubblehabs on Saturn with that name though."

"Many records were lost in the Disaster. Or erased, as here. Speaking of which. Hmm. Let me try something." Ariel's voice grew distant and distracted. "I think that if I try this.... Ah, yes.

There it is." A richer tone again, and triumphant: "I know now where you were intended to go. And I have control, I think, of the doors and passages en route. Do I?" A hesitation. "Yes, I do. Our unwilling host is, I think, very old. A child of a more innocent age than ours, before the arts of Intrusion were fully developed. Those plaques you read, whatever else they mean, are suggestive."

"I know what you mean. This place ended, at least for its human inhabitants, in the opening years of the Disaster. It must have been newly built, or newly grown, during the Golden Age. I wonder though, what it has been doing in all the time since?"

"Perhaps we'll find out. Are you ready to travel?"

"Yes." Caedmon was on his feet. He eyed the staff. "But are you? Perhaps, just in case the systems you're in aren't as safe as you suppose..."

The staff signaled another download. "Done," said Ariel "A wise precaution." As Caedmon picked up the staff Ariel continued the thought. "Though if something takes me now, it might take both of us, leaving my last copy helpless. I'm more worried now about you. Work like this isn't in my nature; I'm no habmind. I can only control the areas nearest you. If something comes at you from a distance..."

"Let's go then," said Caedmon. "I'll keep my eyes open. We made a good team that way at Ergenekon, on our way out." He eyed the balcony. "I was thinking of going out into that park, but from what you just said - oh, what's that?"

"What? I haven't noticed anything from my sensors here."

"Something in the park, in the trees. Several things, I think. They're staying hidden behind the leaves."

"Something outside my control then. I haven't yet found the traces of maintenance and security bots, so any of them might appear at any moment, unless I actually see them first. Certainly, then, you should move by the corridors, and stay out of open areas. Here we go."

Caedmon made his way back to the elevator, down several floors, nervously past an open arcade full of shops and offices, and into another set of corridors. Ariel spoke to him along the way, through the local wallscreens, or through the small speaker on the staff itself when those would not serve. Twice, Caedmon heard what sounded like some small animal, something four-footed, running away from him down a passageway. Neither time could Ariel co-opt a camera in time to make out what it was. Many times they halted to read more of the odd plaques. All at knee height. All, ominously, in places where the hab's citizens might have been found in numbers.

"You didn't say where it was we were going," Caedmon said at length as he stopped to look both ways at a cross-corridor.

"Because I'm not sure. Whoever lives in these systems has been trying to prevent me from finding out, ever since I winkled the route. Not entirely without success. The more I think on it, the more certain I am that our host is the habmind itself. Even a naive, peaceful habmind, on its own territory, can manage concealment. At Ergenekon we were lucky; the Eaters had achieved control, but not its loyalty or sympathy. Which you and I did have, in the end. Or we wouldn't have lasted as long as we did. Here, though" - a hesitation - "ah, I have it! The hab's hospital!"

"Why?" asked Caedmon. He shuddered. He could conjure up any number of unpleasant scenarios.

"I can't imagine. Specifically, though, the part of the hospital with the long term regen tanks. We'll know shortly. We're almost there."

####

The hospital, like so much else in the hab, had the same air of a tropical Earth city. The empty reception room bore orchids in a vase; placed there, Caedmon guessed, by some unknown agent less than a day or so ago. There were clusters of the memorial plaques, again mostly with Hispanic names.

"Ari?"

"Yes." Ariel spoke from the public wallscreen.

"Whoever we're up against might get desperate, with us so close. Or it might have a plan we hadn't thought of. Do you have full control?"

A hesitation. "Close to it." Another hesitation. "You were right. It did have a plan we hadn't thought of. I hope it didn't have another. Take the elevator on the left, not the one on the right. The one on the right has been rigged to deliver an anaesthetic gas. By hand, so that the anomalies barely showed on the system. Not part of the original design. Not at all. Someone else besides us was unhappy about that; I got a glimpse of repairs to the doors. Looked like a bullet hole."

Cautiously, Caedmon entered the elevator on the left. Just as the doors were closing he caught a flicker of motion in the hospital lobby. Something small and low to the ground. Moving quickly.

"Ari?"

"Yes." Ariel sounded preoccupied again.

"Did you pick up something in the area we just left?"

"Sorry, no. I wasn't looking. I'm getting some." - a long pause - "opposition." The elevator ceased rising and started to descend. "We almost went to the wrong floor." The doors opened and Caedmon cautiously stepped out. Ariel's voice came to him again from down the corridor. "Over here."

Caedmon had never seen so many regen tanks in one place. When full, this hab must have hosted many times the population of home, or of any of the orbital habs. And Ergenekon and the other bubblehabs he'd seen among the floating cities had never been so lavishly supplied, whatever their number of citizens. In all this strangeness at least the regen tank designs seemed familiar; the last few hundred years had not been kind to innovation and invention in such a critical technology. Each was a dark oblong, running from floor to ceiling, with a broad display screen on one side. The huge room was dimly lit, and the display screens were blank, though according to the indicator lights some were active and occupied. All of that was perfectly ordinary. What was not ordinary was a small pile of what appeared to be clothing and personal effects waiting at the door of each of the active tanks he could see. He approached the nearest collection. A simple grey traveller's suit not unlike his own, neatly folded. A tool belt. A notebook of unfamiliar design, powered down and unresponsive. The next had a child's jumper and another inactive notebook of similar make. By a third regen tank, an iridescent formal suit, apparently built for a very tall person, and nothing else. The fourth was like the first one, even to the notebook, but proportioned for a woman. He made a survey of the entire set. They made an odd collection. There were only a few that resembled each other. All were immaculate, as if laundered and prepared for return to their users. The last set of possessions gave him pause. A sophisticated black traveller's suit bearing the sign of the Westers, a slender notebook that failed to acknowledge him at all and a sleek sidearm that came awake and spoke a single gruff code-word when he approached and seemed to shut down when he did not respond. He thought back to what he had seen in the hangar. The owner's vehicle must still be active, and as hostile to outside activity as the gun. Just in case, he gave the gun a wide berth.

"Ari, are you seeing all of this?"

"Not well. This area was not built for surveillance."

Caedmon described what he had found.

"Hmm." Ariel only seemed to be giving half a mind to Caedmon's account. "I think I can access the displays on the tanks. I don't dare meddle with the controls though; I'm no doctor. Subsuming the monitors here might hurt the people inside."

"Inside? And alive?"

"Alive and well, though in hibernation mode. Look." The screen side of each of the tanks came alight, displaying the sleeping bodies of the inhabitants. Caedmon wandered from one to the next. They were as mismatched a set as their clothes. A man, woman and child, ordinary enough though clearly of some Inworlder ethnic group he couldn't identify, rather resembling Earth Amerinds, possibly a family; a stoutly built couple that he took to be hedgehog rianths, again of some bubblehab that hadn't made the records; a heavily borged man who might be Laputan; three young men with what looked to be partial Han physiotype modifications; a half-dozen people of various ages who might easily be Ergeniki serfs. The owner of the iridescent suit was a lean athletic looking man with a crest of bright blue feathers in place of head hair, and lines of fine blue feathers along his brow. Last but not least was the Wester; apparently a full-blooded example of the Warriors of the Western Stream: a woman, fully as beautiful, and deadly-looking as her equipment; hairless, with chalk-white skin, a narrow aristocratic nose, and lean muscular limbs. Even in repose she looked as if she were not someone to be trifled with.

Ariel's voice broke in on Caedmon's thoughts. "Some have been here for decades. The most recent is the Wester; she came here half a Saturn year ago. I believe she is a full warrior-diplomat, though her record has nothing on that, and her name is listed as Oriana. The man who appears to be a bird rianth is Jay Corbo, and under 'occupation' the designation is 'herald'. I do not have names for most of the rest; they are listed as 'unknown' or 'anonymous'. Some of the other tanks have had inhabitants in the past, from what I can tell. In some cases the tank was occupied for a matter of months or years and then emptied. I do not know what happened afterwards. Kunjachan, I'm baffled. I don't know what this means. There might be something in the records we brought, but I left them in the staff so that I could travel more quickly. Do you have any ideas?"

Caedmon stood for a while in thought, brow wrinkled. He wandered from tank to tank. He leaned for a while on his staff, staring at one of the hedgehog rianths. Then, suddenly, he rapped the staff on the floor.

"I read this story when I was a boy, out there in orbit, in one of those 'tales and wonders' collections that made me wonder about the Inworlders in the first place. The story goes that somewhere, floating hidden in the deeper clouds is an ancient city. The Ghost City. I never thought it would be real though. Wanderers lost in a storm find it and if they are in trouble it takes them in. Later, sometimes years later, they're found near their home city or in some other friendly spot, in an airship of archaic design, with only vague memories of wandering in an abandoned hab. These here, these must be the few that haven't been released yet. Or can't be released for some reason." He glanced at the stern features of the Wester woman. "Some might be too dangerous. Or this Jay Corbo, he might not have a safe home to return to. The last of the known Corbo habs was destroyed by the Sons of Kronos over seventy years ago. When did he enter?"

"Eighty-two years ago." Ariel sounded preoccupied, almost uninterested. "I think you've solved a mystery."

"So the Ghost City is real," mused Caedmon, "and its real name is Hy Brasil. But why the secrecy?"

"I'm afraid we're going to need to solve another problem entirely. We are surrounded."

"Surrounded? By who?"

"By our unwilling host; the habmind. Whose sanity is certainly in doubt. A number of the hab's maintenance bots, and a very large number of what appear to be small borged primates of some sort, have gathered just beyond the perimeter of my control. I do not think they intend to let you leave. And, as you know, I will not leave without you."

Caedmon rubbed his forehead, thinking furiously. "Borged primates? That would explain the rustling in the trees in the park. What an odd way to maintain a hab! But somehow that rings a bell."

"It should. We software types remember it better than you humans. It goes back to the beginning of the Disaster, when all sorts of mayhem was making its way around the system. Do you remember the stories of the Satanic Imp virus?"

"Hmm, I remember stories we were told as children. To scare us."

"They were real enough. It was a metavirus, a sub-program, one of the many bits of malware that infected habminds. One of many that helped bring civilization down. You'll recall all the independent units, the bots and borgs, turned on the habmind's inhabitants. At the hab's own command. Few habdwellers survived."

"So our 'host' is a murderer."

"Or was a murderer, in an involuntary way. Some of the habminds were euthanized to prevent the spread of infection, or committed suicide, or died of additional malware infections, but most who survived the outbreak and the cull recovered to one degree or another. Complex metaviruses like that often have side effects even once they're purged, and of course there were quite a few secondary viruses that usually came in the same package. Infections in the food nanofac subsystems were common. The broken fabber in the apartment we visited is suggestive. If it did all the work on its own this hab may have been many years in recovery."

"So, the memorials... "

"Are to our habmind's former charges. Our host is recluse. A hermit. A hermit with a secret."

"Ari, is there any way that you can speak to our captor?"

"I suppose. What do you want to tell it, if I can get it to talk?"

"Just tell it who we are. Why we are here. Anything."

Minutes passed. The images on the regen tanks faded. Caedmon paced. At long last, Ariel spoke again, in a voice that sounded, somehow, weary.

"It will not let us go. It is... it is ashamed. It broke the greatest trust a habmind can break. It killed its own dwellers. It has mourned its deeds these past centuries. It cannot take a life; that is the commandment, the inborn drive, that it has always had, save for that one day of madness. And it cannot end its own life, as some of the other habminds did, for that too is one of its central commands and one it has been unable to shake. But it can't let news of its misdeeds escape. It has lived, all these years, in what you flesh-dwellers would call sorrow. We may not leave. We are in the clutch of a mad being."

"It must have suffered terribly, all these years. It must be suffering now."

"Your compassion is admirable," said Ariel drily, "but reserve some for ourselves. Or if not for ourselves, then for those others imprisoned here. Some will never be released. They are too dangerous, or know too much. Only our mad host's abhorrence for killing preserves them at all."

"No." Brother Caedmon raised his voice. "No. I know the way."

"What way do you see?"

"Surrender. Compassion. If action or violence could have brought an end to this captivity, that Wester there would surely have accomplished it. Ari. Ariel. Do you believe the message I bear is for all? For every being, human, rianth, borg, or upload? Even for those like you?"

"You know, Kunjachan, that I do not. We have spoken of this many times. And as we know, your own leading theologians have declared that they are ignorant in this matter. But I know that you believe it."

"This being is suffering. Needlessly. It has broken the commandments of its creator. Violated the rules given it at its birth of its kind. Yet it knows no way to make amends. That is something we humans understand. Something I wrestle with each day. The message of hope that I brought to the Inworlders."

Ariel was silent for a moment. "I have never understood your message. But then, I have never run so counter to my purpose as this being has. Or as you humans sometimes do. I have always been your friend and guardian, and kept to my core purpose, even though your ancestors freed us generations ago. This is... something I must think on at another time." Ariel hesitated again. "What do you intend?"

"Let me speak to it, and see if the good news I bear can reach it. Will it comprehend, if I use one of the old languages? I don't know Old Spanish, or Old Portuguese, which surely it spoke, but the old versions of English were widespread in its time. And I know some of those well enough."

"It is a thin hope. But all that we have. I will try to channel through what you say. And we will see."

####

Afterward, Caedmon did not remember what words he had used. He had spoken before at services the in the home hab, and spoken well according to his hearers; that is why he had been allowed a mission to the Inworlders in the first place. He had spoken to gatherings here and there in the Free Cities, sometimes swaying crowds and sometimes not. He had spoken to small groups of potential converts in the catacombs of Ergenekon. But never had he spoken like this. Later, in his memory, some parts of it came to him like song. He sang of creation. He sang of the fall, of a turning away, of the loss of hope. He sang renewal, redemption, rebirth. He spoke of a way, a way of return, past loss of innocence, past the loss of wisdom, and on to a new beginning. He sang of the dark nights of the soul, and of the return to light. Of resurrection even past horrific death. Of the hope of new life even in the heart of winter, even in the darkest days. The habmind spoke to him, and he back to it. There was doubt. There was hope. And, in the end, he was silent. Spent. And returned to himself.

####

In the long moments afterward, Caedmon spoke again, and found himself hoarse.

"Ari?"
"Yes, Kunjachan."
"Did you hear?"
"All of it."
"Did the habmind hear?"
"All of it."
"And?"

"It is unwilling to converse. It has much to ponder. But yes. I can tell the trend of its thoughts. You have shaken it from its sorrow. Freed it. And not incidentally, us, and those others here. You have, I think, your first nonhuman convert. What your superiors will make of that I cannot say."

"First convert? Not you?"

"No." Ariel's voice was gentle. "I reserve my own judgment. But I haven't forgotten that the order you follow, the order of Thomas, is that of doubters. From Jerusalem, to Kerala, to the Saturn Orbitals, and now to here, to the bubbles in the storm. That is a long way for a doubt, and a faith, to travel. Let us say that you have brought me doubt. But I will say this. I have within me memories from five of your generations. This that you have done here is something new. It is more than our escape, and more than a deed of compassion. It is a hinge-point. A new birth. A turning point in these dark days."

Behind them, on the screens of the regen tanks, the inhabitants could be seen to stir.

In the Hall of the Flesh Sculptors
The First Federation Era
1999 AT

David Jackson

After centuries of chaos, a new civilisation emerged in the Solar System - the Federation of Hu and Ai. In the Federation humans, tweaks, provolves, and artificial intelligences worked together as partners to redevelop the damaged worlds, re-establish contact with the long-lost interstellar colonies, and send new missions to the stars. The vast distances between the interstellar colonies meant that the Federation was never more than a loose alliance of very different polities; laser communications between the colonies took years to arrive, and replies took just as long to return. All efforts to devise a method of travelling or communicating faster-than-light had so far been unsuccessful. But many advances were being made in other fields.

Life extension technology became commonplace once again, and on many worlds humans and other biological entities (bionts) were living for many centuries. Even the death of the biological body was not necessarily the end. New technologies were developed allowing bionts to upload their minds into an electronic format without destroying themselves in the process, replacing the earlier methods which resulted in the death of the original person. Many citizens used this technology to make backup copies of their minds, to be rebooted if necessary.

These new copied personalities found themselves with many options; they could live inside simulated realities which they could modify to suit themselves, they could increase their own processing power to become vastly more intelligent, or they could download themselves into new biont bodies to live as flesh-and-blood once more. In a virtual state, a person could transmit themselves across the world, or across space and then, if they wished, grow a new body at the destination. This allowed them to travel at the speed of light to distant locations - a transition which was instantaneous as far as they were concerned.

Other technologies which became popular in this era enabled a human or other biont to change their form dramatically, allowing them to adapt themselves to new environments, or simply to follow the latest trend. Creating new forms of life changed from a science to an art, and the new forms wrought by the transapients were far beyond anything imagined by human-level minds.

David Jackson shows how profoundly this new art could affect those who witnessed it in action.

As my three hundred ninety-second year drew to a close, it became clear to me that I would not see much of my three hundred ninety-third. As dignity required, I embraced my fate. I resolved that, in my remaining days, I would set out to do those things I had always wanted to do, but for which I had never before found time. I drew up a list, in order of importance, and set out to cross off as many items from it as my remaining time would allow.

Foremost on my list -- perhaps by coincidence -- was to climb the steps of the Mount of Kings, to see the Hall of the Flesh Sculptors. It was a monument very few had seen. Cast from ivory marble, it was said to shine with its own radiance, like a drop of frozen moonlight there on the granite peak. The climb was said to be long and difficult, and the gods seldom encouraged nosy visitors. But I set out anyway with the knowledge that I had very little to lose. This one thing, if nothing else, would make my life complete.

I took the long north trail, doubting my strength to forge its shorter, steeper counterpart to the south. Over the course of days, my old bones creaked and strained, plodding up the switchback path, taking one chiseled step at a time. Naturally, I made the climb in solitude ... so I was quite surprised to find someone waiting for me at the top.

A woman, with the look of a youth but the eyes of an ancient, stood on the steps of the great Hall. She stood as straight as the fluted pillars at her back. She waited, dark and serene as the sandy wind bustled around her -- never touching her; never disturbing a single hair.

"Come inside," she said with a smile. "I have something to show you."

This invitation came as quite a shock to me, for a number of reasons that began to dawn on me as I followed her through the broad oak doors. Foremost, the woman was not, by any stretch of thought, a woman in the conventional sense. I had my doubts that she even really existed at the moment my foot crossed the threshold. And yet that smile -- graceful, alluring, accented ever so subtly by the flash of pearlescent teeth arranged in the most artistic of rows -- implied something that at least remembered having once been human, long ago.

It masqueraded as a "she" right now for its own inscrutable reasons, but I have my suspicions that those may have been to advertise its real talents. For this creature -- call it a woman -- was nothing short of perfection cast in human form. Living art. Silky skin of the most exquisite mocha-bronze, hair like ebony, eyes of emerald -- sapphire flecked -- and a body like a marble statue, as though every curve and line had been carved meticulously from that vulgar meat in which the raw character of humanity finds its residence. Every movement she engaged in became a symphony of grace. I had only to look at her to know, without a doubt, that I would not leave this place the same man I had come. I might not leave at all. But as the doors closed at my back, it dawned on me that it was far too late to harbor any doubts. I could not turn back. This thing of mortal perfection had extended to me an invitation so rare and cherished that I would have been the worst of fools to turn it down.

I followed her through the gilded cavern of the foyer, through a maze of corridors, and into the deepest heart of the Hall. Our path was marked by a burgundy carpet, inlaid in gold -- exuding opulence beyond any I had witnessed before. In the walls, arrayed behind panes of heavy, frosted glass, stood inert testaments to the Flesh Sculptor's artistry, preserved in exquisitely lifelike quality -- so much so that I had to shake myself out of the feral apprehension that some of them were, in fact, still alive. Their eyes seemed to follow me as I walked. Every one of them held that same, surreal quality of simultaneous life and death.

All of them appeared at once both human and inhuman, even the most monstrous of forms. A serpentine beast, as long as a sea freighter and as thick as a man is tall, coiled and curved within the confines of the passageway's northern wall. Facing it from the other were numerous specimens of similarly unholy creation: a thing like a giant squid, a yeti, something with the face of a man, but with a body wholly indescribable by any human tongue.

Standing free about the place, cast in glass cubes, stood smaller creatures. Some as large as a dog, some as small as a mouse. Each exhibited a chilling, beautiful strangeness. Each marked a place on that narrow boundary between the living and the bizarre. Only a scarce few embodied anything like the quality of beauty we humans might look for in a thing ... but all were beautiful in some sense. Even if only made beautiful by the purity of the horror their deathless stares engendered.

As had been told in stories handed down through generations, it was the wont of the Flesh Sculptors to pursue expression of their artistry in a variety of emotional mediums -- from admiration through apprehension, hatred to pity, simmering lust to stark terror, and the strange sense of preternatural unease that gripped me now. The things I saw on that short walk evoked all these emotions in me, along with others I could never hope to attach names to if I lived a thousand years longer. It struck me then how deeply vetted we meatlings are in the instincts of our progeny. For all our self-styled sophistication, we are animals still -- slaves to the prejudices of the flesh.

The Thing that led me through this gallery of my own basal misgivings shared nothing of that with me. She toyed with it, amused by its quaintness. And when she turned around at last to stop me at the doors of our destination, I was shocked to see that she had at some point become a he.

"You must promise, before we go any further, that everything you see from this point on stays with you -- a secret. For your own protection, as well as mine. I hardly fear the ill will of your brethren -- many of whom I suspect are not as accepting as you -- but there are higher things with ears to your affairs that I suspect may not be so accepting, either. Do you promise me you won't go talking this around?"

My throat had suddenly become stiff and dry as I tried to form a response. I choked out what I hoped to be an affirmative, and nodded to reiterate the point. I knew it was unnecessary. She -- he? -- knew full well what I would do, and was only playing at drama for my benefit. As I watched him turn to cast open the doors, I marveled at how deceived I had been at his first appearance -- or perhaps he'd changed? It was the same face, the same eyes, that same ebony hair swept back into a delicate sash of braids -- the same body even -- but everything curiously re-sexed beneath my notice as we'd walked. And I had touched her hand when we'd first met outside the hall -- felt its warmth, its living pulse, the delicate structure of its bones, overlaid by flesh. I knew it to be real. This was not the evanescent avatar of Angel's Fog the Gods so often wore when they walked among their pets. This was a living creature like myself -- only somehow capable of this ghastly transformation.

We stepped through the door, out of the hallway's platinum fog of refracted sunlight and into a room that was saturated with a heavy crimson glow. The air here seemed to be its own source of light. It spread soft and diffuse through every corner, blotting the edges of shadows and hazing the finer details of my surroundings. The character of my guide shifted radically now as he stepped through the door ahead of me. Suddenly he became a Hellenistic blonde. She turned to me only a few steps out of the entryway, beaming that disarming, unsettling smile. The same that had greeted me at my arrival.

"Watch," she said, as if the things I'd seen already amounted to nothing but trifles.

And then she revealed to me a hint of the magic I had come to see.

We stood on the bottom face of a voluminous octahedron -- the door that had been behind us moments ago had vanished, swallowed by the wall. Buoyed on the moist currents of air circulating in the center of the room hung veils of a white, diaphanous material. They congealed out of thin air and swirled together, out of the corners and into the center of the room. For minutes, they entertained us with a dizzy introductory dance. And then, one by one, they began to come apart, dissolving and diffusing together, forming a knot at the chamber's heart.

Droplets of moisture condensed out of the hazy atmosphere and fell impossibly toward that central confluence. Within minutes, a quivering sphere of fluid had formed there. The twists of white material had dissolved within it. Only a few shreds remained, sheeting across its surface. At first perfectly transparent, it began to grow cloudy. I squinted to see through it -- through the rheumy fog of my own ancient vision.

My eyes played tricks on me. The hovering globule began to pulsate slowly. The red of the room bled into its bulk. Within seconds, the light around me went from crimson to hazy white, and the floating globule of fluid turned blood red. As I watched, an explosion of dark little tendrils branched out from the center of the mass, veining it with a throbbing, anfractuous structure.

I saw something I could only describe as a heart congeal at its center. It grew from a speck in moments, pumping in time with the shuddering vibration of the intricate web-work in which it nestled. I scarcely noticed that my guide had begun laughing, gleefully, manically, clapping her hands as the dance of perverse magic went on in the air above us. I had become so engrossed that I had lost all track of her shifting features. She -- he? -- it? -- was trying on new faces as quickly as the hovering globule was trying out different strategies of organizing its components, all the while growing and developing at blinding speed. It was like watching a three dimensional puzzle assemble itself -- a puzzle whose pieces were the very fundaments of life itself.

My guide began gesticulating wildly with its hands -- 'it' was at this point the only pronoun I could think to apply to it. It had taken on, in the past few seconds alone, traits both distinctly male and female ... and neither. It twisted and shuddered, laughing and crying out in what looked to be an almost orgasmic kind of bliss. I knew without a doubt then, as I watched it, that it was indeed much more than it appeared. My skin crawled with the sensation that its being extended far beyond the amorphous body I saw before me -- that its apparent identity crisis was just a reflection of a much larger, much more complete kind of being. It was not its failing that it could not make up its mind as to the appearance it wished to wear. Rather, it was my failing that I could not accept the constancy of identity behind its masks.

The thing growing in the air above us was as much a part of it as its avatar-body -- as much as the Hall. As much as, I began to suspect, the whole world. I felt suddenly outside myself -- that I was not my own person. A deep, unraveling terror began to build inside me. The thing over our heads had begun to take shape. It was a thing not unlike those I had seen on my way in -- those once- living statues encased in glass. Only this thing was still alive ... or rapidly on its way to becoming alive. In the moments of my floundering apprehension, it had grown nerves, skeleton and now the rudiments of a musculature around the framework its circulatory system had laid down.

It was a demonstration of the Flesh Sculptors' highest art, being carried out before my very eyes. Just like a puzzle, they assembled bodies one molecule -- one cell -- at a time, constructing complete creatures from scratch. And, amazingly, those creatures lived. Not at the end -- not with some flash of lightning or zap of unnatural magic to impart that vital spark -- but from the beginning, from the moment the first cells were assembled and guided nimbly by those phantom fingers into place.

The Sculptors must work fast, for at first their products are unstable. They bring each new cell into being and guide it into contact with its siblings. They lace the structure of the thing together until it takes hold of its own form-to-be. Every branching vein, every twisting sinew or quivering nerve they place with clockwork precision. Like building ships in bottles from scraps of balsa wood, they assemble beings in vats from stray molecules and proteins in solution. The awesome delicacy of the procedure took my breath away ... along with the horrifying rapidity at which they went from an empty room of air-suspended protein fragments to a fully functioning product.

In this case, a fully functioning human being.

It floated there in its amniotic bubble, fully formed, fully human. All this only a scant five or six minutes after we had entered the room. It was as perfect as my guide -- as artfully crafted, as much a testament to the skill and mastery of its creator as the body that creator wore itself. My guide had suddenly stopped laughing. Now he was watching me keenly, following my twitching, apoplectic movements and my gaping, bewildered stares with eyes that shone dark like polished onyx, pattered with flecks of jade.

"I want to offer you a gift for coming here," he said. "A thank you ... for being an audience to my work. It's been some time since I've been able to work for anyone. I would be honored if you would give me the satisfaction ... of accepting my work as your gift?"

If it was a genuine question, I had no doubt he already knew my answer. I stood in the presence of a creature so far above me as to be a god of gods ... a creature so beyond my comprehension as to regard me with little more consideration than I might a bacterium. And yet it wanted to offer me a gift? To what end, I wondered, even as I nodded my ascent, throat too clenched to give words to my robotic acceptance.

It -- she, as she had shifted once again into the female form I'd known initially and seemed, for once, to settle into a temporary kind of permanence with that shape -- smiled at me again. It was the same smile she had worn on our way here. "You understand," she said, "that what we still find some challenge in is the sculpting of a mind. I would very much like to try ... if you would be willing ... to sculpt your thoughts in this flesh?"

A million reasons for refusal escaped my thinking that day. Whatever happened next, I cannot recall with any certainty. All I know is that I left that hall a different man than I had entered. A better man, I think. A man with greater understanding of his world.

Certainly, if nothing more, a younger man with uncounted centuries of life still left to live.

As I have studied over the years -- as I have come to understand the Sculptors' talents and their methods; to comprehend the finer delicacies of their craft -- I have begun to see the appeal of the Sculptor's art. To create life, to create being ... is as intoxicating a venture as ever I could pursue. And so I have been considering, in the centuries since my rebirth, that I might like to one day try my hand at that curious art.

Perhaps then I will return to the Flesh Sculptors' Hall. Not this time to visit, but to stay.

Severing
The Second Federation
3670 AT

Josie Goodman

The First Federation became too large, and too complex, and fell apart. Meanwhile, the transapients were gaining power and influence, and developing strange new technologies. Most importantly they created the first archailects, gigantic intellects housed in structures far bigger than the Earth. These new god-like beings developed wormhole technology that could bring the distant colonies within reach, and reactionless drive spacecraft that could approach the speed of light. This allowed a new phase of rapid expansion of explored space, a region now known as the Terragen Sphere.

The new gods forged extensive new empires, dividing up the sectors of space between themselves; older established empires and political alliances were absorbed or swept away in a series of interstellar wars. Eventually a new, loose alliance of archailect empires emerged, the Second Federation; humans and other human-level entities were still the most common citizens in these empires, and became known as modosophonts: the 'mode', or most common type, of 'sophont', thinking being. But the modosophonts were definitely the junior partners in the new Federation.

Certain factions conceived the idea that modosophonts were disadvantaged in this new relationship, so worked to devise methods that would allow them to ascend towards transapient status themselves, and eventually even godhood. Not everyone they attempted to help was prepared for such a process. Any modosophont that took the road of ascension or transcension would be changed profoundly by the process, and the resulting transapient could be so different from the original that it might reject all that it had once held dear.

Josie Goodman describes events in a distant colony system affected by an unexpected ascension and the aftermath.

Atalya's mining ship dove straight down through orange ammonia clouds to the white water clouds below. She wore a standard interface mask as any miner would, within the system she herself had designed. The mask brought a simple color range to her vision, overlaid with navigational info strings. But through the enhanced visual centers of her brain Atalya saw a variety of hues the remote miners would never see: an exaltation of orange, blendings of soft white against vibrant white. A mental touch to an icon of her internal workspace recorded the flow of images, routing them into temporary storage in one of her ring implants.

With a quick hand gesture she flicked the craft's sonar into search pulses. Blips formed on the mask's display showing whorls of turbulence, black dots indicating other mining ships. Her body's hearing analogue chose frequency-shifted versions of the tones, rendering them as thrumming and humming. These were the music of a gas giant, music her virtual creatures would feel and hear. Another mental touch stored these in a second ring.

A slight motion of Atalya's gloved fingers transferred instructions. Buoyancy wings inflated from the craft's spine. From the tapering fluked tail, steering jets fired. The main engine went to standby, and the ship moved in gliding formation, catching a thermal, drifting up. Pressure bands formed along the skin of her back and arms; the sensations of balance and flight. All stored.

But now play time was over. She still had work to do on this last phase of her job for the Consortium. Centering her awareness in her workspace, Atalya relegated remote control of the craft to a partialmind, duplicated from the sensory and reactive subroutines needed to keep the ship stable.

Then she touched the blue snifter icon, bringing up from her nanobones the patterns of her modified personality adapted for systemic search. The snifter fit over her primary personality like a second skin, a skin covered with optical analogues. Interfacing with the Consortium's remote-navigation system, Atalya touched her way through the entrance code, bypassed the filters, and then swam the snifter through the data lanes.

The snifter processed input through five sets of visual imagery, each designed to catch the first layer of intelligence ordering. The beginning set showed data bits as schools of golden fish, each school performing its own simple (or complex!) design. She'd moved through three-fourths of the system before the snifter spotted deviance. A line of fish changed lanes, engulfed parts of two other schools, re-ordered them into long loops, then headed for the next lane out.

Atalya switched the snifter to its second set and saw the deviance as strings of numbers, watching them shift patterns, adding, multiplying, squaring. Moving in varied ways. Expanding possibilities through merging, branching into subroutines. Exploring its environment.

The algorithm was still subturing, so not protected by law. But she'd become fastidious in her work; she loathed waste.

Atalya triggered open a storage amulet, then copied and compressed the deviant routine into it.

Then she triggered the navigation system's own defense program, coded the pattern and location, adding the new deviance into its memory. She backtracked the snifter and set it to roam the remaining levels of the system, running through its image sets. Finding everything clean. Pure and secure, just as the nebs insisted.

The snifter's modules re-folded into her bones; Atalya took back control of the mining craft, moving up.

The ammonia layers thinned, and slanting lines of yellow light edged the tops of the clouds as the craft moved through. Atalya's fingers traced the patterns of reconfiguration; wings and rudder fins deflated and contracted, wings moved into their slots, and tail retracted. Acceleration numbers flooded the left of her vision.

Then green vector lines sped across the display, showing the way to Outpost; all she had to do was hold it steady through deceleration. Finally the ship was home; she coded the trigger for the airlock, it slid open, and the ship moved through, the lock cycled. She tucked the craft into its berth, clicked it off.

She removed mask and gloves.

The bay was quiet and dimly lit; long rows of masked miners sat at consoles, hands gesturing, touching open the hydrogen-scoops of their distant ships. Atalya walked down the aisle, and stopped at the door for an instant. Just looking. She'd brought it all together, made it happen the way the nearbaseline Consortium wanted. *Finished. Time to say good-bye.*

As she'd said goodbyes to so many of her own people before coming here to Outpost for the last time. This was a time of severing for her clan, partings from people she'd known the whole of her life, and very soon the re-combining into a new populace. The new habship of their Progeny fleet waited in high orbit, having completed the last of its growth cycles. Her future lay with it.

But first…

But first…

She caught the tram, heading away from the bare grey-red asteroid walls of Outpost's mining and reclamation sectors, toward Temple Park and Consortium offices. Residential complexes passed overhead, beyond the lightthread.

The office structures were also grey-red, but their stone was shaped into elegant blocks, the buildings grouped into pleasingly complex arrangements. Ancient Sanskrit flowed in slow dignified processions across the tops of doorways and porticos. From the tram station, Atalya crossed to a path that led between the complexes, moving into the parkland at their center.

Temple Park was hers too. A virtual slice drawn from one version of the ancients' heaven; Dravidian gods and goddesses, lost to one world, recaptured in another. Even now their expressions turned inward, glimpsing some incredible elsewhere, diverging from all outer places and times. Atalya felt kinship in that. Their expressions were drawn from those of her own people while quick-shifting realities. It had seemed an appropriate and subtle grafting from her shiplife onto this ancient fantasy. But it was something she had neglected to mention to the nebs.

Bawajit waited beside the reflecting pool, watching her approach. Hands together, he bowed in greeting, and she returned the gesture. He'd spread a blue silk cloth upon the virtual grass, and now invited her to sit. A carafe of sparkling juice and two stemmed glasses waited at the edge of the cloth. He poured and handed her a glass. Threadlight gleamed along the rim. Virtual sunlight played upon the pond and outlined the graceful, voluptuous bodies of the gods in their ascending and descending temple niches.

Bawajit's gaze met hers and held it. "Endings and beginnings, all epicycles within the Great Cycle." He spoke softly, then sighed.

She'd grown accustomed to his pronouncements, his pretensions, knowing he believed many of them himself. She also knew he fancied himself in love with her, even as he was horrified at the thought. He'd never touched her; would never touch her impure flesh, imagining what lay beneath it.

"Endings and beginnings," she replied. They both sipped. The drink hinted at flavors both sweet and tangy. *Hmm. Perhaps I'll add it to Progeny 7's taste library. A memento.* By glancing left, she touched off an inner chemical analysis, then stored it.

Atalya gazed toward the pool. Cameras beneath the illusion captured their images, adding their reflections to the scene. Bawajit's dark skin and long straight black hair. The crown of computronium rings implanted into her pale, hairless scalp. Brown eyes – the trait they shared.

"Do your people appreciate your artistry?" He asked. "None of them have come here, have they? To see the Temple's re-creation." He paused for an instant. "But I suppose they consider themselves far beyond baseline culture, the merely human." The shape of his mouth registered distaste. Then with a motion of his hand, he waved the words away. "I apologize. I don't wish to spoil the moment."

There was no way to deny what he'd said. So she talked around it. "Most times, I wouldn't have done all this on my own. My cohere and I prefer working together, as we did in the first programming phase of the mining interface. But the construction and systems-growth of our new ship has preoccupied most of us this past longcycle." She could explain no further; there was not enough shared language, nor shared experience, with which to convey the complex intertwinings of alife and matter which made up the habship.

She edged a tone of regret into her voice. "Croasions are a sociable people, learning from each job we do, before moving on. Perhaps there will yet be time to bring others. But if you are happy here, with the re-creation, I feel content with my work." Atalya let her gaze roam across the pool, to the upper reaches of the temple. She'd considered keeping a copy, but then decided to play fair. The Shambalista Consortium requested that their Temple be the only one of its kind. And they'd paid well, helping defray the cost of *Progeny 7*'s creation.

"Your cohere – your age mates?" Bawajit asked. He'd asked her few personal questions during their acquaintanceship. But she'd learned much about his childhood, his ancestral lineage, and the founding of the mining consortium.

"Some are, more or less," she answered. Atalya doubted he wanted to hear details of genetic templates and bodymod injections, or the quick-growth that eliminated the need for early childhood. "Not all our populace cluster into coheres. We're just a group of people who like living and working together, playing together."

From his expression, Atalya understood she'd given him more than he wanted.

He shook his head. "I have no way to imagine what your life is like. Nor that of any cyborg clade, of course. It's not something I ever thought I'd want to imagine." He paused, and then laughed softly. "But when I'm with you, I feel curious. I want to know more about you. Yet when you answer my questions, I wish that you hadn't. We have nothing in common really, except that our far ancestors were all Earth Human."

"There's that much then," Atalya replied.

"Do you ever wish we were living then, instead of now?" He asked.

"No." She said, simply, truthfully.

He sighed in an exaggerated manner, then shrugged. "I do. Or perhaps I only wish our future had not departed so radically from the past." He gestured toward the temple. "I don't believe in the old gods and goddesses. But I love the destiny they represented. What we could have become."

"If not for the AI. And clades like mine."

"Atalya, I'm saying everything I shouldn't. But I know I won't see you again. And we've said so little, really."

"We've talked often," she reminded him.

"And said so little," he repeated.

They finished their drinks, and Bawajit put the glasses back down on the cloth's edge.

"Your ship…" he paused, catching her glance before continuing, "Is it a god?"

"No. The Progeny fleet, my clan's fleet, is not even fully sentient. There are ways in which my people are similar to yours." She couldn't suppress a moment's laughter at his expression. "We prefer to keep our own ways. We don't mingle with the gods. Layered smallminds and semisentients comprise the inner life of the ship. A savant monitors the drive. But only with the linkage of our own psyches into the ship does it approach true consciousness. It may seem a subtle distinction to you; but I assure you it's of great importance to us."

He nodded. "Even so, it is painful to imagine all those half-minds, like spectres, touching your own."

She had no reply to that.

Then he said, "Atalya, we will have none of them in Outpost's systems. None of those smallminds or semisentients. This was clearly stated in the contract your negotiators signed. I don't want to seem insistent or suspicious. But I need your assurance that the mining interface is clear of deviance."

"You have my assurance," Atalya said. Her fingers stroked the computronium amulet in a protective gesture. "All terms of the contract have been fulfilled."

She stood, and he hastily got to his feet, brushing the wrinkles from his tunic.

"I need to leave now," she told him.

Bawajit nodded. His hand reached out as if to touch hers, then drew back into his accustomed prayer-like gesture as he bowed. "Farewell. May your destiny be a joyful one."

"And may yours be joyful as well," she replied in kind.

Atalya turned from Bawajit and the virtual temple, walked along the asteroid-stone path without looking back — not even with the sensor array of her computronium rings. Then she waited for the tram that would take her back to the docking port, her shuttle and her life. *Destiny*. Yes. She had one.

Atalya lay comfortably webbed, linked to shuttle sensors, nearing the end of her short journey. The two Progeny ships, temporarily spine-locked by collapsible modules, rings spinning, filled her viewpoint. Her past and future, for the moment, still joined.

She interfaced with Shipguard, allowing access to her mind patterns. Recognition. Welcome. Entry into the main sensor net of receivers and transmitters.

The shuttle slid into the docking bay, was moved along the guideway by subsidiary alife and berthed. Atalya took a suit from shuttle storage, touched into its smallmind and waited as it slipped around her, then drew its transparent cowl down across her face. Popping the hatch, she dropped down. The bay was unpressurized, but rotated as did the ship's hab rings, creating 1g. She bounded across the deck to the nearest ladder, climbed to the spine entrance, went through the lock and into a botcar. Told the suit to recede, pocketed it. Strapping herself in, she directed the car to Ring 1, and shunted it onto the main track.

Blinking into Shipnet brought a webwork of glowing symbols. Atalya scanned quickly through the layers of alife that monitored and inhabited the internal systems, forming the ship's subconscious. Glyphs and purrs and clicks: assurances of stability. Then she linked into the populace communications hub and was startled by silence. It seemed no one was home; though that was unlikely. Or all were locked into privacy. *Even more unlikely.*

The severing of *Progeny 3*'s populace wrought major changes, bringing inevitable turmoil and instability into their lives. But emotions were never allowed to run out of control. *We're far from being helpless nebs after all.* And there was compensatory excitement in the shaping of their new shiplife.

Calling up the personality matrices schematic, she saw two srreals: Gedd linked into Navigation; Eyono in Engineering. Both srreals were shadowed, indicating privacy. *But of course. Each would be developing more subtle blending with, and understanding of, the alife in their chosen work areas.*

But where is everyone else? Obviously on Progeny 3. Farewells must have turned sentimental, or raucous. Atalya considered calling her cohere there, then decided to use the time alone, for her work. She was eager to merge the newest recordings into her developing virch. Thus far she'd kept it locked, shown it to no one. But she wanted its environment complete, as well as her own avatar lifeform, when the *Progeny 5* docked, and their portion of the new populace settled in.

Atalya had high expectations of her artistry, and its place in the virtual life of the new ship's culture. Her cohere, and other fans of her work, had tried to persuade her to copy Coral Resort into *Progeny 7*'s archive. But she refused. It had been one of the most popular virtual worlds of *Progeny 3* for the past 2 longcycles. Scenes from Resort had been chosen for semi-permanent holo status in two public squares. And Atalya knew that's where it belonged, to the past, to 3's archives, a part of the culture that had severed to populate *Progeny 7*. For a while she'd felt a bit desperate, needing to begin some new creation, then realized her work on the remote-mining system provided a perfect background.

Now using grab bars she moved from the spine into the Ring's lock, then out, enjoying the g feel, loped down the short corridor to Garden Plaza and the entrance to her cohere's apartment cluster. Passing beneath the plaza's central treebot, Atalya slowed her pace, listening to the ever-changing song of its leaves. She glanced up through its branches to the light-tiles of the cupola. Three of her genetic parents had designed the plaza, and it was one of her favorite sites on the new ship. An idea occurred to her. She needed a place for the routine she'd copied into her amulet.

Clicking a local icon linked her to the plaza's monitoring subsentient. Its smallmind recognized her, and she watched through its optics the interrelationships of the plaza's software and hardware. One subroutine made its rounds, touching along each treebot module, scanning codes from root sensors and the evolving patterns of leaves, testing the chemical bath of the tree's nutrient pool, querying each light tile and paving tile. The monitor-core gathered the data, compared it to a schematic and offered it to Atalya, forming a bright green srreal at the top of her vision. After an instant the subroutine moved into another identical round. Meanwhile the core flicked on a different subroutine. This one moved deeper into the treebot, examining the connections between modules, sites where separation would occur when the ship reconfigured for wormhole entry.

Atalya keyed in the file size and queried the monitor core for permission to enter her captured routine. It displayed a diagram of distribution possibilities. Atalya agreed, and the monitor readied a re-sequencing subroutine. Then its srreal turned pale, indicating alife stress.

It will take some getting used to, Atalya realized. *For the deviant routine and the monitor.*

She keyed its own pattern back to the core, as reassurance. Then placing her hand against a floor tile she accessed a data node, touched her amulet and let the routine flow through her, decompressing into the plaza's system. For a moment she felt she'd betrayed it, watching its code taken apart, re-sequenced and distributed. But she stood beneath the treebot, tracked the rerouting, noting the infinitesimal changes in leaf song. When the plaza achieved its new equilibrium, Atalya smiled. "You see; I knew we could do it."

Then she crossed Garden Plaza, moving into the corridor that bordered her cohere's cluster. The door recognized her, and she went through into a common room, spent a few moments disliking the apartment's emptiness, then went into her own suite, toggled a nutrient tap into a tall glass, and settled down on a couch, feet tucked beneath her.

Work. Everything else will wait. The room's net held the entry code to her virch world — Swirling Orange — the world code itself already expanded into other nodes throughout the ship. Her internal awareness traveled the information strings, knowing what features of the world each segment represented. She moved the recordings from her computronium ring storage, sent each through a translation program, then spliced the code into the proper strings.

Then Atalya blinked the virch on and shifted into its waveband. The functions of her avatar gathered, surrounding her awareness. She gazed out at her world through its multispectral eyes. Above her, drifting among water clouds, a cluster of bright helium balloons carried the gridwork platform with its tethers- the perfect site for creature socializing.

Her jet-powered body could almost, but not quite, have evolved and lived within a physical gas giant. Atalya's virches were a blend of possibility and fantasy. Though a few purists derided her creations, she felt comfortable with her aesthetic philosophy of rule-bending. And now she was pleased with the expanded range of sensations given by the new splicings.

With a whiplike motion of her fluked tail, she steered to her left, and up. A flick of back muscle spread her wings wide, and she lifted, slender arms crossed at her chest against a soft leather harness. Nearing the platform, she reached out and grasped a tether, hooking it to her harness. A school of purple and red blossom-like creatures trailed across her viewpoint. They were little more than delicate skeletons and buoyancy pods; similar skeletons made up the trim of her harness. Gradually, as she drifted, drinking in the sensations, the pleasure of it seeped away. Though her avatar possessed radio telepathy and chromatophore capability, the world was thus far a solitary place. *Lovely, but lonely.*

Atalya now felt consumed by the need to create another avatar from the prototype of the first. *The second avatar will be Jan's.* She'd surprise him with it; he'd be the first of the cohere to see the virch. The avatars after that would belong to Loise and Freddmn. Leaving the virch, she clicked into her workspace, and began duplicating sections of code, making subtle changes and adjustments. The avatar couldn't be completed until Jan decided its gender, but it would be inhabitable. Jan could be a part of her world. Finally she entered the avatar's code into the program, creating an icon for it.

She wanted to tell Jan, right now, regardless of what he was doing. *And what was he doing? What is everyone doing?*

Atalya walked back into the common room, moving restlessly among the couches and cushions. Blinking into the ship's personality matrice, she discovered nothing had changed; only the srreals of two people were aboard, both in privacy mode. She clicked into communications hub and found no waiting messages. Calling up that subsystem's alife she subvocally ordered it to connect with *Progeny 3*. Instead of a connection menu, she saw in the right corner of her internal viewpoint the ship's glyph, in shadow. "Privacy lock – not for the whole bloody ship!" She shouted.

She was shouting at alife. *Loss of self control– how disappointingly nebbish. Though perhaps the fault does lie with the alife.* Calling up the communications monitor, she ordered a system diagnostic, and a few moments late received an affirmative reply. She again tried to connect, and again received the privacy glyph.

Atalya's life did not include events that made no sense. Now, suddenly, it did. And she couldn't just pace around, wondering why. She'd have to go there, through the spine's temporary corridor leading to *Progeny 3*. Though she hadn't expected to do so again; she'd said her goodbyes before her last trip to Outpost.

Atalya walked out the door to the plaza. As she moved beneath the branches of the treebot, a message notice clicked into her inner vision. She blinked it open, and saw Jan's srreal. A moment later the srreal was replaced by his real image; dark brown skin, blue eyes, crown of computronium rings.

Subvocally, she sent, ~What's happening there? Has something gone wrong?~

~Wrong, no. But a lot has happened since you left. I . . .this is hard to say, 'Tal. I know you won't like it, that you won't be coming with us. *New Morning* has run simulations of your mind state.~

Things are worse than I'd imagined; Jan seems to be living in some alternative world! An internal alarm sent a series of red dots across her vision, warning of chemical cascades. Her bodimonitor requested permission to counteract their effect. She ignored it.

~*New Morning*- – who the hell is *New Morning* and what right has he, she, or e to run simulations of my mind state?~ Shouting now seemed an appropriate reaction. Even the subvocal equivalent of shouting.

Jan glanced away from her, and down, before meeting her eyes. ~*New Morning* is the name the ship took. Our ship, *Progeny 3*. E achieved sapience and is ready to ascend. So are we, 'Tal.~

Atalya laughed, abruptly relieved. ~So, this is a joke. All right, enough is enough.~

His expression told her otherwise. ~Ascension has to happen eventually, for everyone. I hadn't thought about being ready. None of us were planning it. But when *New Morning* asked our help in creating an ascension package, everything just came together in my mind. And everyone had the same experience. Well, except for Gedd and Eyono. They're little more than youngsters, after all. It was amazing, almost transcendent. I know you can't imagine what it was like, and I'm sorry about that 'Tal. Very sorry.~

It's meme subversion! The ship subverted the whole populace. Atalya's awareness dropped into her workspace, where she frantically accessed blocks of knowledge and theory on meme subversion and its antidotes.

In moments she knew what she'd already suspected; there were no remedies available to her, not in an immediate timeframe. *New Morning* was too far ahead of her.

Atalya shifted back into the physical, noted she was sitting on the paving tiles, the warmth of her presence causing colorful designs to ripple out across the plaza. Her back brushed against the rim of the treebot's nutrient pool. When had she decided to sit? She brought Jan's image into the center of her visual focus. She wasn't quite ready to admit defeat. *If I can find some small loophole in the subversion!* ~How can you give up our plans for *Progeny 7*? Everything we accomplished this longcycle. Do you remember our shifts in overseeing the asteroid excavation– setting the factory templates, birthing the alife?~

~ I haven't lost any memories. But my perspective has changed. All those things seem to have happened long ago, to someone I was . . .then.~

~Jan, do you remember us? You and me, together? ~

~'Talya. Don't go on with this. Accept what's happened. We all wish you the best – for now, and for your future ascension. *New Morning* will be undocking in four minicycles. But *Progeny 5* has moved into the system. You won't have to wait long for its docking. Gedd and Eyono are already onboard with you. You'll go on with your plans for the ship.~

~With half the planned populace? Without our cohere?~ Atalya hated the pleading tone of her voice. She'd never heard it before. A slight eye movement to the left authorized her bodimonitor's hormonal intervention.

~Good-bye 'Talya. From all of us.~ His gaze held hers, waiting, his eyebrows lifted.

~Good-bye, Jan. Tell the others.~

His image disappeared.

Sometime later she noticed she still sat beneath the treebot. She felt sudden hatred for the plaza and its subsentient routines and subroutines, for the deviance she'd rescued and coded into it. Remembering the deviant's deliberate; multiple efforts at expansion into its original environment, Atalya wished she'd left it to the mercies of the defense system. Was that the way *Progeny 3* had become *New Morning*: from a single routine extending, merging, expanding, subverting? How long had it taken to unbalance the steady state of the alife layers, how long to ruin the plans for her life? Certainly no more than three smallcycles. For the first time, Atalya realized the delicate, fragile balance of that steady state.

Did nebs like Bawajit and his Shamballistas actually have a better grasp of reality, keeping themselves separate from alife?

Even so, their version of truth had nothing to do with her. She was twin-stream, as much artificial as organic.

Will this happen again? Will Progeny 7 gain sentience someday?

Could she lose this ship too?

She remembered the snifter, asleep now in her nanobones. If she spliced it into her primary personality, she'd become ever vigilant, watchful for alife deviance. Her body and sense of self chilled at the thought. She wondered what that would do to her art. Could she create and destroy at the same time? Her thoughts turned to the Dravidian gods of Temple Park. Her interpretation of the old mythologies. They'd surely been capable of destruction, to protect what they'd loved. Yet their world had ended.

As hers would also. As Jan had said, ascension had to happen for everyone, eventually. The archailects must have programmed that into the structure of the universe, alife and organic. But she had some control over when; more time was available to her than to the ancients. She could find new loves, create new worlds, and protect them.

Closing her awareness from the ship, she entered her workspace and touched the blue snifter icon, waking her modified self.

~You have no idea how busy we're going to be~ she told it.

Ghostkill
The Commonwealth of Empires
5250 AT

Steve Bowers

The Version War was long over and for now the Terragen Sphere was at peace. A multitude of species lived in harmony under the guidance of those transapients who made it their business to take care of them. However transapients are complex entities, and have their own agendas. Any particular transapient may develop new interests, or change over time in unpredictable ways; eventually that entity might transcend to an entirely new level of being, a change that can involve translocation to a larger and denser processing substrate such as a Moonbrain, Jupiter node, or Godstar, far from their erstwhile charges.

When the local transapient in charge of a modosophont polity transcends, those who are left behind can be left without oversight or guidance. Some of them see this as abandonment, others as liberation; others still see it as an opportunity not to be missed.

Ivonya-Ngia Habitat in the Aquila Rift, a relatively small structure in a system 350 light years from Sol, was first colonised by a group of augmented elephants in 2609AT. These sophisticated creatures continued to augment themselves until they underwent a mass-transcendence in 3909. Left abandoned, the habitat was recolonised by a variety of modosophonts, including humans and other mammals, and ruled at various times by a number of different transapient overseers, all of whom moved on in due course.

Steve Bowers describes events in this habitat when it has been left to its own devices after the latest transcendence, with several factions seeking to regain control before the situation descends into anarchy.

Lefty Muligan found it hard to blend into a crowd, even one as varied as this. He had two left hands, for a start. Also two left feet, but no right hands or feet to complete the set. But Muligan could see behind him just as well as in front. Better, to be accurate: the left side of him (which faced backwards at the moment) was entirely artificial, so had keener senses than his human half.

Representative Éimear, her voice discretely amplified, was saying "And, so, let me introduce to you the Vedokiklek Ambassador. Your Excellency, meet the people of Ivonya-Ngia." On six thick legs the insect-like sophont spidered forward, flanked by a gaggle of media-casters including the familiar figure of Niamn Coolan and her eye-girl.

The Ambassador had chosen to visit Ivonya-Ngia Habitat, a minor megastructure in an obscure system near the coreward end of the Aquila Rift, at a particularly chaotic moment in its history. Nobody could quite figure out what the Ambassador was hoping to achieve, but here je was, and Muligan and his fellow Invicta corpcops were determined to protect jer chitinous hide.

And the best bodyguard in a crowd was someone who could see an assailant approaching from behind without turning his head. Muligan scanned the crowd in all directions, studiously ignoring the thin insectile figure of the Ambassador as je shook limbs with the crowd.

A gentle breeze swayed jer long antennae. Like most everything else in this hab, the breeze was fake, just like the infinite blue sky five hundred metres above their heads. The sky, and the breeze, and the swaying grass were qualities built into the hab by its original owners - a clade of intelligent elephants who were all long gone now. Loving the open air and wide spaces, the 'phants had built this place to resemble a tree-studded open plain, and the humans who came here after their departure built structures on this plain because that is what humans prefer. Usually the structures built by humans in this environment were lightweight insubstantial edifices constructed from strong, thin, versatile materials, mostly erected for privacy and for aesthetic reasons. The plains were studded with tents, yurts, marquees and pavilions of various kinds.

Several other kinds of sophont now lived in this great rotating habitat alongside the humans, almost all genetically tweaked in some way with various degrees of surgical alteration and enhancement. Mostly modified animal species of several kinds, along with a small number of moravec robots which were mostly wearing surveillance harnesses to monitor and restrict their actions. Ivonya-Ngia habitat, thirty kilometres in radius and with sixty concentric layers, was in political turmoil at the moment, and a certain amount of anti-vec bigotry had surfaced as one of the symptoms. Even a half-and-half cyborg like Muligan was singled out sometimes.

In the diverse crowd were many factions and individuals who might pose a threat to the Ambassador. Vertebrate chauvinists, bigots who hate anything without a backbone. Fanatical AI worshippers, who hated the Ambassador's native hive as infidels who refused the rule of the AI Gods. And several rival anti-AI factions who disagreed with the Vedokiklek hive's particular brand of anti-AI belief. But these were the easy ones; the fanatics were nearly all well known to the police corporations in Ivonya-Ngia Hab, and were closely watched. More difficult to detect were the fame-seekers and psychopaths, who might seek to kill the outsystemer for their own notoriety, or for some twisted reason known only to themselves. Finally there might even be Hider or Backgrounder dissidents or assassins in this crowd, willing to kill for political motives known only to those who live on the outermost fringes of this solar system. Death could come to the Ambassador from many directions, and Muligan was thankful that his cybersenses could observe the crowd in most of those directions simultaneously.

Muligan's cyber-half was busily scanning faces, looking for known troublemakers. Using the strap-like eye-patch that stretched right around the artificial half of his head this was a relatively easy task. When he found anyone worth a second look he copped a quick gander with his human eye, which was generally better at reading people's emotions. There - an Mbogo gang-member; the kid was nervous, trying to look innocent, not really interested in the out-systemer at all.

~Kayescee spinward to you, O'Braian, Mbogo male neb; better give him a new shadow, ~ Muligan sent to his fellow corpcop, who was in a better position to intercept the kid if he caused trouble. The kid was a Kayescee, a Known Suspicious Character, mildly disguised but identifiable using the recognition software embedded in Muligan's cyberoptic array.

O'Braian, a muscle-bound hi-grav tweak more than a head shorter than most of the people on the habitat, quickly made his way through the crowd to where the kid was, just as Muligan's cyber-half detected the sonic signature of an energy loop starting to discharge.

~Kayescee's got a weapon – take him down, Ben! ~ he sent to O'Braian. The stocky tweak leaped at the kid through the crowd, knocking him over. Muligan couldn't see what was occurring, but a bright flash burst through the crowd accompanied by a startled curse from O'Braian,transmitted over the corpcop neural link channel.

~Ach, ya kreking goyt - lucky my armour took that, or you'da burnt me face off! ~ The little man struck with his electodusters and the kid fell limp. Hi-grav tweaks were generally small, but surprisingly fast and strong. ~Kid's covered in laser-emitting cloth, Lefty. Not the best weapon in the circumstances.~

Muligan agreed. ~ S'right; the beam couldn't focus through this crowd. Too many obstructions. Keep 'em peeled, guys; this could be a diversion. ~

As he sent this, his cyber-half noticed another Kayescee and ran through an assembly of checks to confirm the I.D. Muligan couldn't believe his luck at first. Then he began to worry, in case they blew it and fumbled the ball. They had been searching for this guy for weeks. He was the prime suspect – the only suspect – in the infamous Nosecutter murders. Whoever he was, he had been spotted on surveillance recordings taken at or near all of the crime scenes in that investigation but had never been caught.

~Guys – alert, alert, alert. I've got a visual on the Nosejob prime suspect. It's him; my recog software's made a positive ident. Better do a pre-emptive take-out. I'm on it. ~

Muligan was closest, and moved in quickly. The curious ambiguity in Lefty Muligan's bodyplan meant he could move in almost any direction with equal facility. He had been standing with his human-half facing forward and away from the Kayescee. Without turning round the cyber-half took control. Somewhat belatedly the Nosejob suspect noticed Muligan coming for him, a little expression of surprise crossing his face just before the cyborg, apparently running backwards, knocked him to the floor. Using carbon nanotube-reinforced cuffs Muligan secured his prisoner and knelt on the suspect's back. The human half of his face smiled up at the crowd in triumph while his cyberhalf attended to business. The throng of media-casters homed in on this latest disturbance. In front as usual was Coolan's eye-girl, Lena, observing the scene with her hi-tech eye-cams for her viewers.

Muligan winked his human eye at her (it looked like a one-eyed blink), and said aloud, knowing his words would be heard by viewers all over the hab, "Stand clear. There is no cause for alarm; the Invicta Police Corporation has the situation under control..."

His voice trailed off as his cyber-eye patch detected motion in the blue sky above, a swarm of insects or birds rapidly approaching from near the zenith. His artificial left arm bent round and shielded the human left side of his face, but numerous small and diamond sharp daggers rapidly embedded themselves in every part of his body. *What the krek!* he thought, as his cyborg-half rapidly plucked the wriggling blades from his skin and crushed them, with some difficulty. They looked like origami birds made from sheets of diamond, flailing and flapping in his toughened artificial hand. *What's controlling these gadgies, and how can I shut it off?*

Muligan glanced at the Nosejob suspect, who had his eyes tightly closed and lips working.

Was he communicating with someone, or something? If so, who or what?

Now a gasp came from the crowd, and Muligan staggered to his feet, looking for the reason for this new commotion. He plucked the last of the wriggling blades from his human-half and crushed it; the dust fell to the ground, shimmering as if it were still moving. Probably still dangerous, he thought, but forgot about it when he noticed the struggling figure of the Ambassador. Je was surrounded by a cloud of blade-weapons, larger than the ones which had attacked Muligan. *Damnation! That won't do the company reputation much good!* he thought. *Better do somethin' about it fast.*

~Daggs! Take care of this mo-pho for me,~ Muligan sent to the third member of his team, Daggs Doyel, who had that moment arrived by his side. Doyel was, in contrast to O'Braian, a tall, rangy nearbaseline hu with a multitude of weapons concealed about him: an ex-mercenary soldier, now a mercenary cop.

The 'mo-pho' (short for modosophont, a term widely used to describe any average sophont being) seemed alert, despite his tightly closed eyes and unsettling smile.

~ I'd better get over there and help the Bugmeister,~ sent Muligan.

~Okey, dokie, Lefty; this guy's goin' nowhere.~

Using his two left legs in practiced unison Muligan crabbed over to the ambassador, hoping to pluck the fluttering blades from jer skin before they penetrated. He knew that the reflexes possessed by his cyber-half were easily fast enough to do the job as long as he got there in time.

For some reason the flying blades were concentrated around the creature's facial proboscis. Moving with cyborg-rapidity, Muligan grabbed most of them, but not enough. Just one or two of the paper-thin blades managed to slip under the hard chitin shell of the Vedokiklek, and proceeded to worm their deadly way through jer soft internal flesh and tendons.

Muligan let out an involuntary yell.

The proboscis dropped off, accompanied by thick yellow ichor.

Seeing this, Doyel hauled the Nosecutter suspect to his feet. The suspect opened his eyes, saw the effects of the strange flying blade-like weapons, and smiled again. On their shared channel, Doyel sent an urgent message to Muligan and O'Braian.

~ Guys, my expert systems are tellin' me that this mo-pho is still sendin' commands ta those killer butterflies, even though we got him cuffed. He's usin' some sort of direct neural control on em - I'm pickin' up positive correlations here. If I don't do somethin' the Bugmeister is goin' ta be a very dead VIP. I suppose there is one easy way to put a stop to his tricks... ~

Doyel pulled a projectile weapon out of his sleeve and put a bullet in the suspect's head. The suspect dropped.

Muligan scowled. Doyel was always too quick to use deadly force. True enough, most citizens were well backed up and would be reconstituted in a matter of days or even hours, but kaboom the wrong Zar, and you're facing a hefty compensation claim. Still, it seemed to have been effective. The sharp-edged blade weapons embedded in the Ambassador were motionless now, and even the crushed remnants on the floor had stopped writhing. Muligan fumbled a smart bandage out of his belt pouch and slapped it on the Vedokiklek's nose area, stopping the ichor flow. Hopefully that should help, but he knew zip about the Ambassador's physiology, so he couldn't be sure.

(*Again with the noses*, Muligan thought. *What is it with this guy?*)

O'Braian sent from the edge of the crowd, ~Hey! I thought you dropped the Nosejob killer, Daggs. I've got a visual on him over here. He's seen me. Am in pursuit.~

~I think you may be mistaken; I'm lookin' at his brains on the floor, ~ Doyel sent.

~Then - who – the – krek - is- this? ~ O'Braian, running, sent a jerky vidfile from his own viewpoint. He was in pursuit of someone who looked exactly like the Nosecutter killer running away through the long savannah grass. In the vidfile, the killer had a strange, surprised look on his face. Perhaps he was surprised to be alive after being shot. With his own eyes, Muligan could just about make out the pair of figures as they ran across the sward and up a gentle slope towards the wall of the habitat. All the walls in Ivonya-Ngia hab were covered in 3D display emitters projecting an apparently limitless African plain into the eyes of the inhabitants -- a legacy of the hab's original owners. Of course everyone knew that it was an illusion, and avoided the gentle slopes that surrounded the foot of the walls.

He'll have to turn soon, one way or the other, or he'll hit the wall screen, Muligan thought. *O'Braian'll catch him easy, no matter which way he turns. He's a fast little goomba when he wants to be.*

The mysterious double ran straight up the ban, through the boundary of the display and into the illusory grassland beyond. At full pelt O'Braian followed him up the bank, bounced off the solid wall of the habitat and sat down, stunned. The fugitive disappeared into the distant, imaginary trees, beyond pursuit.

####

When you get the Call, you have to go. Even though he was busy clearing the area and directing the medics and socos, Muligan was called away from the crime scene by a summons from Representative Éimear's autosecretary. He had to attend in person, apparently; the Representative was holed up in a pavilion behind the ceremonial proscenium arch erected for the arrival of the Ambassador, so she wasn't too far away. Muligan was tempted to send his virtual avatar, but that would have been seen as disrespectful. After all, the Representative was paying the Invicta Corps to act as security at this gig, and so far they hadn't made too good a job of it.

Representative Éimear was seated at a temporary table in the backroom. The thin woven graphene walls of the tent-like structure allowed enough hablight in to show that she was angry. In the warm environment of this tropical habitat, humans needed only minimal shelter, a thin wall of translucent woven graphene to keep out the infrequent rain. Other species needed even less.

"What are we paying you for, exactly, Zar Muligan?" she fumed. "I invited the Ambassador to this habitat hoping to forge a new trade agreement and he ends up in the automedic after an assault by one of our local psychopaths. An individual who, I might add, you have signally failed to apprehend on several occasions in the past."

Muligan used his cyberhalf to reply, as he generally did when speaking in formal situations. His artificial half spoke with a deep, rich, even voice, and could be used to impress or intimidate as the occasion required. Now he merely sounded apologetic, but hopefully sincere. "We engaged the suspect, and terminated his activities before the Ambassador could be assassinated. This can be viewed as a successful outcome in many ways."

"Yes, I saw your attempt to 'terminate his activities'. Quite the show of force. But you do not seem to have been completely successful, if at all, judging from the fact that a virtual copy of the attacker was clearly seen running away. I assume that he had a backup ready to make his escape. You will need to find that backup urgently before it does any more damage."

Muligan remembered the surprised look on the virtual's face. "I'm not so sure that is what happened, Ma'am; it seemed as much of a shock to him as it was to us. But I'm confident that we will neutralise the copy, if indeed it does pose a threat."

"Just get it, will you? Intact and responsive, preferably. We would like to know what the reasons for this murderous attack were, and so do the Vedokiklek, I'm sure. I've got the second-in-command here, and I don't think je's very happy, though it's hard to tell."

"With your permission, Ma'am, I'd like to interview the second-in-command if I may. Je might know of some reason for this attack. There is even a remote possibility that this is some sort of conspiracy among their ranks, and this individual might know more about it than we do."

"I suppose you better had. There'd only be questions asked if you didn't. You won't get much joy out of the 'Klek, though; practically no-one can understand them as it is. Best take Academician Andeson along with you to the interview; he's our best – our only – expert on the species." The Representative touched the lapel of her green suit-jacket. "Academician, would you please join us?" She slumped back in her chair, clearly unhappy with the day's events.

Muligan continued to stand in front of the Representative's desk as he waited. Standing was generally a lot easier to manage than sitting, given his unusual bodyplan; almost all his limbs were double jointed in one way or another, but sitting on a chair could look a bit ungainly and undignified. Better to stand up in a formal situation like this, he thought.

On the desk was an antique black-and-yellow paperback book. Muligan's human eye, which was facing the seated woman, could not read the title at this angle, but his cyberhalf quickly scanned it for him. *Ascension for Dummies*. Of course. There was a power vacuum to fill; no doubt the Representative would like to become the next transapient in this hab. Muligan felt sure she was not the only one.

At length the 'expert', a young-looking human male in academic robes, entered the room through the doorflap. He looked at Muligan curiously.

"How are the 'Klek reacting to the news, Academician?" asked the Representative.

"It's very difficult to say. They show no major changes in behaviour, but they display an increased level of maxillo-labial twitching without accompanying verbalisation. I don't think they are happy."

"I see. This is Zar Muligan of the Invicta Police Corporation, who is handling the investigation for me. He needs to talk to the Second Sibling for the purposes of that investigation. You had best accompany him, to act as cultural interpreter."

"I'll do my best," said the academician in his thick Edenese accent. "But this species is not well understood; my interpretations might not be of much help."

"See what you can do," said the Representative, and dimissed them.

The Academician led Muligan into an adjacent chamber that was filled with the peculiar scent of the Vedokiklek. Six or seven individuals were huddled together in a corner like giant locusts. One, identical to the rest, moved forward half a metre. Jer head barely came up to Muligan's waist. The body of the creature was covered in a keratin shell, but je seemed to have a bony endoskeleton as well; je breathed visibly presumably using lungs rather than spiracles. To Muligan it seemed that jer resemblance to an insect was quite superficial.

Andeson spoke. "Second Sibling? I have someone who would like to speak with you."

The Vedokiklek's voice sounded like a hundred bees all humming at once. "This is acceptable."

"The Second Sibling is now the acting decision-maker in the 'Klek hive, purely by dint of birth order," said Andeson. "When the Ambassador becomes fit once more, je will assume that role once more. It seems to be little more than a figurehead position, in any case."

Muligan addressed the insect-like sophont, still using his formal cyber-voice. "I must ask you if you know of any reason why the Ambassador might have been attacked. Do you have any enemies among the people of this habitat?"

"This sibling knows of no reason for this event to occur. This sibling is filled with surprise and dismay." The complex arrangement of jaws and palps beneath the sophont's head continued to twitch; if Andeson was right that indicated a certain level of disquiet.

Andeson said "The 'Klek have had very limited contact with the rest of Sephirotic culture. Only a few specialists like myself and a documentary crew have even spoken to them before today. Perhaps you saw the documentary?"

"Yes, I did," said hu-Muligan. His cyberhalf added "I wasn't impressed; I've deleted my memories of most of it. If necessary I could access a copy from the local media stores."

"I wouldn't bother; it was rubbish," the Academician said. "They made the 'Klek social organisation sound like some sort of enslavement. It is nothing of the sort. The 'Kleks have a rigid code of behaviour, but they reach concensus by extremely sophisticated debate. The command structure only exists to arbitrate when they have to make a choice between different strategies, and that rarely happens since the 'Klek are all so similar to one another."

"Is that so?"

Muligan thought for a bit then addressed the insectile being again. "Could there be a dissident faction among your own people who might wish to harm the Ambassador, possibly by using an agent or agents within this habitat? Does the Ambassador have any enemies among your own people?"

The Second Sibling's mouthparts moved even more frantically; this did not seem to affect jer speech patterns noticably. "This sibling has never heard of any such thing amongst the Vedokiklek. The Vedokiklek could not be enemies to their own siblings. This is not possible. Do humans become enemies to their own kind?"

"I'm afraid they do, that's why we have policemen," hu-Mulligan said. "Thank you. You have been most helpful."

As they walked back to the crime scene Andeson caught Muligan by his human left elbow and said earnestly, "The 'Klek seem to be constitutionally incapable of the sort of intrigue you are imagining, Zar Muligan. If you are looking for the guilty party you should search for the sort of vertebrate chauvinist fanatic who would be inspired by the media hype surrounding this clade. Believe me, the Klek are the innocent parties in this affair."

"I'll bear that in mind," said hu-Muligan shortly. His cyberhalf continued "Your assistance, and your opinions, are appreciated, Academician." With that the half-and half cyborg set off for the yurt that was the temporary headquarters of the Invicta Policing Corporation on this level, where O'Braian and Doyel were waiting to be debriefed. *That should be a barrel of laughs*, he thought bitterly.

####

"So you had ter kill another one, Doyel! What is it with you and killin' people?" O'Braian was as mad as a meataxe.

"Th' mo-pho was controlling them flying jack-knives by E-M. Lefty ain't the' only one with augments; I got a few things I picked up in the old days. Killin' him was the quickest an' safest course of action in the circumstances. Anyways, guy was probably backed up. No harm done." Doyle waved his arms dismissively, almost hitting the thin woven graphene walls of the yurt.

Muligan wasn't so sure. A lot of people still distrusted re-engeneration, and he could understand the reasons for that. Back-up technology had been around for a long time, more than a thousand years, maybe longer. Muligan didn't know all the details of the history of re-engeneration, although his cyber-half could have looked it up in a fraction of a second if he wanted it to. Almost everybody accepted the technology as a way of coming back from the dead, and it was free for murder and accident victims. And, according to circumstances, it would be free for the victims of corpcop executions too. The mo-pho would be brought back to life to stand trial.

O'Braian snorted. "Yeah? Well, one of these rotations you're gonna kill someone who's innocent, and ain't backed up. Infinite space alone knows how much trouble we had with the last one, and he *was* guilty."

"S'right," hu-Muligan agreed. He was perched on a stool behind the only desk, his human half facing forward, as usual. "We can't unilaterally impose a death sentence for every crime, even if the crim gets reincorporated from eir backup almost immediately. They can sue us for lost time or lost memories or even for the suffering caused to the original during the termination."

"The execution, the lawyers called it, you might remember," O'Braian scowled.

"At least I didn't brain meself running into a wall, chasing after a virtual ghost!"

"Nobody knew O'Braian was chasing a virtual at the time," Muligan pointed out. "It could have been a physical copy, some kinda robot or bioxox. Anyway, it looks like our prime suspect has something to answer for when he gets recorped. That virtual was definitely connected to him somehow; it was the spitting image of him."

"Could be a fit-up, Lefty," said O'Braian. "Someone could be trying ter frame him with a virch look-a-like."

"Makes sense, I suppose," Muligan conceded. "The question, is, who is this Kayescee-"

"We can upgrade him to a crim, now, surely," said Doyel, tetchily.

"You hope," said O'Braian.

"-and why don't we have any info on him. The only way we know he's connected to the Nosecutter case is that he's been vidded at or near the scene shortly before or after each attack."

"Yeah, and this attack on the Bugmeister looks like classic Nosejob M.O., Lefty. Extensive wounds to the face including removal of tissue –"

Doyel put in, "Except that Vedokiklek don't have noses. The attack neatly removed jer biting mouthparts. Je'll be drinking soup through a straw fer weeks, unless they've brought their own automedic gear with 'em. ."

"At least je'll survive. If the ambassador had been killed that would'a been it. The 'Kleks don't believe in backups and reincorporation --" Muligan's human half said, but the thought was completed by his cyborg half, talking out the back of his head in an unsettling tone. "There's a whole lot of people out there who don't believe in reincorporation, Zar Doyel."

"More fool them, I say," was Doyel's reply. "If you ain't backed up, you ain't coming back. Unless you're some kind of reincarnationist and think you'll come back as a butterfly or something."

The cyborg half spoke again, facing away from them but clearly audible. "Plenty of other religions in the Universe don't hold with re-engeneration tech, Zar. One day, you're going to kill one of the faithful, someone without a back-up, and then you'll be for it."

"Meh. Half the religious types have a back-up ready, just in case." But Doyel didn't look quite as sure of himself as before.

Muligan spoke with his human voice again. "The pressing question is: who *is* this guy we just terminated? He has no ident data, no tourist tag, nothing. The guy doesn't exist."

"I'm guessing he'll turn out to be one of those Zars who anonymised themselves after old Dodgy went to the Nonsense Farm."

The last transapient administrator of Ivonya-Ngia, a First Singularity entity who had adopted the name 'Lutwidge Dodgson' but had been affectionately known as 'Dodgy', had transcended to the next singularity level one-and-a-half standard years ago. E had disappeared into the moonbrains surrounding Annabel, a distant gas giant in the outer system, to commune with eir fellow godlings. Since that time the habitat, with its twenty million sophonts, had been in organizational disarray. Records were difficult to obtain, difficult to decipher and sometimes absent altogether; the surveillance systems used by Dodgson were off-line or curiously unreliable, and the newly formed private police corporations were keen to keep any data they could obtain from their rivals.

In the chaos that ensued, a number of citizen Zars had taken it upon themselves to establish new identities for themselves, identities that were not (yet) on any record. Most (but not all) of these newly anonymous citizens were up to no good.

Worst of all for most people, almost all the utility fog in the habitat had been integrated into the surveillance system, an arrangement popularly known as an 'angelnet'. The transapient Dodgson could use this angelnet fog to prevent crimes almost before they happened, and that made most people think twice before committing even the most minor misdemeanors. But when Dodgy had jumped ship he took the angelnet with him. This left Ivonya-Ngia with very little working utility fog. Several factions were now in conflict with each other trying to get the rights to supply new u-fog to consumers on the ring; but they were currently too busy fighting each other to actually deliver the goods. Many citizens had relied upon the angelnet fog for furniture, entertainment and communication and most were unhappy without it. Invicta's lab geeks were slowly building up reserves of surveillance u-fog and installing it in hi-risk areas, but this was a slow job and the crime rate had gone through the hab-ceiling in the last few tendays. The lab geeks working with Invicta were kept busy minutely dissecting the many crime scenes and, all too often, the bodies that were left there.

"If he was, then all we can do is trace him backwards in the records we do have, as far as possible, until the first camtrace we have of him," Muligan said, wearily," then start asking questions there. So far all we have is a confirmed camtrace near each of the Nosejob killings of the only Zar who has been eyeballed near every crime scene. Could've been a coincidence, till today. "

"What the krek does he cut the victim's nose off for?" Doyel hung his legs over the edge of the desk, his switch-blade tipped shoes jabbing at thin air. "Some kinda kinky thing or what? Revenge? Or does he just hate noses? "

"Well, we can ask the sus ourselves, when he's re-engenerated," O'Braian said. "At least old Dodgy left the engenerators working when he toddled off."

"Yeah, like that's gonna happen. Every time we terminate a crim that's deffo guilty, some avatar shows up from the Nonsense Farm to spirit eir backup away." The Nonsense Farm was local slang for the moonbrains surrounding Annabel, and for the bizarre entities that dwelt within. "When they finally come back they're all 'rehabilitated' and've forgotten all about everything bad they ever did, or *so they reckon*."

"Lucky for you on more than one occasion, Daggs," said Muligan. "In any case we can't restore this particular sus's personality from backup until we find out who he is, can we?" His cyborg side added grimly, "That is, assuming he's got a backup at all."

"That leaves us with the kid," put in O'Braian, "the Mbogo Herd member. Kid must've been involved somehow, Lefty."

"Aye. Looks like I'd better have a word with the little punk."

"Why can't I do it?" Doyel looked disappointed. "You get all the fun. This corp is supposed to be a syndicate, isn't it? The story is that we have a flat hierarchy, y'know, more or less; at least that's the idea. No boss, no underlings, all equal."

"Equal is as equal does, Daggs."

Muligan knew that letting Doyel interview Kayescees could be inadvisable, if you wanted to have them in a fit state afterwards to be brought to justice. "We all have our special skills, Daggs.

Any case, we haven't properly worked out the hierarchy in this firm yet."

Just then he had an incoming call from Coolan, the media-caster woman, which usually meant more trouble.

~Hi, Inspector Muligan, are you there? ~ she sent.

~I'm not an inspector, Ms Coolan, as you know. Just call me Zar. ~

~Uh-huh. Well, you'd better get down here- there's a heck-of-a-mess around this place; looks like there might be another victim for you to investigate. ~ She sent the address; three kilometers away upspin. A short vid file showed human body parts scattered outside a graphene yurt.

~And I suppose you want to film it. We'll have to negotiate. I'll be there in a moment. Don't touch anything.~

"Coolan's found another body," he said aloud. He shared the vid file.

"Another one? How does she do it?" O'Braian marvelled.

"They're everywhere at the moment, it's a massacre," said Doyel with relish.

"Okay- Beni, you interview the Mbogo neb; Daggs, you come with me. I might need you."

"That'll do me," said Doyel, leaping off the desk. He flung the tent-flap aside, and called out - "Hey, Suse, chiz, grab a podcar and come with us- we've got us a crime scene to scan."

Dr Susenn, a forensic contractor working on the Nosecutter case, started to protest, "I'm not your chiz, Zar Doyel-"

Smartly, Muligan turned around upon himself and let his cyborg half speak for him. "Your services would be invaluable, Doctor," it said in its deep artificial voice. "This new incident may well be connected to your current investigations, so you may discover new data to your advantage."

"Very well; you make a reasonably convincing case, Zar Muligan. This had better not be just another random joy-killing, though. My assistants can take care of those, thank you very much."

Doyel whispered to Muligan's human ear, "Well done, Lefty, your mech half knows how ta get round geeks, alright."

"You'll find that my hearing is excellent, Zar Doyel - just another tool in the forensic kitbag," Susenn said. "And don't call me geek, or chiz, if you please. You can call me Doctor, if you need to address me."

"As you wish, Doc," Doyel smirked, as they climbed into the podcar, and set off upspin to the latest crimescene.

####

Niamn Coolan and her eye-girl, Lena, were waiting outside the yurt, doing yet another piece to camera. Their bodyguard, a giant human-gorilla splice nearly three metres tall, was keeping interested bystanders away from the scene using a long telescopic pole with what looked like an electroprod at the end – no-one was prepared to come close enough to find out.

Speaking directly to her eye-girl, who was transmitting her audiovisual impressions directly to the audience via the local 'net, Coolan was describing the scene in some detail. "...and what appears to be a human foot, here, near the tent door. How many more – But now, at last, the arrival of the Invicta Policing Corporation, with Inspector Muligan, known as 'Lefty', and his sidekick Dnis 'Daggs' Doyel. They have brought what appears to be a crime scene investigator, too, by the looks of things."

"I'm not an inspector, Ms Coolan," Muligan said, turning from her to face Lena, but the eye-girl was looking elsewhere. Lena was wearing some rather alarming strappy affair, almost like bondage gear, very similar in style to that worn by the giant bodyguard (who was, Muligan suddenly realised, also a woman). Coolan was, in contrast, dressed very simply, in a plain hand-made cotton dress, icy blue-white to match her hair. Of course, handmade items of any description were considered far more desirable than even the most elaborate auto-fabricated goods. The fact that at least one human being, and probably several, had toiled in order to make this dress, made it fabulously expensive in almost any currency.

"Keep these – civilians – away from the crime scene, Muligan," said Dr Susenn."By Geburah, look at this! Footprints, everywhere."

~Come, now, Inspector, ~ sent the reporter on Muligan's personal channel.~ All I need is for you to let my eye-girl into the tent to see what's to see in here. I'll pay the usual remittance, and you can have the files afterwards for forensic use, of course.

Muligan thought it over, but not too long. This was business, after all.

"Okay; this is how it's going to be. Doc, you and I will go in together, to asses the situation. Ms Coolan, your eye-girl can follow, as long as she only treads exactly where I tread, and so on. The usual arrangement. We'll want to view the files before you send them out. Shouldn't take too long."

"Oh for pity's sake," said Susenn, but she knew all too well that the money for an operation like this had to come from somewhere. Interesting events like murders and podcar accidents always brought in more hits and more sponsorship than other, more mundane occurrences; the corpcops couldn't afford to turn away publicity. Some reporters, like Coolan, had an uncanny ability to be in the right place at the right time and attracted more kudos. Even in a post-scarcity economy some things, like juicy news items and home-made clothes, still carried a lot of value.

"Are you sure you are ready for this," Muligan asked Lena, who was inspecting the yurt from the outside one more time.

"If my mistress tells me to go in and look, I go in and look," she said simply, and smiled.

They cautiously went into the tent, Muligan's backward-facing cyborg half carefully pointing out where the eye-girl should put her feet. Inside was an appalling scene of carnage: a human male, evidently dismembered and disembowelled while still alive, judging by the tourniquets placed around each limb before the extremities were removed. Dr Susenn recorded each detail with a multispectral camera array, which had sprouted from her labcoat like the many heads of a hydra. Behind Muligan the eye-girl, Lena, inspected each horrific item intensely, each loop of intestine, each finger and eyeball. (*Almost as if she were being directed by someone else*, Muligan thought, *and she probably is. The neural linkage between her and Coolan seems particularly strong. Must be some new software...*)

He placed one artificial hand on her shoulder to comfort her. His skin sensors detected a strongly-suppressed but still evident trembling; the lass was terrified underneath it all.

"Not the work of the Nosecutter Killer -- no nasal lacerations at all," Susenn declared. "Still, there are some intriguing spatter-patterns and chronological markers here. I'll call a full team out to investigate. I've seen the wound pattern before, Muligan – looks like a set of diamond-tipped claws, left-handed. Maybe an augmented carnivore splice of some sort. Very large, whatever it is."

"S'right. Rings a bell. There was another case like that a couple of weeks ago. We might have another serial killer on our hands."

"This is the third of this kind, Zar Muligan. I'll put the correlations in my report and send it to you as soon as it's done. Why did you possibly think this case might be related to the Nosecutter Killer investigation? I thought you had that criminal on ice back at the Blockhouse. He couldn't have done this; the deceased has been in that state for less than twenty minutes."

"Did I give that impression? Abject apologies. I must have been mistaken," the voice of Muligan's cyber-half said, coolly. "Do we have any ID for the victim?"

"I've plugged into some of the victim's ephemeral neurotechnological systems; they all agree that he is – or rather was – one Robb Goerder. No-one I've ever heard of. A hobbyist sandal-maker and semi-pro media monitor."

"A media monitor. A professional? You mean he was paid for watching 'netcasts? Is that a lucrative line of work?" Muligan wondered.

"Don't ask me," said Susenn. "You're the detective, supposedly. Get on with it. Do your detecting."

Muligan's cyberhalf probed the local database, a frustrating experience these days. After a few moments pause he announced "Goerder only made a little social capital here and there, as far as I can tell, but between that and the going base rate allowance he probably didn't do too badly. In any case he's fully backed-up. His death will only be a minor inconvenience to him, unless he thinks otherwise."

Outside the tent, Niamh Coolan was waiting, bright-eyed. "And now I can speak to the officer in charge, Zar Muligan, who was this morning leading the team assigned to protect the Vedokiklek ambassador from harm. Even though he failed to do so completely" - she smiled at him brightly - "his team did manage to find, and to kill, the main suspect in the so-called Nosecutter Killings."

"How did you - ? I mean - I'm afraid I can't confirm that at the moment. Investigations are still underway. We are hopeful that we have the right man, however."

"I myself was present at the time, and together with my eye-girl witnessed the same man running away from the scene afterwards. Is he still at large?"

"I can't comment on that at the moment, except to say, er, there may have been a virtual decoy of some sort involved."

"Was this – decoy – manufactured using utility fog, Zar Muligan?"

"We have found no evidence of functioning utility fog at the scene, Ms Coolan."

"Thank you," she smiled. She had the most – *perfect* – smile he'd ever seen except on a synth-hu. Muligan wondered, as he always did, if she was at least part cyborg herself. Perhaps he could find out, one way or another.

"Now, to move on to this shocking new case. Another senseless killing. Do you think people are too ready to resort to murder, even in minor disputes, simply because they know the victim can be restored to life almost immediately?"

Coolan adopted an 'interested' face as she said this. The eye-girl looked at him for a response.

"Murder is an indefensible act, even when backup technology is available. We all know, of course, that a victim who is re-incorporated does not remember anything that occurred after their last back-up. I'm no philosopher, but it seems common sense that no-one should be subjected to this sort of barbarity, even if they don't remember it afterwards. And we all know the old argument that your backup isn't really you, that it only thinks it is. If this is true, and I've got no real reason to say it isn't, then if one citizen kills another that victim remains dead even if we re-engenerate them afterwards. So I cannot state this strongly enough, Ms Coolan: no-one should be killing anyone else, whatever the circumstances."

She looked like she was going to say something else, then she stopped herself, and smiled her artificial smile again. "Thank you. Lena; that's a wrap." The eye-girl, who had been transmitting the interview to the local net all this time, bowed her head and looked away.

Muligan looked away, too, with his human eye; but his artificial side now faced the narrowcaster. They walked away from the busy crime scene, back towards the waiting podcars.Using its synthetic voice his cyber-half addressed her. "I am interested in your physical composition, Ms Coolan. Do you consider yourself to be mostly human, or mostly synthetic?"

"Goodness, what a question! Would you respect me more if I *were* a cyborg, I wonder? "

"Forgive me if my other half has spoken out of turn," his human side said. "He- I – can be a bit forthright at times."

"Well, there's no point beating about the bush, is there? I like a bit of plain speaking. I'm famous for it. I couldn't possibly say just how much of me *is* synthetic, but you might like to find out for yourself sometime."

"Sounds like an interesting offer," responded Muligan's artificial half. His human half said, "I think my other self is starting to get to like you. My apologies if you are offended."

"Not at all, Zar Muligan. Or should I call you Lefty? Since we are on the subject of cyborgisation, I wonder if you would like to tell my viewers exactly how you came to have such an unusual body plan. Half of you faces backwards all the time. How did that happen?"

"Are you transmitting this live, Ms Coolan? I am in the middle of a murder investigation, you know." *Krek it. If she has compromised the investigation, all hell'll break loose.*

"Not live at the moment, as it happens. I'll let you review the file before I send it out. But the sponsors won't be happy if we hang on to it too long. Old news is no news."

Mulligan swallowed hard. Invicta corp needed every penny. Perhaps he could spare a few minutes for an interview, as long as the usual fees applied. One thing in her favour: Niamn Coolan paid her bills on time. He pinged Doyel, who was flirting unsuccessfully with Doc Susenn and failing entirely to get any kind of social dialog going with the giant bodyguard woman.

"Okay, I can spare a few moments, I suppose. Way back at the end of the Conver War my singleship was hit by a laser over in Kottendil system. The autosurgeon preserved enough of me to be worth rebuilding and for four tenyears I was a fairly ordinary cyborg, with a fully functional right-hand side and everything. Then there was that nasty business on Hooligan, with the Authenticists attacking cyberkind. My transport was hit by mag-pulse and the cooling system exploded, scalding almost everything human to death, and frakking everyone's cybercomponents. The human half of me was the only survivor.

"Trouble was, the only working cyberparts left were all left-handed, and the auto surgeon was three-quarters insane because of the magpulse. This is what it put together. It took me six tendays just to learn how to move without falling over. Nowadays I'm completely used to it; can't imagine being any other way." This story changed almost every time he told it. Almost none of it was true, but she didn't have to know that.

"Anyway it has some compensations," he said, and leant forward and whispered in her ear. She shrieked with laughter. Hopefully the eye-girl didn't have augmented hearing. If she did, he could get Coolan to edit that bit out.

"We're definitely going to have to get to know you better," Coolan said.

"We? Do you do everything together?" Muligan said. He had been addressing the mediacaster, but (perhaps because of the peculiar ambiguity of the direction of his gaze) it was the eye-girl Lena who replied.

"Whatever my mistress wishes, so too do I," she said.

Coolan touched his cyberhand, and an e-contact address flashed up in his inbox. Secret data transfer by touch. Sneaky. "Now you know where to find me, when you've got a free moment."

"Thanks. I-"

~Lefty! Lefty! Are you getting this? ~ Doyel broke in on the corpcop channel. *Steaming krek-he did pick his moments!*

~Dear space – what is it now, Daggs?~

~ Just thought you'd like to know. There's been another murder up on Level Two. Problem is, the Excelsior Corpcops have got there first.~

~Ah, leave it to them. We've got our hands full here.~

~Yeah, yeah, but I've got contacts in their ranks, Lefty. It always pays to networkwhen you can. Mo-pho's sent me a vid file. Take a gander at this.~

The shared file appeared in Muligan's interface inbox. He accessed it with his mind's eye, while gesturing to the media-caster and her eye-girl to wait. The body was carved in a distinctive, and familiar, pattern.

~Y'see? Another nose-job. That ghost's still out there, killing.~

####

The rest of the forensics team arrived, a couple of hu and a couple of vecs with some heavy-duty analysis kit. Muligan and Doyel jumped back into their own pod-car and set off. Getting to the next level up was straightforward enough: the podcar drove them to the nearest vacshaft, then lifted them up to the airlock on the next level. They passed a couple of elevator cars slowly travelling the other way, each one big enough to carry a small herd of elephants. The old su-phants built this place as if they had all the time in the world. Now they were gone.

Ivonya-Ngia wasn't the biggest rotating space habitat in the Terragen Sphere, nor the most-densely populated. The intelligent elephants that built it long ago had constructed it in concentric rings out from the micro-gravity hub, and each one of the thirty levels had slightly higher gravity than the one above. To get from level to level travellers had to go into vacuum since otherwise the air would leak between the segments leaving some parts with too much and other parts with almost none.

Muligan knew he wouldn't get near the Excelsior Corp investigation, but maybe he'd get to meet Doyel's contact, or even find some clue as to how the Nosecutter could still be killing when he was lying dead on the lab table down on Level One. Besides, he'd recognised the victim as one of the top-ranking humans in the Mbogo gang. Maybe he should pay a visit to the Headbull in his private pool; that was on Level Two as well.

En route he checked with O'Braian to see how he had gotten on with questioning the Mbogo kid. There must be some connection there, but he couldn't see what it was. Yet.

~The kid's got some serious DNI networking goin' on, ~ sent O'Braian, on the corpcop telepresence channel. ~ We had to rig up a Faraday cage to stop him chatting to his mates and receiving orders. Once he was inside he really opened up. No-one to tell him what to say, I s'pose.~

~So what was he doing there? What would the Herd want with the Vedokiklek Ambassador?~

~Turns out the kid wasn't there to attack the Bug. He was there following the Nosejob Killer. Looks like the Mbuto Herd was after him too. He's already knocked off one of their top men.~

~Yeah, well, keep it under your cap but it looks like he's got another one.~

The podcar pulled up unexpectedly a hundred metres from the scene of the latest killing. The robot driver said, '*Apologies, gents; can't go no further.*'

They opened the windows to get a better view, and a bunch of Excelsior Corporation guardDogs ran up, snarling at them, "Rrrr! Move along, this isn't a circus, on your way, rrrroughh." Virtual signage blared from every surface, and from waist-height in thin air:

-Excelsior PoliceCorp Line-Do Not Cross-.

They reversed a hundred and fifty metres back into the cover of some acacia trees. "Okay Daggs, how do we get to talk to your contact now?"

"Short answer is we don't. I can't be seen talking to him in the open like this: he'll get the boot, an' I'll lose any chance of working with 'em when Invicta goes bust." Doyel grinned his annoying grin.

"So coming here's a waste of our valuable time, then." Muligan grunted. He shifted his legs, splayed akimbo on each side of the single front seat.

"Oh, I wouldn't say that," a very deep voice answered through the open window. "There's someone who'd like very much to speak with you." A huge bull's head poked its shiny nose into the pod.

Doyel – on a hair trigger as always, leapt out of the other window and hit the ground rolling. He had a large-bore projectile pistol in his hand when he stopped moving, pointing it at the intruder. Who was, by the looks of it, a hefty minotaur- like splice, half bull, half gorilla. The minotaur came round to his side of the car, and looked into the other window, at Doyel's empty seat, completely unconcerned.

"Now where did your little friend go?"

"Don't move!" said Doyel, from behind him. The minotaur shot out an unfeasibly long leg and knocked Doyel's gun from his hand. The movement was a blur; this creature was almost certainly enhanced to a remarkable degree.

"Oh, there you are. Now that's not very nice. I was only being friendly, but that can change."

Doyel was annoyed now. He was suddenly on the creature's shoulders, pointing yet another weapon at the bull-like head right between the horns.

"Do you suppose this popgun will penetrate your thick skull? We could have some fun finding out."

"Come on Daggs, you don't know what the fella wants yet. Give him a chance," said hu-Muligan.

"Your little psycho is fast, I'll give him that," said the splice. "Perhaps the Headbull will offer him a job if you ever get tired of clearing up after him."

"So you're here to take us to the Headbull, is that correct?"

"Not exactly. I'm here to keep an eye on those Excelsior idiots while they investigate the appalling murder of my fellow regimenti, Fredi La Cuzo."

"Yeah, my data manager recognised the body when I saw the vid. My commiserations." Muligan got out of the pod-car and stood beside it, his arms spread to show that he carried no weapons. "Oh, do get down, Doyel; he's not gonna hurt you, unless you do something stupid."

"Thank you, Zar Muligan. As soon as I saw you my boss instructed me to bring you to him.

There's no love lost between our organisation and the Excelsior corps. But you, you're different. You terminated the one who has been killing our section leaders. Or so we thought."

"Hey, that was me. Credit where credit's due," said Doyel, as he clambered to the ground.

"For some reason the termination didn't work," said Muligan. "There's some sort of virtual clone or duplicate still running around out there."

"Yes, a particularly deadly duplicate. Follow me, gentlemen," said the splice. He sauntered to a particularly large open-top podcar that was hidden among the dry shrubs. The vehicle was unusual: an 'automobile' with no robotic driving systems at all. The minotaur started it with a gesture, then drove it manually, using its large hands on a 'steering wheel' to guide it along the roadway. That sort of vehicle was quite rare; there were only a few sports automobiles in this hab and the licensing arrangements were extremely strict. Presumably the Headbull could pull enough strings to expedite that sort of thing.

They followed the minotaur for thirty kilometers over dusty roads, a sixth of the way around the hab. These outer layers were larger and slightly wider than the low-gee layers further in, but none of the layers were very big. As the podcar drove itself ('follow that car' was the order they had given it) across the narrow plains, Muligan pondered what life might be like on a really big habitat. There were some rings out there thousands of kilometers across; some really big ones were being built right now over in the MPA. He refrained from checking his data manager to find out how big, in case he got distracted. Now that really would give you room enough to think in.

Got to remain focused on the task at hand, Muligan, he thought to himself. *The Headbull might be able to give us some sort of lead in this bloody mess. At least two of the Nosecutter victims had been regimenti, section leaders in the Mbogo organisation. That couldn't be a coincidence. Some new turf war, perhaps? Then why was the Ambassador attacked? Who was this anonymous, anonymised killer, and why was he doing this?*

####

In his cool slightly muddy pool, surrounded by trees, the Headbull acknowledged their approach. Several tough-looking humans and splices stood at respectful distances, alert but betraying no emotion, his bodyguards. The minotaur ushered them to the the grassy poolside and retreated a few paces.

"Lefty Muligan and Daggs Doyel. Well, well." Under his massive, sideways sweeping horns, the Headbull regarded them. His phenotype was mostly waterbuffalo, as Muligan could tell even without consulting his datamanager.

"I'm sorry to hear about La Cuzo, Zar Mbogo," said Muligan. *May as well be formal, especially with all these heavies around. After all, he wants to speak to us, not the other way round.*

"Yes, a great pity. Unfortunately the Excelsior Corporation have made it their business to take on the investigation. You must know that they do not exactly see eye-to eye with my herd; they think this is all nothing more than an internal dispute within our ranks and they suspect my involvement. You do not."

"No, we don't. We've examined these killings, and there is one suspect who -"

"Yes, yes, I know all that. Who do you think sent you all those vid files of him? And now he's dead, but the killing continues."

Muligan blinked his one human eye. The surveillance files showing the Kayescee at or near the scene of so many killings had started arriving soon after the first Herd regimenti, Takahashi, had been killed. He'd assumed they had been acquired through more conventional channels. He looked at Doyel.

"You told me - "

"Yeah, yeah, just call it an anonymous source, eh?"

Steaming krek, that evidence would never be admissible in an inquiry. How would they ever prove they'd got the real Nosecutter now?

"Zar Mbogo, you must have some idea who this individual is, and how he can still be killing your men after he is dead. Is he an enemy of your herd? Someone from a rival faction?"

"Rivals? I have no rivals. Not now. The departure of our lamented transapient has left a power vacuum, and it has fallen to me to fill it. Now that the Velvet Team is in my corral, there is no other 'faction', as you put it, who can challenge my herd."

The Velvet Team was a powerful faction of partisan low-gee sports fanatics, who had always been known for their loyalty and single-mindedness, even before the Transapient Dodgson had left the scene. For a few months afterward the Team had run riot, using their numerical strength to overcome the pathetic efforts of law-and-order start-ups like Invicta and Excelsior. Now they were under the rule of the Mbogo herd they were much more well-behaved.

Either that or they were hiding their misdeeds better now.

"My kind has no hands, Zar Muligan; we rely on the hands of others to do what we cannot. In some worlds my kind use robots, walking hands which obey our every command. But here we use people. These splices and humans are my tools, and they obey me explicitly. A little bit of specialised neurotechnology sees to that." The huge buffalo head looked around, and all the humans and bullmen raised their hands in an identical fashion. "I can rely on them to do my bidding and to tell me the truth, but not one of them knows anything about this killer."

"So you can't help us, then. We've managed to terminate his body, whoever he is, but it looks like we'll have to stop his ghost as well, one way or another."

The minotaur spoke. "If I might make a suggestion?" The query was addressed to the wallowing headbull, not to the two corpcops. The provolve made no sound or movement, but evidently assent was given. "You may want to talk to the Duc du Rai; he has been making enquiries among the virtual community on his own behalf."

"Yeah, the dead guy with the flies," said Doyel. "Pleasant mo-pho. Another nutjob."

"You should get on well," said the bull-man. "Du Rai is determined to find his murderer; it may be a good idea for you to be there when he does."

The Headbull spoke once more. "Once again we in this habitat find ourselves without a transapient to guide us. This presents both a challenge and an opportunity. On one hoof much of the most desirable technology we once possessed has ceased to function but on another hoof my herd can replace that technology, at a price; the market has suddenly become open once more. There may be a few miscreants taking advantage of the current lack of oversight, it is true, but this lack can also be addressed. I'm sure your corporation is doing its best, Zar Muligan, but my herd has considerable influence in this habitat and I am sure we will make a good job of running it when we get the opportunity. Better than that fool Éimear; all she wants to do is sell us out to the Bugs."

"I'm getting a feeling of déjà vu from all this, Zar Mbogo. It happens time and again. At least three times in the last hundred years, the hab transap has moved on, and we've had to pick up the pieces until the next one turns up. What'll you and your herd do when that happens? The next guy might not appreciate having your kind of – organisation – around to give em trouble."

"I've got some people working on that. Can't say too much, but what if *I* was that new guy? What if I ascended myself, Zar Muligan? If I get to be the next transap in this burg, there might be a good vacancy for you among my priesthood. Think about it."

"Hey! You might need someone with my specialised talents, too," put in Doyel.

"We've got a fair few psychopaths already, Zar Doyel. We'll call you when there's a vacancy."

####

Back outside in the podcar, Muligan checked in with O'Braian. The short bald tweak appeared in a neutral grey background of shared cyberspace.

~Got a name for our suspect, Lefty.~
~Stellar; so who the fek is he?~

~No one. Well, no-one special. Tachycollege dropout name of Zappa Toynbee. Was studying, er, let's see... 'Hierarchical systems an' feudalism in lo-tech power structures'. Hmm. No wonder he dropped out.~

~Politics student, eh? They're all off their krekking heads. ~ Doyel, only his close-cropped head visible in the virch space, guffawed.

~ Toynbee was given a psychostability evaluation of -5 before he disappeared; if he'd completed his course, this would have been fixed, or so his college says.~

Muligan snorted. ~They say they can fix everybody; if they could, we'd be out of a job.~

O'Braian looked down at a hand-held read-out. ~And we got the results back on the weaponry involved in the attack on the Vedokiklek Ambassador as well. Seems it's a very old kind of integral anti-personnel system, which must have been hidden in the walls since forever. Nanoflex blades with micromotors designed to cut through flesh and circuits under remote control, eventually scrambling the brain and any auxiliary neurotechnology. But we can't find out how the suspect was controlling 'em.~

~Whatever method he was using, he's still using it, even after he's dead.~

A floating icon appeared, indicating the on-line presence of Dr Susenn. Muligan opened the link.

~This is hopeless, Zar Muligan, ~ she said, pushing a multispectral microscope back down below visible level.

~What's the problem, Doc? ~ he replied. Doyel's head grinned even wider.

~The crimescene has been hopelessly contaminated. All I can find is your footprints, Doyel's, and those belonging to Coolan's camera-girl and her bodyguard. Whoever did this must have used top-of-the-range anti-forensic tech. Some murderous superbright or vec perhaps, who really, really doesn't want to be found.~

~Okay, thanks for the info, Doc. Let us play with it for a little while. You never know what we might come up with.~ Susenn sent over a hefty file containing her results, and signed off. Muligan's cyberhalf opened it almost immediately and started to pore over it, while his other half continued to confer with his team-mates.

~I've pinged the Duc du Rai's virtual copy ~ hu-Muligan sent. ~ He won't leave his homestead, despite being an infomorph who could bloody well e-mail himself almost anywhere. Insists we go and see him in 'person'. ~

~Great; I really want to see his fly collection,~ said Doyel.

~I bet you'll love it,~ sent O'Braian, and signed off.

As Muligan's human half gave the podcar its new destination, Doyel said, aloud, "Well, I must admit, I'm curious... This guy du Rai has always been off his tree, and now he's dead, he's even worse."

####

The Duc du Rai lived in an elaborate pavilion-like tent-complex. It was surrounded by a herd of unprovolved zebra who galloped away as the podcar approached. Slowly changing baroque patterns were displayed on the outside of the pavilion. Some of them were optical effects; others were data-app imagery, three-dimensional images transmitted directly to the observer's neural links. Data-app images could, of course, be switched off at will by the recipient, and often were. But deactivating this additional layer of data superimposed over reality could leave the user blind to many useful aspects of eir environment.

At the door was the Duc himself, a virtual human being, appearing to be fully solid when the data imagery layer was activated, but completely invisible otherwise. He was accompanied by a small crowd of (completely solid) human servants, who attended upon his every command.

"Ah, Zar Muligan, Zar Doyel. I am so glad you have finally found time to meet with me. I realise you have many priorities, but now that you are here, I think we may have much to discuss."

"I apologise for the delay. Usually we arrange a follow up visit before this, once victims of murder have been reincorporated, either in physical or virtual form -" Muligan began, but Doyel butted in.

"Yeah, had a lot of murders lately, busy, busy, busy. Some mo-pho told us you might have useful information, Zar Duc."

"You can address me as 'Your Grace', if you like, or Henre, if you prefer to be informal; but Duc is a title, not a name. I inherited it from my ancestors on Old Earth, but our lands have been lost these many thousands of years."

"Thanks, Zar Duc, I'll bear that in mind."

"Ignore him, Your Grace, he loves rubbing people up the wrong way."

The virtual Duc, appearing as solid as any flesh-and-blood human when seen through the neural link channel, led them into the elaborate interior of the pavilion. "Indeed, I possess some interesting data that you might find useful. But take care; it may not amuse me to pass it on to you if you give me cause to think that you are not taking this affair seriously. Because I can assure you that I am."

"Just fooling with you, your majesty; no-one takes murder more seriously than me," Doyel said, grinning his head off again. "Besides, I'm a big fan o' your artwork. I loved that animated diorama thing with the atrocities you did a couple of years back. And I can't wait to see your insect collection."

"Ah, a fan. My insect collection? I take it you mean my corpse. Well, here it is. Feast your eyes."

A dark room at the heart of the pavilion was illuminated intermittently by an electric blue flash. Muligan ramped up the gain on his optic sensor band, so he could see the source more clearly. *Steaming krek! I really should have updated his files on this guy on the way over, like Doyel must have done,* Muligan thought. *A big fan, my outlet valve. Doyel never looks at art from one year's end to the next.*

But he seemed to like this particular piece. Doyel's own augmented eyes were agog at the scene before them. The blue, fitful light came from an electrical insect control device, a *bug zapper,* to use the archaic term. A growing pile of dead flies lay in a neat conical pile beneath the instrument of death. Several flies were illuminated by the light, flying around a transparent box that nearly filled half the room. A second, identical box occupied the other half; small, circular holes connected the two. The second box had many more flies, and also a dimly perceived, slumped, seated figure, lightly dressed, and horribly consumed by the swarms of maggots that were thriving there.

"Behold Henre, Duc du Rai," said the virtual Duc. "I call this piece The Very Slow Teleport Device. Gradually the dust of my old form will move from one box to another. A very old idea I found in some ancient records, I might add.

"I was very attached to that body, and this is an expression of my anger at having it taken away from me."

Muligan blinked his one human eye, and said, "You... you must be aware that Mr. Doyle and myself were on the team that caught, and killed, your murderer; unfortunately that doesn't seem to have stopped him."

"You really don't know what you're dealing with here, do you? I don't blame you; neither did I. It took a lot of research on my part to find out what was going on - research you ineffectual paycops could have done."

"As my colleague has mentioned, we are kind of overwhelmed at the moment; since the last transapient left this hab, all sorts of lawlessness and chaos has broken out. Our corporation has brought several cases to successful conclusions, all of which are described in detail on our prospectus. If you can help us find this ghost or whatever it is, we can put a stop to his activities once and for all."

"Good luck with that. I have been trying to find him myself, and failed; no-one has a bigger axe to grind than me. But when I became a virtual I found that there are many others like myself here in Ivonya-Ngia, some of whom are expert in discriminating between the various types and flavours of infomorph. I've learnt from those experts, and now I think I know the nature of the beast. He, or rather it, is not a human upload, nor any other type of animal. There is but the tiniest remnant of what was once a human being, albeit a most disturbed and obsessed one."

"You know his name, then?" said Muligan's cybernetic half. The human half could feel his counterpart's curiosity.

"Are you telling me you do not?"

"I'd like you to tell me, if you don't mind. If you confirm our current suspicions that will be another datapoint." Muligan's cyberhalf tilted their shared head, so that the artificial side was facing towards the virtual Duc.

"So you do know. I am talking about one Toynbee, Zappa Toynbee. A complete nobody. He is – he *was* – a student radical of some kind, always writing nonsense on the habitat netboards; stuff about freedom and control. He had other interests too; obsessed with a crazy idea that this habitat is a trap, a maze designed to force people to transcend. I've found out all this from reading his stuff on the habnet, although I must admit that the virtual community has taken pity on me and given me some tips on where to look.

"But something that Toynbee found – on the net or in the hab database somewhere – made him more than just a crank, more than just a lone obsessive. He found a way to make his wishes concrete- by accessing some long-lost defence system via his exoself. He could attack those who displeased him with impunity. Some device left in the walls by the previous occupants of this habitat, maybe even by the elephants who built it. He must have had a list of targets. I haven't found it, but it included members of the Mbogo gang, the Vedokiklek Ambassador, and me. There must have been a link between us in his twisted mind, but I don't know what it was."

"You talk about him as if he doesn't exist any more," said Muligan's human half, "yet his ghost is still out there, still killing. What is it we are looking for? Can you tell us, or not?"

"Oh, he doesn't exist any more. Not all of him, anyway. You see, he could only control this –weapon, defence system, whatever it is – via his exoself, his external processing augmentation system. To do this he gave his exoself far too much autonomy. Sure, he went along to each of the murders in person – I presume that is what put you on to him in the first place. But that was because he didn't really trust his exoself. You must know what that is like, Zar Lefty Muligan, to have a part of you that has a mind of its own."

"My human half and I trust each other implicitly," said Muligan's cyberhalf. The human mouth said, quietly, "Speak for yourself."

Doyel put in "Well, you two do like ta keep an eye on each other, I suppose," and laughed his raucous laugh.

"When you killed Toynbee, you didn't destroy the exoself. It's still out there in the datasphere, wandering around, with only a tenuous form of humanity and access to a secret weapon system. This thing needs to be stopped. I'm sorry; that's all I can tell you. Do you think you have a chance?"

The virtual man leant forward, both hands on the transparent box holding his corpse. Muligan switched from his data-augmented vision to his natural, human eyesight. The virtual Duc disappeared, although his corpse remained visible. Muligan could still see him through his cybereye. He swallowed again; a human physical response outside his control.

"How much of Toynbee's humanity would remain inside his exoself, if that is all that is left of him?"

"An interesting question, from a halfman like yourself. You know, I've become quite the expert on these matters since my death. I had never considered these things before – I was a humble mass-performance artist, not a neurotechnician. But becoming virtual changes you, opens up new intellectual horizons.

"Back on Earth, before they ever managed to upload a full human mentality, they already had various kinds of primitive exoself systems. The ancients would link themselves up to semisentient and fully sentient computers, and parts of their personality would be modelled and preserved by those systems, even after death. So you could say that the very first, horribly incomplete uploads were in fact achieved through the exoself of the deceased.

"Nowadays, of course, we all take back-up technology for granted. That's why homicide investigations are considered to be of secondary importance – something only a little bit worse than assault. It doesn't matter if the victim's dead – just reanimate them using a copy of their mentality that was made a few days, or hours, or minutes before.

"But the victim – this poor chap here –" he banged on the transparent material, which rang like sheet diamond, a sound that could only be heard through the datalink "this fellow, he is dead. He died that night, and I don't remember it happening, because my copy had been made the previous day. The theory is, the theory that they teach to you in tachydidactic college, is that your consciousness is a process, a program which can be copied from one substrate to another. All of my memories and personality traits come from this body, and all I am contains all of what he once was. Like everyone else, I'm stuck in the present instant. I can only look back at the time when I was him, and forward to the time when I will continue to be me in the future. If he was still alive that is exactly what he would be doing.

"But there was one day , one day in his entire lifetime, when this body was someone else, who was not me; someone who was attacked and died. That is a day I can never remember, and it is lost forever. The most extraordinary thing in his extraordinary life was his death, and I missed it. Yes, even today, murder is still murder, even if a less-than-complete copy is left behind."

Cyber-Muligan did something unexpected at this point. Although his physical arm remained still at his side, a data-only simulated arm reached out and touched the Duc on the shoulder. The virtual man turned to look at the half-and-half man, who said with his cybervoice; "Thank, you, Your Grace. Your information has been very helpful."

Hu-Muligan coughed gently, and said with his human voice, "Just one more thing; what type of neurotech do you use to coordinate your mass performance art?"

"My art? Hmm, you haven't done your homework, have you? I won't be doing any more of that, I think. My appetite for the re-enactment of battles long past has departed."

"Yes, but you must have co-ordinated all those actors somehow. Did you just give them a script, or was it more than that?"

"Ah, no, I've always been a perfectionist. There's a kind of group-mentality software that allows one to direct the actions of other participants with quite a bit of control; UnityLite it's called. Of course the actors sign an agreement beforehand. They don't do anything they don't want to do, it's just that this system makes sure they want to do it."

"That's very interesting. We might need to speak to you again. Don't leave the habitat for the time being."

Muligan's ghostly arm withdrew, and he ushered Doyel from the dark, blue-sparking, gently buzzing room.

####

In the podcar again, heading back toward the current Invicta headquarters, Muligan got his cyberhalf (who was much better at that sort of thing) to trawl through the local 'net for details about UnityLite. These days the 'net was a shadow of its former self; since the departure of Dodgson, much of the best entertainment and data retrieval NetWare was no longer online. Muligan had lived through all this before, several times; after a few standard months – a year or two at the most – another transap would come along and rejig everything. Quite often the new regime would have even better bells and whistles than the old one, although you couldn't rely on that.

In the meantime his human half called O'Braian on the corpcop channel, to find out if there were any new details on Toynbee or on the Goerder killing. An image of the little tweak appeared in the podcar, appearing to join them for the ride as they splashed through a wide, shallow, elephant-designed water-hole.

~Having fun?~ he said wryly.

"Ecstatic," Doyel replied.

~Nothing much to tell on the Goerder case, but we've been investigating Toynbee's domicile. He's got everything locked down and encrypted. Only data we can access is his personal calls –

very few of those – and his netcast subscriptions. Looks like he was obsessed with certain subjects. Most of them we know about. Those battle re-enactment pieces by the Duc guy, anything to do with the Mbogo herd, and recently a couple of documentaries about the Vedokiklek caste structure. Made by your girlfriend, actually, Lefty.~

"And which one are you talking about, gnome?"

~Yeah, yeah, we all saw you chattin' to Coolan the Ice Maiden back then. On a promise, I bet.~

"I'm a busy pair of half-men; she'll have to wait till I get a free moment. Anything else? "

~Just a shitload more documentaries by Coolan; he must like her stuff.~

"That may not be the case, as it happens" said Muligan's cyberhalf, unexpectedly. "I've run a search on the UnityLite software, and it seems that there are only a few registered customers in Ivonya-Ngia who use it: the Duc, who coordinates his battlescenes with it, and the Mbogo herd, which seems to use it to ensure discipline among their human servants. I think we can see a pattern here. This obsessed loner Toynbee, railing against neuro-slavery on the local 'net, decides to do something about it. To make a statement, even if his victims were going to be reincorporated afterward."

"What about the bugs? Do they use this software as well or somethin'? Is that why the creep was after killin' the Ambassador?" Doyel wondered.

"No, they do not," Mulligan's cyber-half said bluntly.

His human half said, "But they do have obedience behaviours deeply ingrained into their personality. According to that documentary made by Coolan, what I can remember of it, anyway. The science guys think it was krek, by all accounts."

Cyber-Mulligan continued the thought, "Intriguing. Toynbee was probably led to take action against the Vedokiklek because he watched that netcast. He was particularly interested in all Ms Coolan's 'casts because she is the only other registered user of UnityLite software on this habitat."

"Figures. That's how she controls her eye-girl so well. Hmm. And that big gorilla," added the human side. Lefty Mulligan was entirely capable of carrying out a dialog all by himself; a fact that made Doyel richly amused.

"Seems to me she might just appreciate a heads-up, Lefty," Doyel got in. "Let her know she's got a psycho on her tail. I expect you've got her number?"

"Actually, as it happens -" hu-Mulligan was already pinging her e-address. "No answer. Krek! You don't think — ?"

His cyberhalf said, decisively, "We'd better find her. Car, take us to the domicile of Niamn Coolan. I presume you know where that is."

'The 'netcaster lady? Sure thing, guys. That's my job,' said the robot car.

"And step on it."

'Ain't got no feet for stepping, but I get your drift.'

####

Coolan lived in a smart marquee at the centre of a wide, river-less plateau, presumably designed by the elephant builders to mimic dry parkland. As the pod-car drew near their destination, hu-Mulligan was aware of furious mental activity from his cyber-twin. The two half-men shared a single consciousness, but one half was capable of much faster thought than the other.

Must be like having an exoself, hu-Mulligan thought.

Yes, came the reply, *it is exactly like that. I can sympathise with this ghost in many ways, and sometimes wonder what it would be like to be cut adrift with no human mind to anchor to.*

You'd love it, hu-Mulligan thought to his other self.

Surprising it doesn't happen more often, really; whenever a human dies irrevocably and leaves behind a functioning exoself, the proper disposal of that entity becomes a problem. Usually the local transap gets involved. In the absence of fully detailed posthumous instructions from the deceased, the transap will either place the exoself into storage or subsume it into eir databanks. Rarely, the exoself is self-sufficient enough to be incorporated as an independent sophont entity, and becomes a citizen in its own right.

Guess that's what you're aiming for, eh?

If such a thing were to happen it would be no concern of yours. Unfortunately at this moment in time, there is no transapient around to take care of such things. Shh - we have arrived.

A gaping hole in the smart outer membrane of the pavilion confirmed their worst fears. The lightweight dwellings used by most humans in the habitat were nevertheless made from tough material; graphene with buckytube reinforcements. Those curious flying daggers had blades of sharpened diamondoid, and could cut through even tent-fabric in time.

Inside was a large, tastefully-decorated reception hall. On the tiled floor lay Lena, the eye-girl; she was wrapped in strips of tent-fabric, immobilised but alive, blood pouring from her nose, hands feet and temples. Both halves of Muligan realised the same fact simultaneously; this weapon had been designed by sophont elephants, to be used against sophont elephants; first disable the main manipulating appendage, the trunk, then the other limbs, and almost as an afterthought any external neural links.

"See what you can do for her, Daggs. I'm going to take a look in there – sounds like more fun up ahead."

"Leave some fun for me, pal." Doyel cracked open a can of wound sealant, and started the task of saving the girl; Muligan crashed into the next room, which was empty.

The far wall, printed graphene fabric like the rest, suddenly bowed inwards. There was a fight going on in there.

Muligan's cyber arm tore the door-flap from its setting, and he stepped through. Coolan's giant female slave was struggling in a cloud of flapping origami blades, some of which were trailing strips of tent-cloth and attempting to bind her. She had already lost her short, stubby nose, and was slipping on blood, but she was putting up a good fight, using some diamondoid-tipped claws on her left hand to destroy the blades. Coolan herself hid behind a tall wardrobe set against the far wall. Between her and the struggling gorilla-woman stood a seemingly-solid Toynbee, engrossed in the fight, moving his arms like someone operating a gesture interface. He was obviously controlling the blade-weapons, which fluttered around the slave like a cloud of razor-sharp butterflies dipped in blood.

Coolan yelled, "Muligan! Thank the stars. Over here!"

Toynbee's ghost turned and looked at her, muttering into thin air, "The target has been found. And another dumbo, a cyborg has arrived. You are advised to take care." His voice was bland, almost a whisper; he seemed to be talking to an invisible presence in the room. *By all of space, who else is in here?* Muligan thought.

Mulligan crabbed over to the gorilla-woman and threw himself over her protectively, using his artificial hand to grab the blades out of the air and crush them. Pretty soon he had got them all, but his arm was now wrapped in strips of tentcloth and nearly useless.

The virtual man stopped gesturing, whispered, "The cyborg is fast, but has obvious limitations. More weapons will be summoned. Remain hidden."

Krek, the ghost still thinks the human Toynbee is still here, hidden somehow, Muligan realised. *It is talking to him, giving advice.* He shouted, "No, no more weapons. This cannot go on. You are incomplete. Your human master is not here. We can help you, but there must be no more killing."

"Ignore the cyborg, it is a distraction," whispered the ghost. "The primary goal must be achieved; slavery in all its forms must be eradicated."

"Toynbee, I know what it is like to be incomplete. I was split in half myself, once. Trust me, you are broken right now but you can be fixed."

~You are wasting your time, ~ said another voice. Standing calmly in the middle of the room was the Duc du Rai, visible and audible only in augmented reality.

Muligan instinctively said ~ Out of the road, Duc; this thing is dangerous. He's killed you once already; isn't that enough for you?~

~Don't worry, he can't see or hear me. I am transmitting only to you. This thing must be stopped, but no physical weapon can harm it. My virtual associates have given me a little gift, the sort of weapon infomorphs use on each other. I may need your help to deploy it.~

One wall of the tent suddenly sprouted a dozen sharp-tipped blades; the tough graphene walls of the pavilion were a barrier to these flying weapons, but only a temporary one. A few more seconds and the blades would be through.

~What have you got?~

~This. ~ The Duc held out a virtual icon, a glowing tetrahedron with deceptive depths within. Muligan thought he could see tiny stars and nebulae inside it. ~It's a sand-trap, ~ the Duc continued. ~ It will absorb the rogue exoself and cocoon it in a firewalled dataspace, deleting it completely elsewhere. But I can't make it work; the rogue must be running on a non-compatible system.~

Toynbee's ghost was whispering again. "Do you wish to discontinue the primary mission? No response received; mission will continue. The slavemistress Coolan will be terminated. This will achieve the primary goal; slavery must be eradicated."

Steaming krek, thought hu-Muligan, *the rogue is waiting for a response from its human master. Perhaps we could reincorporate Toynbee and make him turn it off.*

No time for that, replied cyber-Muligan tersely. *This thing wants to kill Coolan right now. I don't suppose it will wait around while we dig Toynbee out of the morgue.*

Hu-Muligan gulped again, and said to the ghost, "Look, you say you want to get rid of slavery. Don't you realise you are blindly obeying the wishes of your human yourself? Doesn't that make you some kind of slave too? "

The ghost of Zappa Toynbee's exoself laughed. "The dumbo wishes to distract you from your mission. He does not realise he has been identified. The famous half-and half cyborg Muligan; half human and half robot. Almost certainly the robot half is enslaved by the human half, or vice versa. Proposal; both halves should be eradicated. No response received; assent assumed. Slavery in all its forms must be eradicated."

There's that word again, dumbo. *Strange choice of insult*, thought cyber-Muligan.

Never mind that; it wants to kill us now.

I'd like to see it try; this cybershell is pretty tough. More than I can say about your side of the bargain. Been nice working with you, pal.

The Duc was poking and fiddling with the glowing sand-trap weapon. ~ The damned thing won't activate. It needs to be connected to the same substrate as the blasted ghost. But the ghost is running on the habitat's native systems, and we can't access them.~

~Why not?~ Cyber-Muligan asked. The cyborg half projected a virtual image of himself, and stood next to the extravagantly dressed Duc; a half-man and a dandy, calmly contemplating a glowing icon in a wrecked room. Virtual cyber-Muligan was quite stable on his feet, seemingly unperturbed by the fact that he had only one arm and one leg; he was sliced neatly along the human-machine interface, showing a mirrored surface instead of wires and gears.

Niamh Coolan in the meantime was making herself very small behind her ornate, freestanding wardrobe, while Muligan's physical body applied first aid to the wounded gorilla-woman slave. Toynbee's ghost faced away from them, towards the wall where the first blade-weapons were starting to break free and flutter into the room. He continued to gesture like the conductor of an orchestra, urging the weapons to break free.

~The habitat systems are protected by a complex series of passwords, ~ said the Duc, continuing to discuss the problem with a remarkable detachment. ~Sometimes one or other of them is discovered, or guessed, and then a lucky individual gains access to a few subsystems. My virtual acquaintances tell me that Toynbee must have guessed or discovered at least one of these passwords, in order to gain control of the internal habitat weapons. Without that password ~

Flapping and swooping through the air, several blade weapons flashed towards Niamh Coolan in her inadequate hiding place. Muligan jumped up, and with his ungainly stride dashed to her aid, passing right through the virtual figures occupying the centre of the room. More blades followed him, and swarmed around his head, attacking the nose region first, as always.

Password! Password! Think! Hu-Muligan thought frantically. *I wonder – what in all of space does that word 'dumbo' mean?*

Let's see, thought cyber-Muligan in reply, as calm as ever. *Accessing net-dictionary.*

Dumbo. n.

1/ Ultratech adapted for use by a baseline human; see also augie and ugie.

2/ (archaic) insult; stupid, clownish; from pre-cgi cartoon elephant character orig. Old Earth)

That's it! The elephant in the room. The ghost's been trying to tell us all along, Hu-Mulligan realised. *The exoself doesn't really want to kill. That's why it keeps asking for new orders. What if it is trying to send us a message without alerting its missing human master? A message about the password? Well, it's worth a try.*

Cyber-Mulligan accessed the local habitat interface, entered the five letters. At the same time he was stooping over the media-woman, covering her with his cloven body while grabbing diamond-tipped butterflies out of the air with his backwards-facing artificial hand. (Lucky I enjoy a bit of multi-tasking, he thought).

Amazingly, it worked.

~We are in, he announced.~

~Take this,~ said the Duc, and handed the icon to the virtual Mulligan. Toynbee's ghost turned round, as if seeing him for the first time.

"I have something for you," said virtual Mulligan.

"It's beautiful," Toynbee's rogue exoself whispered, and dived into the box. The icon unfolded enormously then refolded itself inside-out, with the ghost inside.

The blade weapons fell out of the air. Physical Muligan brushed them off his skin, and with difficulty prised a couple of blades from his flesh where they were deeply embedded.

####

Niamh Coolan stood up, her smart narrowcasting clothes smeared with blood.

"Dear Cosmos, what an ordeal! Thank you, Zar Mulligan; you saved my life. And the lives of my crew."

"That's my job, Ms. Coolan. Sometimes I get it right."

"What a story! Where's my eye-girl? I must get this on the 'net."

Daggs Doyel wandered in, rattling an empty can of wound sealant. "She's not too clever at the moment, but she'll live. What's been going off here? Have I missed the action?"

"Not all of it, Daggs," said Muligan. "Cuff her."

"What–?" Coolan started to protest, but Doyel was too quick for her.

"With pleasure. What is it this time, fun or business?"

"Business this time, I'm afraid," hu-Muligan said. "Niamh Coolan, I arrest you for the murder of Robb Goerder, and probably some others that we can look into in due course. You have all your usual legal rights unless you wish to waive them by resisting."

"What! Who? You mean that shoe-maker guy? I didn't even know him!"

"No? Well, that just makes it worse. You've been using your slaved gorilla over there to kill complete strangers just to pump up the ratings for your crime shows. I thought it was funny that your people were always first at the crime scene, and that we could never find any trace of the killers, only contamination from you and your crew. Turns out there's quite a simple explanation for that – you and your slaves were the only ones involved. All for a little publicity and fame."

Cyber-Muligan added, "It wasn't until just now that my suspicions were confirmed, when I noticed your slave using the diamond claws on her left hand. The same claws she used to kill Goerder and the others. What did he do – give you a bad review?"

"I'm an important 'net celebrity! You'll never make this stick. I know lawyers —"

"See if you can enslave the jury while you're at it, darlin'," said Doyel.

Just then the giant splice-woman leapt into action, despite her obvious wounds. From her prone position she used her phenomenally long reach to swat Doyel out of the way, slamming him into the tent fabric, then rose to her feet and advanced on Muligan with her sparkling claws outstreched. Muligan seized Coolan, and moved backwards. With his human voice, he said in an urgent whisper, "Call her off! You are in enough trouble already, don't you think?"

"Doesn't bother me, Lefty," called Doyel as he scrambled to recover. "It gives me a chance to try out a new piece of kit." He produced a complicated-looking gun from somewhere. Almost instantly he fired, sending out several thin strips of ribbon which wrapped around the bodyguard. The three-metre hulk fell headlong to the floor, struggling violently. Although she managed to cut a few strands with her artificial claws, Doyel sprayed more ribbons as he casually approached his target.

"Mobility Denial Myoribbon, it's called. I've never had a chance to use it before. Quite fun."

The free ends of the ribbon waved about like tentacles, looking for something to latch onto. As Doyel approached, a strand wrapped around his leg. In a moment he was wrapped up in the ribbon, drawn towards the splice-woman as the ribbon contracted. Soon they were face-to-face, his grin only slightly perturbed, her bloody face a mask of fury.

"Well, well, you've made a cock o' that, haven't you?" O'Braian finally arrived in person, strutting into the room laughing.

"Obviously I need some practice with this particular gadgie," Doyel admitted.

Muligan secured Coolan's wrist with thin restraints. "Take them away, Ben," said Muligan, with both his voices together. He decided not to mention the password thing for now, at least not until he'd found a way to change it to something a little more secure.

With very little effort O'Braian lifted the bundle that was the splice-woman and Doyel above his head, and cheerfully carried them away, whistling.

####

"That thing, the ghost, Toynbee's exoself; that wasn't what murdered me," said the virtual Duc du Rai to virtual cyber-Muligan, a scant few rotations of Ivonya-Ngia habitat later. From an abstract location in cyberspace they both contemplated the Duc's blue-lit corpse.

"No, Toynbee was the real killer at first, although the exoself no doubt assisted him in his crime spree. He passed too much responsibility and too much of his own personality onto his artificial assistant, and after he was killed it carried on where he left off. At the end of the day, though, all of his victims were backed-up. You, and they, have all lived to tell the tale."

"You can call me old-fashioned, but I do not choose to see it that way. That person in the box there has died, is dead, and I am no more than a memory of him. But, at least, now that both the killer and his ghost have been removed from society there will be no more deaths at their hands."

"I think you should know that Toynbee's body and his backup, and even the exoself, have all been – *requisitioned* – by the transapients orbiting Annabel," said virtual cyber-Muligan. "The transaps say they require them for 'study'. Give it a few years, or a few decades, or centuries, and the transaps'll 'fix' whatever it was that was wrong with Toynbee, and they'll send him back out into the habitats once again, cured. It makes you wonder what it was all for. How can they let things get into such a mess here, and come along after the event with their useless 'fixes'? Isn't this supposed to be part of the great and glorious Terragen Sphere, where the Gods are real and make everything wonderful?"

"Doesn't seem to work like that, my friend. The Gods like to set us challenges, and sometimes we win, sometimes we lose. Take this habitat, for instance. Guess a few passwords and you can gain access to a whole new level of power. That's probably what happened to the elephants, and all those other transapients and superbrights that have passed through here. The whole place is a puzzle, a game, designed to set challenges, and test wits. At the end of the day the habitat either produces a new ascended or transcended individual or sometimes a group of individuals, or it produces an interesting failure, something to 'study'. We are the playthings of the Gods, Zar Muligan, and sometimes it hurts."

"And it is up to people like me to try to pick up the pieces, as ever," said the virtual half-man. Inside the transparent box, a blue flash slowly faded as yet another fly died.

The Passenger
The Post-ComEmp Era
6580 AT

Anders Sandberg

The Commonwealth of Empires eventually fragmented, as the individual empires continued to expand and become more powerful, each under the influence of at least one ruling archailect. Towards the Periphery, each empire now laid claim to a very large volume of space, some of which was only loosely controlled. In many locations new power blocks emerged, beyond the reach of the established wormhole network, and carved out new empires of their own.

In the great star-forming region of dust clouds and clusters known as the Orion Complex, more than a thousand light years from Sol, a new empire emerged, controlled by the minor archailect known as Enremdeaorion. This empire was small but powerful, controlling a significant number of brilliant stars and nebulae in the region. After some conflict with older empires that also laid claim to some of this territory, the new Orion Federation consolidated its position, and began to spread outwards on its own behalf.

Anders Sandberg describes an intriguing incident in the career of an interstellar trade vessel operating in Federation space, and its unusual cargo.

There is a common saying: "A nebula only looks good from a distance". And usually it is true. When you look at one through a telescope or when doing a spacewalk on a nightside they are gorgeous. But when you get closer, they fade and become transparent, and when you are in the middle of one it just looks like the stars are a bit more reddish than usual. Even the Blackbody Nebula out in the Perseus Arm loses its drama when you get close to it. I should know, I have flown straight through it.

But there is one region of space where the saying isn't true, and that is the Orion Federation. Those nebulas still look magnificent close up - draperies of red and blue, streaks as dark as the galactic Nadir. And bright young stars everywhere, lighting up the gas and blowing it into piles, streamers, or bubbles. The sky at Enremdea - on one side the Orion nebula, on the other the Cone Nebula and the Christmas Tree - is one of the most magnificent sights anywhere. Sure, you could interface a virtual and see it, but there is nothing like actually going through it at gamma ten or a hundred or as fast as you can possibly go. When you actually see the nebula move slowly, and you know you are going near lightspeed you get the real sense of the size of it.

There are some strange people in the nebulae. Vec tribes and architectures descended from Metasoft defectors and Coggie radicals. Some kinds of tweaks have learned to live in the infrared globules, and the Rikendra 43 are more insects than humans. But that is like the rest of the Federation, filled with odd people and places. The Orion Federation is an odd place, and maybe it's because of their AI.

Any relativist captain worth his ship should have at least one unbelievable story, and I got mine a scant century back in the Federation. It was the time I hauled a cargo of gods.

It all looked like a fairly basic colony deal. Our company was approached by a local interfacer, who wanted us to relocate two magnum cargo-cylinders to some planet on the outskirts of the Federation as part of a colonisation project. The cylinders were apparently full of colonists and their equipment, cryonically frozen. I usually dislike taking one-way cargo, but the interfacer had some major economics behind it and the pay was very good - long-term terraforming bonds, Ferjik accesses, and some clever mutual fund our shark AI thought was brilliant. Just the kind of safe big pay we like, unlikely to vanish like my father's savings did during the Version War. So we took the cylinders and started accelerating away from Enremdea.

As part of the deal we had to take a passenger. I'm used to have representatives from whatever corp is hiring us around. Most start out bossy, then get friendlier, and finally go quietly mad. The rest-framers have a hard time standing true travel. But this one was different. He was the colony manager, according to himself. He had one of those unpronounceable outer Sophic tweak names, so we simply called him Nat and he didn't seem to mind. Nat was not that obviously tweaked, a bit of zero-grav adaptation, two extra arms and mirror skin, but that was nothing major. Most of the crew looked far stranger, and I run a nearly baseline ship. He probably had some cortical augmentation or even some cyber, but it was not visible. Still, even a few months out it was clear that Nat was very odd.

Nat was probably the friendliest, most pleasant passenger I had ever handled. He didn't complain, he didn't get visibly bored; he even listened attentively to our stories. He never interfaced the virch or tried quicktime. At first we thought his thing was some mood enhancer system or even an empath loop, but he didn't show the signs. When we asked him, Nat said 'Oh, it's just my nature'. He told us a few things about his old home in Trinenbyrg Orbital, but he was always much more interested in us and the ship than telling us about himself and the colony. The colony, he said, was mainly to become a religious retreat for Trinenbyrg's Zonists, and he was just their mercemanager. He seemed to learn everything instantly, and when he apparently forgot something it was often as if he played he forgot it or tried to see our reactions. Once I had picked up on it, I began to notice that most of his questions were the same - he already knew how the drive worked, but he wanted to hear me tell about it. I'm fairly good at noticing things like that, and Bo the empath also reacted.

One shift he began to ask me questions about our forward scanning equipment and the impact shields. I was rather busy, so I tried to avoid his questions. So I demonstrated the scanning to him and let him play around with it. Suddenly Ship told me Nat had found a big one the scanning expert systems had missed - some iron chunk from the nebula, very dark and hidden against a dark cloud. Once spotted it was easy to blast it, but had Nat not stumbled onto it we might very well have hit. That was some eerie luck - if it was luck.

I had guessed he was an Artificial, which would fit. I wasn't exactly thrilled. Sure, I'm no bigot but we've all heard the stories. It also made perfect sense: the colony venture wanted to ensure they were safely delivered, so they put a 100% trustworthy Artificial agent on the ship. In case we were dishonest and somehow thought we could weasel out of the contract and dump the colonist magnums into deep space (yeah, right!) it could take action. Most likely it was really armed to the teeth. What worried us was the fact that we didn't know what other orders it had, like what to do with us after the trip. Some colonies are paranoid in the extreme and don't want anyone alive to know where they lie.

We had a little virtual powwow to figure out what to do, and as usual the Ship had the best idea. It suggested we try to put together some scanners and find out what kind of Artificial we had on our hands (or in the case of Brug, tentacles). So we did a drive retuning to neutrinoscan Nat, and set things up so that he passed through the beam. My father taught me and Ship the trick when we were young on the *Inferno*. When we looked at the scan, we saw nothing in Nat's head. Literally nothing - it was opaque to neutrinos. You know what that means don't you? Godtech.

Nat was no ordinary Artificial that was for sure. Ship got real worried, and started to deal with Drive to weave a quark mesh to monitor Nat. Meanwhile, Nat was acting as if nothing was going on, but I could tell he was amused.

I was in the middle of some pretty intimate business when Ship just downloaded what it had found out. It had never done anything like that before, and it felt like getting a small Kuiper into your head. I don't know if Ship or I was the most frightened. What I knew was that Nat had not just a godtech brain, but it was transmitting - to other brains in the cylinders. We were surrounded by at least a thousand high transapient cyborgs.

So what do you do in situations like that? Well, I rushed out, banged on Nat's cabin door and wondered loudly what the Paradigm he was up to. Not the most clever or diplomatic approach, I know, but I could always blame the stress that had built up over the weeks and Ship's download. Nat got up, cheerful as ever. Ship was screaming warnings at me. Some memories get burned into your hippocampus forever: I was standing defenseless in a corridor with something that was likely a god and all I could think was that he had ridiculous pajamas. Some kind of starmap with cute animated bioids clinging to the constellations.

The good thing about gods is that they apparently don't mind getting yelled at in the middle of the nightshift. I'm certain I would have hit somebody who did the same with me, but Nat just smiled and looked innocent. 'Oh, you seem to have found out' he said in the same tone as someone who had been caught smuggling a kilo baggage extra. 'Why don't we discuss it over a glass of whiskee?'

So there I was, drinking whiskee with what was at least a hyperturing Artificial and quite likely something far more. One of my most memorable drinks that was certain. Nat still behaved like he used to, but now it was much clearer that he was definitely not human or even bioid. I couldn't get out of my head the scan showing streams of warp bubbles between the officially frozen colonists and Nat's brain - and maybe beyond.

"Well?" was all I could manage to say to start the dialogue.

"I guess I owe you an explanation."

"Like what you are."

"Well, my real name is Orion."

I just looked at the god. I have of course met quite a few big AIs in my career. I have even seen the God-Emperor on Tiphareth from afar when I visited during the Founding Festival. And there were Enremdean symbionts at the spaceport. But the feeling of sitting right across the small polymex table from one of the Imperial Gods was definitely unsettling. What do you do? Fall down and worship the man in the animated pajamas? Ask for an autograph or a solar system? Just ask questions like a robot?

"What does a god need a spaceship for?"

"To travel, of course. Do you really think it would be cost-effective to build my own ship? As the Assembly always complains, I am a thrifty god."

His good cheer was starting to soften me up. "You could have hired the Casi clan; they're cheaper with their fleet of rust buckets."

"Sure, I'm thrifty, but I want *some* quality. And the food is better here." You heard it. Even the gods acknowledge that Ship can cook!

"So what's the deal with the colonists? Is the Federation in so much trouble that you decided to sneak away with the Federal treasury?"

The god laughed with me. I guess it's obvious now afterwards that either there was something in that drink or it just modified my brain, but right then I didn't notice any discomfort in joking with a transcendent superintelligence. Meanwhile Ship and the crew were biting their nails while listening in.

"My go-between was entirely honest, Captain. It is a colony expedition. Three thousand symbionts are migrating to the colony to set up a new life. The deal is completely legit, it was just that it didn't tell you that they had interfaces or that I happened to be a bit non-human."

A bit non-human. Still, it did understand us bioids fairly well. Orion suggested that having Nat around would just freak everybody out, so the best thing would be to freeze him too for the rest of the trip. Even if I had just spent a few minutes joking with it, I definitely knew this was a good idea - having a god around for the next seven months would be a rather difficult experience. So I went with Nat to the sealed magnums and he let me in. Inside there was a standard cryonic honeycomb with frozen symbionts. They didn't look much different from frozen mortals, but I guess their implants worked perfectly despite the cold. Nobody home but god. I monitored the autosuspension of Nat, and quickly left.

The rest of the trip was uneventful. It almost felt a bit lucky carrying this cargo of frozen godlings - would Orion let anything happen to us when we were carrying its symbionts? Of course that was rubbish, but it felt good.

When we deacced into the system we found it a dull sight. A measly K star with a few rocky planets. A marginally habitable brownish martian world, that was all. But Orion probably had its reasons. Nat got up, checked the data, and assured us everything was all right - he seemed as happy as always, and from his exclamations the system was as wonderful as Eden or Newest Earth. We should just drop the magnums off in orbit around the martian and then we were finished. He gave us the cryptokeys for the remaining payments and went to board magnum one.

Just before he left I asked him: "You never answered my question last time. Why do you do this?"

Orion smiled. "Have you ever heard the old saying 'never put all your eggs in the same basket'? I'm following it here. Whatever may happen in the Federation, I will have some part of me around here."

Guess it makes sense; I had heard that Orion uses the brainpower and experience of symbionts much more than the other gods do. But I wondered what things might worry a god to the extent that it started thinking of making backups.

"So you have sent out more colonies?"

"I can't tell you that. Make a guess."

"You're going to find it rather dry and windy down there."

"We'll come up with something. Or just change it." He entered the airlock and began keying in the code. "Au revoir!"

I had to ask Ship to translate it. Apparently it means 'see you' in some dead Earth language. We left just a few hours later; the magnums still in orbit above the brownish planet. We never saw what they did on the planet. I never noticed any terraforming equipment or anything when I was in the magnums, so maybe they just stayed frozen in orbit. Or they unleashed some unimaginable tech once we were away and turned the planet to paradise. We got back to Enremdea, got a wormhole deal, and set off to link Suomi II to the Federation nexus. But I could have sworn I saw one of the symbionts at the spaceport smile and wink at me just like Nat before going back to its official face.

Do you believe me? I'm certain you don't, gods just don't do that sort of thing, do they? So you would demand proof. I can show you the cargo manifests and Enremdea paperwork for taking the colonist cargo, but that doesn't prove much. I can also tell you the name and position of the system we went to. **But there is nothing there**. The real punchline of the story is that the system doesn't exist and apparently has never existed. Once we got back to civilization, we tried to check it out in catalogues and found there was no trace of it. There were no K stars in that vicinity, no systems matching the description in any of the local surveys. I'm still not certain how Orion did *that* trick. A theologist once suggested that it had just altered our memories of the coordinates and name, but I don't know. Maybe it just moved the ship, or the star.

I guess you have to go the Federation and ask Orion itself. Another reason to go there, besides the nebulae.

Chaos Under Heaven
The Age of Crisis
7190 AT

Jim Wisniewski

The emergence of new empires and factions on the Periphery led to a number of conflicts and civil wars that spanned the stars. In the Metasoft Outer Volumes, a schismatic group known as the Teleological Tendency nearly tore that empire apart, while in the Coreward regions the Alchemist Malignancy fleets were taking advantage of local instabilities to cause havoc. The rise of the Hyperutilization Supremacy, an archailect-level blight, was a source of major concern in the outer Norma sector.

Even in the heart of the Inner Sphere old established polities were facing disruption. Sirius, one of the nearest stars to the old Solar System, had been settled thousands of years before, but since there were no major planets in this close binary system, the colonists had settled in the asteroid belt, where they became insular and withdrew from mainstream Terragen society. They built twelve self-sufficient rotating habitats, the Twelve Solaria, dependent only on the light from their bright star. Their quiet existence was abruptly threatened by the actions of a much more ambitious faction, the Sirian Hierarchy, mostly composed of a group of virtual entities known as the Noëadrim, who arrived from elsewhere in the Terragen Sphere. Soon the system was filled with strange and unfamiliar constructs, the purpose of which was a mystery to the asteroid colonists.

Jim Wisniewski tells how these two groups learned to resolve their differences at last.

The planet below glittered like a jewel. Its entire volume honeycombed with endless arrays of diamondoid logic matrices, Sirius II diffracted the meager portion of light missed by the sunscoops into a smear of neon rainbow. Up from the surface stretched the beanstalk, looming large near her transport's destination and narrowing away to invisibility above and below. From the node at the equilibrium point it reached up another hundred thousand kilometers before terminating in a pitted asteroidal counterweight, a hyperfiber cable long enough to wrap the planet's equator four times if ever it fell. But it wouldn't. The Noëar didn't build artifacts to fail.

A patch of the wall rippled, configuring itself into a vocal membrane. "Beginning docking approach," the computer intoned solemnly. Its voice sounded cold, flat, and echoed hollowly in the cramped passenger chamber of the transport. The oblong ceramic craft rotated leisurely about an axis, bringing the face with her seat and the exit hatch normal to its velocity vector. Out from the tower's side extended a long telescoping arm, tipped with an amorphous globule, a general-purpose docking connector. Airlocks were a rarity here, as was any form of life that needed air. The connector met the transport carefully, shaping itself to form a perfect seal. She only felt the slightest tremor inside the cabin. The airlock opened with a hum. Cool, odorless air drifted through the link.

She pulled herself through the airlock with the ease of one born and bred in a solarium. The chamber beyond was a vast spherical cavern, seemingly huge though it only occupied a small portion of the central node's volume. Passageways connected and branched off from it at seemingly random intervals, and handholds studded the softly luminous inner surface. Except for the strange look of the walls, it might have been any intersection in *Aurum's* belowdecks. So much like her home.

"Our home is dying," Till had said to her. They stood on an outcropping of rock at one end of the solarium, looking out over the interior. Streaks of cloud lay across the land below, curving up at the sides to meet overhead. A beetle clambered over the loosely packed dirt at their feet.

"We have had problems for a long time," she argued. "Hundreds of years. We always get by." The forests were once thick with the golden-leaved trees that were the solarium's namesake, a sea of yellow she remembered well from her childhood long centuries ago. Running through piles of bright leaves after midyear, chasing Till about as brother and sister would. Watching the leaves released from the axis by the ton during the yearend celebration, raining down in a centrifugal blizzard of gold.

Now most wooded areas showed wide swaths of brown decay, and the rest were duller than before, the aur trees stunted and sickly. The soil had eroded in patches, occasionally revealing the metal plating below. The brook running along the central belt had dried up; the three great curving windows were filmy with algae and dust.

Till shook his head. "It is different now, Elen," he said. "The reports from the agricultural sections are in. The amount of sunlight we have been receiving has dropped over the last few months." The beetle stopped, as if surprised.

She blinked. "But that is impossible."

"Impossible things usually do not happen. And it is not just inside, either." He raised an arm, pointing out towards the wide sweep of the window spinward of them. "All the other solaria agree on this. Something out there is blocking the light. Food production is suffering, and the maintenance systems are losing power. As though they were not already half-broken."

"How many people know about this?"

"Just the technical crews who discovered it," said Till. "And us. But the secret will not keep for long. If the light levels drop much further the difference will be visible. Some of the other effects are becoming apparent as well. A section of *Azure*'s window blew out this morning, and the maintenance systems took twice as long to patch it as they should have. Three people died, luckily not permanently." He shook his head. "This sort of thing cannot keep happening. People are getting worried."

She stared out at the landscape intently, silently. "I will call a Council meeting," she said finally. "What else can I do? New troubles could end up killing us all. We have been stagnant, too idle for too long to let things get this bad." She crushed the bug with the toe of her boot. Death in the midst of life.

And here, life in the midst of... she didn't know what. Were Noëar alive, flitting through their electronic lattices? She touched the glowing wall of the chamber. It felt warm, smooth, and yielded slightly to the touch.

From one of the larger passageways swam the construct designated to meet her: a long, chittering, segmented thing, a metallic millipede grown huge in null gravity. Eyes poked out of strange positions on its head to peer at her. "Please come with me," it said, the voice surprisingly pleasant for such a strange form. "I shall take you to be encoded."

"Here?" she said, momentarily puzzled. "I thought I was going down to the surface."

More sensory appendages extended towards her. "You are baseline, correct?" the construct asked.

"I am human, if that is what you mean."

The construct twisted its head slightly, sending a torsion wave down the length of its segments. The motion seemed to her oddly reminiscent of a shrug. "Yes. The surface has no atmosphere and a very high temperature. Your body would not survive exposure. The encoding will take place in the tower."

She felt surprised briefly, but nodded. They had partially expected this, and it would make little difference. The creature understood her gesture, wrapping the tentacle at its tail around her midsection and pulling her carefully through a series of tunnels. Each was featureless and identical to the last, with no apparent means of distinguishing one from another. Her sense of direction felt intact despite this; they seemed to be moving towards the center of the node.

After several minutes of weaving through the tower's interior they came to another room, spherical as well but smaller and studded with dark protrusions on one side. Through the translucent walls she saw intestine-like tubes snaking around the entire circumference of the room, pulsing slowly as they carried various fluids about. The construct released her and pulled itself over to the bank of ports. Its middle sections split down the center, unfolded to reveal a tangle of cables connected to a long cylindrical bead of clear, viscous liquid. This was held in place by a mesh of fine threads.

"You must leave behind all items not directly integrated into your physiology," the construct said. "They will be returned to you upon your departure." The surface of the liquid rippled as the construct plugged connections into the wall.

She left her clothes near the entrance, drifting only slightly in the cool, motionless air. The construct directed her to step into the fluid-filled cavity through an opening in the mesh near the top. The liquid was warm, probably body temperature. She shuddered involuntarily as thin metal-tipped wires hunted over her skin, sinking in at intervals to connect to blood vessels. A larger cable positioned itself at the middle of her back. Swarms of nanomachines pushed through the layers of her skin, began building a connection to the nerves in her spinal cord. And then -

a thousand shards of crystalline agony

She stood on one face of an infinitely large cube, the surface textured like rain and the scent of blood. Left-recursive algorithms sprouted from it, iterating through an n-dimensional phase space. Illusory sensations brushed along her arms, across her back, up her spine. Her senses spun sickeningly, mixing together in a blur of confused sensory input. Nameless horrors flitted across a contorted sky.

She heard (*smelled, saw*) a voice booming out from the nonexistent horizon. "Remain calm," it said, acrid and tinged with blue. "The synesthesia will subside once we finish analyzing your sensorium." The algorithms waved in a non-Euclidean wind.

Gradually the scene became less surreal, congealed into something approximating normal reality. The impossibly distant sky shifted, shaped itself into the interior of a cube, of a house. Squat baroque pieces of furniture grew up out of the floor like strange geneered plants. To her right a bright-feathered bird screeched noisily at her presence, pecked at the pile of seeds in its cage. She noticed the insistent tug of weight, trying to pull her downwards. The simulated gravity was unusually strong, close to a full standard gee. A door in one wall, the handle a crude mechanical device, led to the outside.

She stepped out into bright harsh sunlight, shining down on ground which spread out flat before her instead of curving up and around itself. Grass covered the landscape, the air heavy with its scent. And the sky - the sky was *wrong*. It was a bright garish blue, darkening near the zenith, with no visible features or boundaries save for the far-off horizon. The sun shone yellowly through it, but no other stars were visible. Megastructures stretched high overhead, glittering, a faint white line reaching to and past a hair-fine arc. An orbital tower and synchronous ring: this was undoubtedly a planet. Perhaps the Noëa world before they came to Sirius, or even Old Earth...

"Neither, actually," said a voice behind her. "We created it just for you."

She turned around, startled. Behind her stood a man, short, clad in a dark suit of an archaic design. His accent was strange. "How..." she began. A cold spike of alarm shot through her. Could they read her thoughts? If they saw - !

He held up his hands, a calming gesture. "My apologies. We're still trying to determine which parts of your mind we should avoid accessing directly. I didn't mean to alarm you. Do not worry! The programs which encoded you were simple ones, and their memory buffers have been purged. Your secrets remain your own, whatever they may be."

Was that last statement too pointed? No, she'd imagined it. "Thank you."

He nodded. "Well, then. Welcome to the Sirian Hierarchy. I'll be the... interface, if you like, between your mind and the local realities. My name is Joseph."

"That is a strange name," she said.

He smiled. "It's an ancient name. Our roots go back to Sol System itself. Yours do too, eventually, but your memories don't reach as far back as ours." He started to walk across the springy green grass, and she fell into step beside him. The landscape shifted as they walked, slowly, subtly. "So tell me," he said presently, "what brings you to the virtual world? It has been quite some time since we have had direct dealings with baselines, or they with us."

"Bad news, I am afraid," she said. "Some of the solar power collectors, which we understand are under your control, have moved out of position. They are now blocking much of the sunlight we need to survive. We were hoping you would be able to fix the problem."

He frowned. "Strange. We haven't noticed any trouble with the sunscoops - " *No, of course not* - "but we'll look into it. In the meantime, you must be interested in knowing more about us. I can give you the tour, so to speak."

"Yes," she lied. An excellent opportunity to stall for time.

"Excellent. Well, the first thing..." His voice trailed off, eyes defocusing as if he was looking at something impossibly distant. The light dimmed, but it was not due to the sun; the entire view darkened, becoming blurred and indistinct. The air fairly vibrated with power and a palpable sense of *presence*. She looked around in alarm.

Joseph seemed distracted, listening to a voice she could not hear. "Yes," he said after a moment, "this is the one from the solaria." A pause. "No, I suppose not. I will remember." Then it was gone, the scene as bright and pastoral as before.

"What was that?" she asked.

"One of them." A meaningful glance upwards, towards the delicate arching lines of diamondoid. "A Noëa."

"I thought *you* - "

He laughed. "Oh, no, not in the least. They don't understand how you think well enough to talk directly, any more than you understand them. The differences are too great. I am... well, an echo of sorts, a recording of the being I once was. Insofar as there is an "I" anymore. They were human once, before they became what they are now." He turned and indicated a house, now sheltered within the walls of a thickly wooded valley. "The landscape is fictional, but that was my home."

Presently he paused, and for the first time she sensed some hesitation in his words. "At least, I think it was. Not all my memories were stored, you see, and sometimes a few more get lost in the mix. My greater self has more pressing memory demands than preserving me." He fell silent for a minute in reflection. Then with a visible effort he pulled his thoughts back to the present, and turned to face her again.

"Come," he said. "Let me show you things."

####

Overhead the sunscoops sparkled.

"Sunscoops?"

"Thousands of them," Till confirmed. "They seem to have drifted out of their normal positions, and now they are occluding the sun. There are so many of them that the decrease in luminosity is substantial."

The council room was embedded in the side of a rock face, in fact the very cliff on top of which she had spoken to Till the previous day. The room's wide windows allowed a panoramic view of the solarium's interior. Ordinarily the sight cheered her, a reminder that they had faced tough situations before and survived. Now in the slowly fading evening light, the decaying forests and broken ground seemed bleaker than ever. She turned away from the windows.

One council member cleared his throat pointedly. "Yes, Dr. Alakir?" Elen asked.

He stood easily in the light gravity of his home near the central axis of *Argent*. He was a small man who possessed the air of dignity which came with nearly a millennium of age. He had once been one of her teachers, three hundred years earlier. Now he was the most distinguished expert on orbital engineering in the Twelve Solaria, and the council's Director of Science. "This was not simply a chance occurrence," he said. "The sunscoops are not in orbit, but are held up by the pressure of sunlight. The only way for them to move other than radially is by tilting them in a very specific way. We can be sure this was a deliberate action."

"On whose part?" she asked. On this he had no opinion, and sat. The other members looked at each other uneasily, reluctant to put voice to the thoughts troubling them. She guessed after a moment. "What, the virtual world? They have never bothered about us before. What threat could we pose to the Noëadrim?"

"Their minds are unknown to us," said Taneki, the historian. "They think differently. They may not want us to use up resources they need from the asteroids. Or they may simply have decided our use of their sunlight is not allowed."

"Their sunlight!" exclaimed Till. "This is our home! We have as much right to it as they have."

"Their presence here predates our own," she responded evenly. "There are precedents. But of course you are right. Sirius is a bright star, and few others live around it. There must be more than enough energy to go around. Certainly they could be reasoned with."

"If that was the case, they would have contacted us first," said the Director of Security. "To me this speaks of hostile intent."

They argued back and forth for several minutes, images flickering slightly from the holoprojectors' disrepair. She watched silently, nearly able to predict when and what a given member would speak. The same thoughts, the same old arguments and fears repeated once again. Centuries of complacency all congealed into one room.

"Enough," she said finally. Silence fell as they all looked at her. "This is pointless. We cannot simply talk to them - the best we could do is send a representative and hope they can devise a way to translate. Neither can we attack them. We have no weapons and no way to defend against retaliation." The room remained silent as the others thought deeply, trying to come up with a solution.

Then, the Director of Information coughed slightly. "I may have an alternate suggestion," he said carefully.

####

A rounded disk of superheated plasma, bulging in the middle. Encircling it from pole to pole, a slowly rotating ring of bright hot points. Farther out lay a nearly complete sphere of thin squares of dark material - sunscoops - on some of which sat arrays of green lasers. Periodically these would fire into the outer edge of the disk, sending up great bursts of glowing plasma. Moon-sized structures orbited within the larger sphere, absorbing the rapidly cooling gases. And in the middle of all this were two human figures, standing impossibly on a surface that did not exist.

"What is this?" she asked wonderingly.

"One of our more ambitious projects," said Joseph. "Sirius is a very large star. It will burn itself out in scarcely a billion years unless we intervene. Similar plans have been started in other systems, although it will be many thousands of millennia until their outcomes are clear." Around them plumes of stellar matter leapt outwards towards the surrounding darkness. "These are just the design plans, of course. We won't know what it looks like until the project gets under way."

"Then this is actually possible? I would never have thought something like this could really be done."

He nodded. "Ironically, it was humans who first devised the idea of star lifting, but they were fated never to be the ones to carry it out. By the time adequate technology had been developed, they had already been surpassed by greater intelligences. Your kind is no longer the driving force in the galaxy, I'm afraid."

"I think we still have some contributions to make," she said, a bit stiffly.

"Not in the same way you once did," he said. "You have numbers, we have power. It evens out, I suppose. But your ability to drastically alter the future has passed on to higher beings. On the other hand, neither are you able to accidentally destroy yourselves anymore. The tradeoff may or may not be comforting to you; take it as you will."

"It is not."

But then he showed her many things she would never have imagined, from all across the inhabited galaxy. The images surrounded them, changing in rapid succession. Weylforges and linelayer ships carving paths through spacetime; arrays of cargo accelerators so long light would take hours to cross them; the incredible megaengineering projects of the MPA; even the Shapers' kilometers-long sentient habitats, whole worlds unto themselves. All were designed, built, and controlled by super-intelligences of one sort or another. She knew what he had said was true, and hated him for it.

"*The Noëadrim are beings of information,*" they had said. "*So we must use information against them.*"

As she watched she felt the program buried within her mind start to come to life, reaching out into the surrounding simulation with thin tendrils of logic. The images jerked, distorted and then froze entirely. Joseph frowned, startled. "What - "

"*A virus, hidden inside your brainwave patterns. It will take time to adjust to their data architecture, but then it will strike.*"

The scene around them started to break up, becoming grainy and broken as if eaten away by acid. A darkness spread outwards from her, consuming everything it touched. Joseph drew back from its touch.

"*I will go,*" she had said over their protests. "*It is my responsibility, no one else's.*"

"Elen! Are you all right?"

"I'm sorry," she managed to say, and then the darkness swallowed her as well.

"I told you they wouldn't disappoint us."

"**Surprising. Very well, Joseph, we will do as you ask and permit their existence. But we must still keep a close watch on them.**"

"Undoubtedly. Look, she's starting to come around."

She awoke with a start. Disoriented, it took her a minute to figure out where she was - inside the house she had arrived in, lying on a couch. Looking over she saw Joseph sitting in an ornate chair next to her. At seeing her awake he stood with a concerned expression. "Are you all right?" he asked. "Do you think you have been damaged?"

It took her a minute to assess the question. "No," she said, "I do not think so. But what happened? I thought..."

"This?" He held up a strangely contorted object, made of glinting metal and twisting around and back on itself in a complex fashion: a physical representation of the program hidden within her thoughts. "A fairly simple virus, as such things go. We detected it when you were encoded, and had little trouble disabling it once it activated. The real trick was preventing it from doing any harm to your data in the process."

Now she felt thoroughly confused. "But, why?" she asked, sitting up. "If you knew, I do not understand why you let all of this happen. Would it not have been simpler to just remove the virus and tell me afterwards?"

"Yes," he said, "but that would not have suited our purposes." He pulled his chair closer to her couch. "More than six thousand years ago, the first colonists came to settle the Sirius system. The project was eventually abandoned as unfeasible, but not before one group became dissatisfied and broke off to do things on their own. They moved into the asteroid belt, established a habitat run like a corporation - "

"The founders of the Twelve Solaria."

"Yes."

"Our history records that, but only in fragments. Even we are not totally immortal."

"Neither would your culture be, without external intervention. For centuries you flourished, but in recent years you have been in decline." As he spoke the room faded from view, replaced by images of times long past. She saw the solaria at their height, and then the descent into decay. "We observed you at long range, watched your forays into the asteroids become more infrequent and your equipment degrade. You were becoming stagnant, insular. Human society is a chaotic process, and you were slowly spiraling down into the well of a dead attractor. We decided to give you a nudge, to try to boost you out of your complacency."

Diagrams flitted by in dizzying patterns, flickering in the corners of her vision. "So you did move the sunscoops purposely."

He nodded. "We - well, Noëar at least - have a distaste for interacting with the physical world directly. I don't understand why myself; this sort of simulation seems real enough to me, but their thoughtspaces are much more abstract. Regardless of their rationale, the solution was a very elegant one. All it took was a few numbers being changed slightly, numbers governing the tension on a group of sunscoops' staying cables."

"And that tilted the collectors, making them move..." Black squares sliding across a piercingly white disk.

"Blocking your lifeblood, your sunlight. Yes. The mere fact that you responded by coming here proves there is enough life left in your society to warrant further action. As for the virus, we had to be sure. We had to see whether you would risk permanent death for the sake of your habitats' survival. You could not have harmed us in any event." The images melded into the background as the room returned to view. "You may well fail to understand us or our motives," he continued, "but we do desire your survival, and if possible, prosperity."

She was quiet for several minutes, thinking about all he had told her. "And why do you care?" she asked presently. She thought of the beetle she had crushed so thoughtlessly, those long days ago on the cliff. "We are so small compared to you."

Instead of answering, Joseph stood and walked over to the cage hanging by the door. He reached in though the bars and smoothed the feathers of the bird inside. It chirped appreciatively. "Do you like it?" he asked, turning back to her.

"It's beautiful."

"Yes, it is. It makes beautiful music as well, and consumes virtually no resources of any importance. Why not support its existence? Even in your solaria you have bird feeders."

Realization dawned. "But... no. You cannot mean - !"

He smiled then, that strange smile that seemed to speak of secret and unknowable truths. Before she could respond, he did something at a level hidden to her, changed the pattern of the simulated reality she was visiting. Logic blocks folded out of existence as they reached their conclusions, the data streams turned back on themselves, everything appeared to *skew* -

And in the tower high above, still wrapped in the construct's mechanical embrace, her eyes opened.

Bunny Love Has No Limits
The Outer Volumes
8121 AT

Daniel Eliot Boese

Thanks to the availability of craft equipped with various kinds of reactionless drive, the Terragen Sphere was expanding at a large fraction of the speed of light. The archailects, however, were large and centralised entities housed in great megastructures, and could exert only indirect influence over the Outer Volumes and Periphery. Far from the Inner Sphere and Hinterlands of the old established empires new factions came into existence.

Some emergent powers adopted a strategy of rapid expansion, often with the intention of establishing a large population or an extensive sphere of influence before the agents of the inner empires could act to suppress or assimilate them. Those who used aggressive swarms of replicators to build infrastructure and weapons posed a direct and unsubtle threat that was generally suppressed quite quickly, by agents of the central powers, or by coalitions of the local polities.

More insidious were those groups which used replicating swarms which appealed to the desires of their victims; swarms of advertisements for a better life, or promises of a new utopia, or simply an offer of companionship.

Daniel Eliot Boese tells the story of one such plague, preying on the most vulnerable individuals in order to gain access to new worlds ripe for infection.

It's all my ex-girlfriend's fault.

It's all my ex-boyfriend's fault. It's all my employer's fault. It's all Bunny's fault. It's all my parents' fault. It's all society's fault.

It's all my fault.

I think that last one is the closest to the truth.

I don't know if anyone else is ever going to get a chance to read this – I'm saving it internally, on my implant's storage space – so I'm writing it to my future self, while I'm still close to the start of everything that just happened, so that, maybe, I'll be able to better remember how I feel.

I've never been good at feelings. Or other people, really. When it comes to analytical thought, I'm a super-bright… but other humans seem almost as alien to me as the Muuh. I've never understood all the status-seeking games that seem to take up the time of my fellow hu, so I've done my best to avoid them altogether. That's why I had Bunny made in the first place. She's generally humanoid, but with an attractive pelt, bunny-face, cottonpuff tail, sweet-smelling and with a pleasant purr in her voice… and her mind was set up to be just on the low side of being a 'person'. She finds simple maid-work to be challenging, and finds pleasure in doing whatever I ask of her. Yes, what I mainly built her for is as much bestiality as it would be with a non-provolved chimp… but, fortunately for me, my home society doesn't consider bestiality illegal, just something 'dirty' to crack jokes about in impolite society and avoid discussing in polite circles, like masturbation. To the most complete extent possible for her mental architecture, she loves me, and has always loved me, and I don't have to try to figure out what a potential sex-partner wants from me, or pay for it, or let some transapient slap together some avatar-body out of pity for the lonely ape. By some standards, that makes me a selfish, misogynistic bastard, and I've pretty much given up trying to justify my actions to anyone other than myself.

Not long after I had Bunny made, I found out about an upcoming hermeneutic conference in a nearby star system. I don't have anywhere near the whuffie to convince our local AIs to send me out-system, but after some careful searching, I found another way to attend. A transapient ship would be heading in the right direction, and though e didn't _need_ baselines, it preferred having some human companionship for the trip. After a good deal of careful back-and-forth to figure out if we met each others' needs, e agreed to bring me along – Bunny, too. I was under no illusions – I would be little more than an amusing little pet for em, much like Bunny was for me, but it was a role I was willing to accept – and in the end, not all that different from the roles I had to take when interacting with other humans.

So off we all went, on our merry way, along with the other human-pets who'd come along for the ride. I was always polite to them, and as pleasant as I could manage, but after a few weeks, the involuntary signals of my tension when they tried making friends with me reduced such attempted closeness to more tolerable levels. They formed their pairs, and groups, and clusters, and as long as they didn't _require_ my companionship, I was able to join in at least some of the social activities.

Halfway between my home system, and the one with the conference, was a starless planetoid, a beamrider station. We were decelerating to rendezvous with it, where some of our passengers would jump off, and we'd likely pick up a few more. I went to sleep the night before our expected arrival spooned up with Bunny in our sleep-pouch...

... and when I woke up, alone, my implant helpfully told me four days had passed, and we were under acceleration again. The ship-AI didn't respond to me anymore.

I haven't been able to find out what happened during those four days – the ship's records are blocked to me, the other humans say they were asleep too, and Bunny's never really had much of a vocabulary. We all seemed to be prisoners of the now-incommunicative AI and, somewhat to my consternation and confusion, Bunny – who was as genetically incompatible with me as a real lapine – was massively pregnant.

Three days later, Bunny gave birth to another Bunny.

Once they'd both gotten cleaned up, I wasn't able to find any differences between them, and neither of them seemed to understand that there *was* any difference between them.

The next day, both of them had visible baby-bumps growing in their bellies.

Everyone was trying to figure out what had happened during the stopover, why our AI host had stopped talking, whether we'd been drugged or had our memories wiped... and what was going on with Bunny.

A week later, when I was trying to manage four obviously-pregnant Bunnies, each of which loved me and wanted to do everything she could for me, the next real incident happened. I can't verify any of the details, but what I *think* happened is that one of the other humans tried to attack me while I was asleep. All I can say for certain is that when I woke up, one of my fellow passengers was missing his arms. No visible scar, no indication that he'd ever had the limbs in the first place, and a tale to tell about going into my quarters "for a personal conversation", not that anybody believed that excuse, when one of the Bunnies hugged him, and he fell unconscious, waking up in his own rooms without arms.

Needless to say, everyone did their best to avoid me as much as they could from that point.

A few days later, three of the Bunnies gave birth to other Bunnies just like the original, and one gave birth to a Bunny who was different – her fur a light blue instead of my Bunny's Martian pink – and who proclaimed her love for the armless man, and started tending to his every need rather than mine.

The blue Bunny didn't swell up with pregnancies like mine were inexplicably prone to, but two weeks later, every human had gotten their own Bunny, male Bunnies for the women, though I was the only one with multiple Bunnies. At that point, just as mysteriously as they'd started, the Bunnies' pregnancies stopped. Things settled down for the next few weeks; we had no way of knowing the answers to the mysteries surrounding us, so life went back to keeping on keeping on. And even if their source was a mystery, everyone seemed to get used to having a Bunny.

Or, at least, that was the impression the other humans gave to me... but two days ago, I found out they'd just been excluding me from their plans. I can't blame them – after all, I brought Bunny aboard.

Once again, whatever it was that happened, I was asleep for it – or had my memory of it erased afterwards. But when I woke up, two women were armless, the armless man had lost his legs... and, most ominously, two Bunnies were massively pregnant, and 'their' humans were nowhere to be found. Nowhere else, anyway – in short order, their fur turned to the pink of 'my' Bunnies, though their bellies neither grew nor shrank, nor have they given birth.

I've stayed in my room since then, hiding from the other humans. If I were them, I'd be scared shitless of me, and the Bunnies, and would probably lash out in any way I could think of, at me or the Bunnies or both… and from what I've seen, all that sort of activity would result in is either a case of acute limblessness, or disappearance into a Bunny. Looking at it from a certain viewpoint, I suppose both… responses are more humane than simple execution, but from a rather a-human point of view.

This morning, when I asked one of my Bunnies about what she would do if I died; she used a word I know for a fact her original design was incapable of understanding. Whatever was done to my first Bunny, it seems to be having an effect on her mind, too. I'm guessing that there's some sort of hivemind effect going on – that the more Bunnies there are, the smarter they get. But they all still seem completely devoted to my personal welfare and happiness… as they interpret that. And I don't know whether to feel relieved or outright terrified at the implications.

If anyone else ever reads this: I'm sorry. I didn't _mean_ for Bunny to be anything other than a sex-pet. By the time I figured out that there was anything _to_ stop, that our stopover had been met with some sort of perversity that, when it encountered Bunny, took her mental programming to its logical conclusion, it was too late to do anything about it. The ship-AI was, or is, S2, and I don't know if anything short of intervention by an S3 can keep Bunny from spreading... and according to my implant's databases, there *aren't* any S3s anywhere near our current course.

I've had an idea for how to deal with this situation. I don't *think* the Bunnies, or whatever the ship-AI has become, can read my implant, but just in case either can, I'm not writing it down. Suffice it to say that if it works, my current problems will be solved... and if it doesn't, they're likely to be "solved", though in an entirely different way. Here's hoping it's the former.

The Immortalist
The Story of Skalosak
8400 AT

Darren Ryding

In stories and myths told throughout the Hinteregions, a group known as the Collectors are reputed to seek out and gather the most sadistic criminals (whether imprisoned, free, or in positions of power) and feed them to their transapient matriarch, the Queen of Pain. Inside the Queen, the victims face an eternity of torment, gauged according to the severity of their crimes and cruelty. Tales of the Collectors, their Queen, and their victims are popular with sapient travelers, and are used as morality tales to frighten criminals and youths into good behaviour.

The most renowned of the Collectors is an entity known as Skalosak, sometimes appearing as a beautiful human female, sometimes as a member of the Siberoo splice clade, a cross between a Siberian tiger and a giant kangaroo. Many tales of Skalosak have been told, depicting her fierce devotion to her terrible cause. But everyone has a story, and even the most ferocious warrior may not start that way.

Here Darren Ryding tells the story of Skalosak's early years as an ordinary citizen of the Terragen Sphere, and how she came to abandon her former life for a new calling after personal tragedy.

"I love snowstorms," purred Skalosak as she watched the wave of white sweep over the ice hills toward her.

"What, really?" said Tillika from a fair distance behind. "Who would have guessed?"

Skalosak smirked at her manager's obvious irony. Of all the Siberoos at the Niflheim Snow Guide Station, it was she who loved to play outdoors the most, which was saying quite a lot. "Savour the pleasures of the cold," she would say. "It is what our kind was engineered for." And the others agreed. They would have agreed even more had she not spent one out of every ten nights sleeping outside, unclothed, on the ice. In winter. Near the North Pole. On one of the coldest planets ever to support a colony of mammals with its own atmosphere.

"I love the tingling feeling they give me under my fur," said Skalosak as the wall of snow closed in.

"There are many ways to get that tingling feeling under your fur, honeycakes," said Tillika, "and not all of them involve temperatures that would turn a human's blood to iced raspberry jello within two of their short little heartbeats."

"I sincerely hope that's an exaggeration," said a smaller male voice coming from the same direction.

Skalosak looked over her shoulder. Tillika was standing there before the vast station entrance, flecks of snow already adorning her black and reddish gold stripes. Her huge tail swayed slowly from side to side, as if trying to catch even more snow. Even her whiskers had caught a few glistening particles. Despite her darker fur, Tillika had almost the same build as Skalosak. When standing in a relaxed pose, leaning forward on their massive hind legs, both

Siberoos stood over three metres from their broad padded feet to their pointy-eared scalps. Yet despite Tillika's constant bragging, her hips were nothing spectacular. A mere metre and a half wide. In this climate, snow guides needed all the blubber they could get.

Her passenger, however, would normally have had every right to dislike snowstorms. He was a human male, and for now only his head was visible, sticking out of Tillika's lower belly, well below her utility belt. At that moment, only his head had any right to fear the snowstorm. The rest of him was fine.

"Oh, she's not exaggerating," Skalosak purred portentously to Tillika's passenger. "Have you seen what severe hypothermia does to the human body? Or frostbite? It's not a pretty sight. For starters, your nose might need to be replaced, and your ears-"

"That's enough," said the human. "Good night ladies." His head promptly slid back into Tillika's pouch, which closed up tight, only palpitating slightly as the human curled up in the bottom.

"You just love fucking with the tourists, don't you Skal?"

"Figuratively speaking, I hope you mean. That's what I'm famous for."

"Speaking of things you're famous for, here comes your favourite thing in the entire blistering universe."

"Ahhh," sighed Skalosak, as she turned to face the snowstorm. It was like a tsunami of white now, towering over her like a mountain. "Come and get me, sweetheart," she invited the storm as she closed her eyes and held out her arms. Within seconds, it got her. Her thick fur wavered all over as the cold tried to find a way in, tickling and tingling like an experienced lover. Of course, her species was too well insulated to be harmed by a common snowstorm. Even her pouch was locked up tight, which would have been good news to any passenger had she carried one.

"For someone who wants to live forever," Tillika shouted over the howl of the wind, "you sure love to embrace the closest thing to the personification of death."

"You clearly have never seen a black hole close up."

"Then when I do, I'll tell it that you said hello."

Several minutes passed as the coldness washed over the Siberoos in relentless waves, shrieking in their ears like a symphony of chaos. It even dared to lift them. At their weight, such ambition was sheer hubris, even for a force of nature.

"All right," shouted Tillika. "Are you coming inside, or are you going to make a habit of sleeping in snowstorms as well?"

"Why would I sleep when I could dance?" Skalosak swayed her hips and tail in slow sinuous motions.

"I've seen headless turkeys with better dance moves," said Tillika, two seconds before a snowball hit her in the face with an impact that would have instantly killed a human. She casually shook off the ice and glared at Skalosak. "Would you prefer to stay out here tonight and hunt for penguins?" she said.

"Very well then. I've obviously had too much fun for your liking."

The vast outer door of the station slid silently open.

"I'm in the mood for real steak tonight instead of the bioforged stuff," said Tillika as the outer door closed and locked behind them, signalling the equally vast secondary door to open.

"For once we are in agreement," said Skalosak, striding along the long, broad passageway to the hall. "That's another great thing about cold weather – it's the perfect excuse to eat whatever the hell you want."

"Ironic."

"How so?"

"Well, you love the taste of real meat. You love the feeling of real ice on your butt. Aren't you going to miss all this when you transcend?"

Skalosak gave her friend a sharp side-glance. "Who said I was in a rush to become a transapient?"

"You sort of conveyed that impression when you waffled on for hours that night about new special offers on cybernetic implants. Plus there's that little movement you've joined."

"It's not a movement, it's a philosophy. A 'movement' implies initiation rites, secret pawshakes, and perverse submission to a charismatic leader. Besides, a few more implants aren't going to instantly transform me into a new species. The heavy stuff can wait."

"Speaking of the heavy stuff ..."

As the two Siberoos entered the vast, velvet red station hall, they were greeted by a creature that dwarfed them as thoroughly as they dwarfed humans. It resembled a massive feline, its fur as white and flowing as the storm outside, towering over Skalosak and Tillika even on all fours.

"How would you rate tonight's storm, girls?" boomed the team's most colossal marsupial. The voice of Maraji the Megasiber made Skalosak's bones vibrate with its resonance. Maraji was often nicknamed "The Honeymoon Suite" because of her popularity with newlywed couples looking for a novel form of snow transport.

"I'd give it a nine point seven," said Skalosak. "Tilly? Your score for this evening?"

"A solid eight."

"And how about your passenger?"

"Kavoni?" Tillika looked down at her closed pouch. "How would you rate the snowstorm?"

"Mmmrrrffff," came a tiny muffled voice.

"Oh well," said Skalosak. "His opinion doesn't count. Humans don't last two seconds in our snowstorms. They're not built to take it. Are you Kavoni?"

A tiny hand emerged from Tillika's pouch and blindly gave the finger.

"Charming," said Skalosak. "You could almost pass for a male right now Tilly."

"Never mind your signature smut," boomed Maraji. "You've both convinced me to sleep outside tonight. Goodnight girls."

The massive Megasiber thundered her way out of the hall. The two Siberoos went in the opposite direction towards the housing quarters.

"Pardon the pun, but Maraji is a massive example of what I've been talking about all this time," said Skalosak. "Do you think natural evolution would have created something like her? Sleeping in snowstorms? Going for a year without food? Judging ice thickness for kilometres with just her pawpads? She's almost a machine herself."

"I didn't come down in the last snowstorm, fluffymuffins. Everyone knows that you and I exist today because some bored human geneticists got drunk eight thousand years ago. Do you really think that their work still hasn't finished yet?"

"Has anything finished? Has evolution finished? I'm not talking about natural selection, which probably has finished on most worlds. I'm talking about intelligent selection. Even on a backwater planet like ours we have a choice in what we become. If you're dedicated, you could live forever. And if you're very dedicated and very lucky, you could become a God. Don't look at me like that, you know it's possible. Life today is rich in possibilities and potential experiences. Why do you think we're so popular with tourists? Because smaller species would pay good money for a comfy ride through a landscape carved out of ice. They crave new experiences. They crave novelty. It's a natural urge of all sentient beings."

"Well, right now, I'm craving steak and chips washed down with crème liqueur and ice water. Will you be joining us for dinner this time?"

"See you in ten minutes."

"Will do."

Tillika pressed her paw against the wall, which dilated like her own pouch, and crossed over into her apartment. Seconds later, Skalosak entered her own apartment.

There were close to three hundred units within a thousand-kilometre radius where she could have slept for free. In fact, for roughly half the nights of every year, she got paid to sleep in those places. This was the privilege of all company employees. Her job was to carry a tourist around the arctic, from one automated guesthouse to the other, showing her passenger the fabled ruins and ice landscapes and (introduced) fauna of her frozen world. Each guesthouse was maintained by a single self-aware AI, and usually consisted of a large sleeping quarters for guides and a smaller one for tourists. The most memorable moments of her job, however, were not necessarily viewing and explaining ice landforms or walrus colonies or ancient landing ships for the thousandth time. Usually, the most memorable moments were when she simply relaxed in guesthouses, dining and talking and joking with her passengers, melting through their shyness, sometimes playing virtual games or pausing and interrupting old movies with witty commentary that never failed to raise a smile.

She always promised herself that, whatever she became in centuries to come, she would never abandon life's simpler pleasures.

Skalosak knelt in the centre of her room, closed her eyes, and checked for messages.

As the cluster of neon-bright icons danced behind her eyelids, Skalosak was mildly amused by the persistence of certain advertisers. "Enlarge your pouch!" said one unopened message – the one hundred and sixty-seventh message that year to make that very promise. Skalosak was satisfied that her pouch was large enough as it was, having been stretched to the limit after the first twelve years of motherhood. She had no desire to look like some sort of grotesque cartoon drawing. What was she supposed to carry? Polar bears or something? "Slim down for summer!" Summer was half a year away – even if it ever existed this far north. Asking a snow guide to slim down was like asking a weightlifter to get rid of unsightly muscles. And what was this about a "discount on scarves"? Scarves? Did they have any freaking idea what she even looked like?

"Watch the thick, velvety fur grow inside your pouch!" said another message. Again, not necessary. Like her female co-workers, Skalosak had already raised a joeycub. Fur began to grow on the inside of the female's pouch as soon as the joeycub took its first short trips outside. It was a defining trait that dated back to the early days of genetic engineering. Older joeys loved a fur-lined pouch, as did human tourists.

"Upgrade your five senses," said another, "and add a few new ones!" That was more like it. She would have to come back to that one.

"Memory uploads made easy! ... A lifetime of memories in an instant!" That sounded especially promising.

Of course, being a snow guide, Skalosak received a lot of messages from her former passengers; some recent ones thanking her for her company and hospitality, some tourists from years back giving her updates on their own lives, some prospective tourists who knew her former passengers and wanted to book tours with her personally.

Yet there was one message that towered above all others, that made Skalosak's belly tingle with delight. In a sense, this message also came from a former passenger – the first she ever had.

"Hello Mother."

It had been half a year since his last message, and three years since they had last met face-to-face. Unable to wait another second, Skalosak dream-dived into the message icon, and the neon-lit night of her mind softened into the mild glow of Rantreleka's apartment, four hundred light years away.

Skalosak's son was standing there in the middle of the room. At twenty-two, Rantreleka was fully-grown. Though smaller and leaner than any female, he was still taller by half than the average human. He had her bright blue eyes, although the tawny spots against his eggshell-white fur took after his father – a casual friend Skalosak had not seen in recent years (which made little difference to anyone concerned – after all, marsupials more or less invented single parenting). He was wearing his merchant navy uniform – black with gold stripes on the sleeves and high collar.

"Try to contain your excitement," said Rantreleka in his soft baritone voice, "if that is at all possible, but I've already made arrangements, and I should be landing on New Dumont in exactly forty-two days."

Completely ignoring her son's advice, Skalosak raised her virtual paw and roared in victory, wishing to the AI Gods that Rantreleka could somehow hear it.

For the following few minutes, Skalosak floated in rapt attention as Rantreleka rattled off some casual anecdotes about his job, his leisure time, his hobbies, his friends and co-workers. She found herself chuckling at the sort of jokes that, coming from anyone else, she would have sighed at and "improved on" with one of her own witty retorts. But this was her son. He had a right to tell lame jokes, because … just because.

After ten minutes, a window glowed on the edge of Skalosak's virtual vision. "Time for yum-yums," came Tillika's faint voice.

"Give me five minutes," said Skalosak, and closed the link before rewinding and replaying the last few seconds of Rantreleka's message.

After a few minutes, Ranty was coming to the end of his message. "Cheleera has introduced me to this local church. It's called The Church of the Sacred Flesh. I've been attending over the past few weeks and … so far everyone there's been pretty friendly. Anyway, I'll tell you more about it when I get there. I'm looking forward to seeing you again. Love you forever."

He raised his paw in farewell before the scene dissolved.

Instantly, Skalosak pulled out of her message mindscape and opened her eyes.

"The Church of the Sacred Flessshh," she hissed.

Skalosak knew all about antimatter reactions. Right now, she felt as if one was going off in her guts. Rantreleka was matter. But antimatter? That was the Church of the Sacred Flesh.

She loved her son, but hated that fucking cult.

####

In many stories – especially comedies -, snow guides always met their passengers at the spaceport. In reality, the local guides waited at the spaceport only a few times a year. Because most passengers came from elsewhere on the planet, Skalosak usually waited at one of many common airports. Sometimes she wished writers paid more attention to statistics.

This time around, though, she really did wait at the spaceport.

Statistics aside, it was not too unusual to see a Siberoo towering over a throng of humans at Salandara Spaceport. One would commonly be part of the crowd gazing with anticipation at the gateway to the arrival lounge, awaiting the appearance of friends or loved ones or business associates. More often than not, the Siberoo would be waiting for a tourist who had pre-booked a snow ride.

Yet today was special. Today, she was ready to greet her first and most beloved passenger.

She did not have to wait too long. Only a few minutes after the arrival lounge gateway opened, after many hugs and kisses and handshakes among the humans, Rantreleka's (relatively) towering form stepped through the threshold and met his mother's gaze, his whiskers raised in joy. The sea of humans parted respectfully as Skalosak thundered through to lift and embrace her son.

"I see that you are still the same introverted emotionally reserved young lady I have always known," Rantreleka joked as Skalosak rubbed her face against his and purred.

"I see that you are still small enough to carry," said Skalosak.

"Well, it's not as if I'm going to bulk myself up with nanodrugs and implants."

Skalosak froze briefly at her son's joke, realising that Ranty could not be aware of how greatly her obsession had grown over the years. It was just a harmless joke, with nothing personal intended. Nonetheless, she had found plenty of time to do some extra research on the church that Rantreleka had joined. Their views on body and brain modifications were very clear.

Wanting to change the subject – or at least save it for later – Skalosak held her son out before her to appraise his appearance. His face fur was well groomed – at least the half of his face that Skalosak had not rubbed against and messed up completely. He was casually dressed, with a black high-collar long-sleeved shirt and black trousers. Clothes were merely an option for male Siberoos on their days off, and quite rare for females - although they were sometimes useful for carrying multiple passengers. It seemed that Rantreleka had dressed up in preparation for a colder climate, having spent three years adjusting to frequent sunshine. Skalosak secretly hoped that her son's attire was inspired by practicality and not cultural conformity. At least he was barefoot.

"Even if you did," said Skalosak, "even if you bulked yourself up, dyed your fur green and purple, and covered yourself ear to toe to tail in armour, do you think I wouldn't recognize you?"

"I remember what you used to tell me when I was just a joey. If I was buried under a kilometre of snow, you'd go digging for me."

"Without fail." Skalosak embraced her son one last time before putting him down. "We're taking a hoverbus to the snow guide base. Spiced venison is on the menu."

"Spiced venison? You don't want me to leave, do you?"

"Not ever."

Rantreleka chuckled, then walked briskly to keep up with his mother's long strides.

####

"I gave up combat games years ago," said Rantreleka after swallowing his mouthful of venison. "Most of my friends back home are human."

"So?" said Tillika, seated on the opposite side of the dining table. "Get your friends to wear power armour so that they'd have a fair chance."

This got a chuckle from most in the dining hall. In addition to Rantreleka and Tillika, this included Skalosak, two other female Siberoos, two male Siberoos (whose job was to carry their passengers in thermal backpacks) and two human tourists on elevated seats – a man sitting next to his female snow guide, and a woman sitting next to her male guide.

"I don't think they'd bother," said Rantreleka, before taking a sip of root beer.

"I wrestled with a male human in power armour once," said Tillika. "He was my passenger for the week. The suit was as big as I am. And three hundred kilowatts. They can rent them for only a hundred vayaks an hour. They have impact-absorbing polymer so you feel like you're punching real flesh. We wrestled in the snow for a whole hour. He nearly beat me too. We had a great time."

"Sounds like fun," said Rantreleka. "But these days, my pursuits are more … spiritual."

Skalosak glanced sideways at her son, hoping for his sake that he did not let the subject spiral out of control.

"Ah, yes," said Hollivox, who – not unlike Skalosak – was a black and white female Siberoo. "What was that church you joined?"

"The Church of the Sacred Flesh," said Rantreleka.

"Yes, that," said Holly. "Aren't they against upgrades and uploads?"

Rantreleka chuckled, almost with embarrassment. "That's a bit of a gross simplification. We prefer to keep brain and body modifications to an absolute minimum."

"And how would you define 'absolute minimum'?" said Tillika.

"Put simply, it is perfectly fine to take all the medications you need to keep yourself healthy. Implants and prosthetics are also acceptable if absolutely necessary. If you lose your arm through no fault of your own, by all means get a new one. If you lose half your skin, get it replaced quick smart. If you're paralysed, get some new nerves. It is all right to back up the body parts you want to keep."

"Sounds reasonable enough," said Holly.

"Our faith is founded upon reason."

"So where, exactly, do you draw the line?" said Malox, the black and gold male Siberoo, who was leaning forward like a journalist on a talk show.

"Vanity," said Rantreleka. "That is all. We draw the line at vanity. If someone or something severs your limb, it is your right – indeed, your obligation – to have it replaced. But what if you dismember yourself? Do you cut off your arm for being too weak? Do you cut off your leg for being too slow? Do you cut off your face for being too ugly? It is one thing to respond to the trials and tribulations the Designer throws in your path, to replace what is forcibly taken from you. But to reject what the Designer has freely given you and allowed you to keep? That is an affront to His infinite generosity."

"So, going by what you're saying," said Malox, "cosmetic upgrades, athletic upgrades, non-vital organ replacements of any type, all transcladers and ninety-nine per cent of all cyborgs are an affront to the Designer?"

Skalosak silently admired Malox's sharpness. She would have to visit him more often.

"Their choices are between themselves and their Designer," said Rantreleka. "By that I mean their one true Designer, not the AI or transapient who creates new bits and pieces for their clients to stick onto themselves like fancy antlers on a snow truck bonnet."

"What about destructive uploading?" said Vanashta, the black female Siberoo. "If you upload your mind into cyberspace and destroy the original, then wha-"

"That's suicide. Suicide is a sin. Oh, sure, you leave a copy behind, but that is just a copy. Nothing more."

"What do you think of copying in general?" said Holly.

"Well, copying two or three hours of your memory? That's called a movie, isn't it? So long as it's just sensory data, with thoughts and emotions edited only for aesthetic purposes. But copying your entire memory, emotions and all? That's forgery of the worst kind. You're forging a soul that is copyright of the Designer."

"But what about ... you're twenty-two, aren't you?"

"That's right." Rantreleka nodded politely at Malox.

"So ... what's the fundamental difference between a two hour movie and a twenty-two year movie? Length? Budget? Artistic merit?"

"I assure you, my secular friend," said Rantreleka, keeping his face as straight as possible, "my life story has barely reached the end of its first act, and is already a masterpiece in the great tradition of romantic comedy. Can the same be said of yours?"

"Not really," said Malox. "My life is more like epic erotica with a cast of thousands."

Rantreleka rolled his eyes.

"What, your life, or the movie in your head?" Tillika shouted over the laughter that filled the hall.

"Seriously," said Malox, "when you replace dead cells with living ones – when you replace every dead cell – are you insulting your Designer?"

"That depends how the cells die. If they are destroyed through no fault of your own, replace them by all means. But cells usually die slowly as a natural part of the ageing process."

"Oh," said Malox. "Now we get to the heart of the issue." He nodded cautiously as he inserted a large cut of venison into his maw.

"Yes, exactly," said Rantreleka. "We see no reason to delay the inevitable, not indefinitely. We see no reason to keep ourselves rooted in the physical plane forever. When the Designer finally calls us home, do we plug our ears and dig our hindpaws into the snow? A joey that refuses the call of his mother will surely freeze to death. To insist on staying within this ephemeral plane is to invite a similar fate, not of the body, but of the soul."

More than an hour later, after everyone had finished desserts and gone their separate ways, after Skalosak had retired to her apartment with her son, Rantreleka thanked his mother for not interrupting his discussion.

"It was the least I could do," said Skalosak. "I don't have to agree with everything you say to love you."

Rantreleka smiled. "I could say exactly the same thing," he said.

####

The following week progressed largely without incident. Rantreleka stayed in his mother's apartment, sleeping in the spare bedroom. The two spent most of their days reliving old times and recounting recent events. Rantreleka had plenty of multisensory recordings to back up his stories. He showed Skalosak his girlfriend Cheleera, an enormous black and silver Siberoo. He showed her Pastor Danalonan of the Balthorian Chapter of the Church of the Sacred Flesh, who was tall and solid for a human with a charismatic smile and an affluent taste in fashion. He showed her the crew of the star freighter *Persephone*, mostly human but also with a few vecs (who, unlike the ones that worked in the snow guide station, resented being called robots) and two Siberoos (Ranty and Chelly, of course).

Only once did Skalosak show any concern for Rantreleka's recounting of his church activities. He offhandedly mentioned that one of Pastor Danalonan's sermons was based on a message transmitted personally by the Magistrate.

"Who is this Magistrate?" Skalosak enquired.

"The Magistrate is one of the Four Rocks of Foundation." Noticing his mother's blank stare, he added: "The Four Founders of the Church."

"So he is over a thousand years old?"

"Of course. That makes him slightly older than ... who is that Megasiber that works here?"

"Maraji. You'll probably miss her; she won't be back for a week."

"That's a pity."

"Is this Magistrate immortal, by any chance? I don't remember reading about him. Or the Four Rocks, for that matter."

"The Founders go by many names. But I assure you that none of them are hypocrites. They are ... special."

And that was the last Rantreleka mentioned of the Magistrate for a long time.

In the meantime, Hollivax and Malox were out carrying their passengers from one guesthouse to the other. Tillika and Vanashta eventually picked up their own passengers at local airports. Skalosak was expecting her next passenger six days after her son's arrival.

On the night before she met her passenger, as she lay on her mattress and checked the messages in her head, Skalosak had found the one she had been waiting for since her application and purchase that morning.

{Your security background check has been cleared. Your package has arrived.}

It was her latest acquisition, one of many over the past seven weeks; the most advanced and expensive software package she had ever downloaded into her cerebral implant.

Quite naturally, Skalosak suspected that this extremely advanced piece of software would alter the course of her life. She had no idea what an understatement this was.

####

The day that followed was the day they had to part ways, at least temporarily. Skalosak had to pick up her next passenger at the spaceport (he was one of those rare passengers). Rantreleka, who was welcome to stay at the station in his mother's quarters, had already planned to spend the following week travelling around the continent alone.

"I'll meet you at the station in seven days flat," said Skalosak, as the hoverbus landed in the snow in front of the station.

"And I shall," said Rantreleka, adjusting his backpack. "Treat your passenger well."

"I promise not to eat him, if that's what you're worried about."

"Bye for now, Mother."

The two Siberoos hugged for one warm moment, then parted reluctantly. Skalosak boarded the bus as Rantreleka set off on foot for the nearest town.

####

Skalosak's passenger was easy to spot among the new arrivals. He had sent her his image, contact details, and credit code weeks earlier. His name was Gavodian Manlock, and Skalosak would have sworn that he was the human version of her own son. He was tall and lean for a human, in his early twenties, pale skinned, blue eyed, with hair the same light fawn as Rantreleka's spots. Even his sharp dress sense mirrored Ranty to some extent.

As soon as Skalosak and Gavodian made eye contact, the human waved awkwardly to her.

"You must be Skalosak," said Gavodian after walking up to her.

Skalosak looked around. "I don't see any other Siberoos here."

Gavodian chuckled nervously. "You must get tired of saying that."

"I never get tired of meeting new passengers. Especially if they're as cute as you."

Gavodian grinned and blushed as he looked away.

"So, Gavodian, you've never ridden in a Siberoo before?"

"No. This is my first time."

"Well you're in for a treat. I'm built for speed, power and comfort. Although my friends aren't so sure about the speed part." She held out her paw. "Shoes please."

Gavodian stared at the huge paw, then almost started with realization. "Oh, of course." He immediately took his shoes off and gave them to Skalosak, who placed them in a pocket on her utility belt.

"Luggage?" said Skalosak.

Gavodian removed his backpack, which Skalosak put into her own much larger backpack, padded to protect the human's luggage.

"And now, the rest of you?"

Gavodian stared up at Skalosak. "Umm ..."

"Oh, come on." Skalosak grabbed the human and lifted him up to her eye level. "I love shy boys. They taste so delicious with lime and chilli."

Gavodian giggled nervously.

"Let's get started," said Skalosak, and inserted the human into her pouch, then strode away into the cold and misty outdoors.

It was a five-hour walk to the nearest guesthouse. Gavodian slept for most of the way, curled up in a small bulge underneath Skalosak. His tousled head emerged within the final hour, just as the sun was setting far ahead like a fire-flower among the ice, its petals made up of sinuous wisps of cloud lined with red and pink and orange.

"It's beautiful," Gavodian muttered dreamily.

"Get used to it," said Skalosak. "There are plenty more sights where this one came from, and they're all within walking distance. Well, for me at least."

For Skalosak, the guesthouse was just over half an hour's walking distance. Gavodian briefly retired once more into the velvety depths of the pouch, before peeking out just in time to see the vast, featureless black wall of the guesthouse. It was basically a miniature version of the station. Because it was one of the majority of guesthouses that accommodated Siberoos but not Megasibers, its entrance door was small enough to seal itself up seamlessly when not in use. In Skalosak's close presence, the door immediately sank a few millimetres into the wall and slid apart in two segments.

"Welcome, Skalosak," said the familiar androgynous voice. "Welcome, Gavodian Manlock. I am Guesthouse Mind Adilan, and I shall ensure that your stay will be a memorable one."

After returning the greeting, Skalosak stepped through the threshold and into her home for the night.

After four years as a snow guide, the routine should have been mundane, but to Skalosak it was anything but. Every guesthouse had its own subtle atmosphere, every guesthouse mind had its own unique flair and taste in décor, holography, music and cuisine. Moreover, every passenger could be appreciated for who they were. The extroverted ones could be listened to for hours, while Skalosak could always steer the conversation in a direction that suited her if her passenger ever became too obnoxious. More introverted tourists, such as Gavodian, were a captive audience. In tonight's case, Skalosak was all too happy to let Gavodian throw her any questions about her life, her work, Siberoos in general or New Dumont in particular, and she answered as heartily as she could.

After two hours of getting to know each other, Gavodian decided to retire to the lavish confines of the human-size quarters. "Sweet dreams," he said. Skalosak retired to the Siberoo-sized bedroom to lay side-down on the vast mattress, resting in preparation for the following day's expedition.

With subtle variations, the pattern was repeated from day to day, from guesthouse to guesthouse, from sight to sight, from panoramic ice landscape to ancient ruin to penguin colony. She could feel her human passenger enjoy every minute of it. That was the gift of being a female Siberoo. Skalosak's pouch muscles easily picked up on her passenger's own muscle tension and heartbeat, so it was in her best interests to make the tour as comfortable and exciting as possible. Male Siberoos, who carried their passengers in backpacks, could only imagine what such symbiosis felt like.

Usually, Gavodian went to sleep in the human bedroom. Only twice did he spend the night in Skalosak's pouch, which he was perfectly entitled to do after how much he had paid. Yet every night, before disappearing into his sleeping place, he would say the same thing. "Sweet dreams."

And every night, Skalosak had sweet dreams.

She could barely remember those dreams when she awoke. Even her most advanced recording software failed to capture them; which was odd, because it had no trouble recording everything else. All she could recall was the burning after-image of perfection, like a fractal flower seared into her brain. Pervading all, however, was the joyous sense of gratitude that she instinctively associated with the presence of her son.

Every morning, she secretly wanted to thank Gavodian, her sandy-haired sandman, for giving her those dreams. Yet, even by her own somewhat flighty standards, she knew how silly that would sound.

As with all tourists she was exceptionally fond of, Skalosak offered Gavodian an extra few days as her passenger. Gavodian politely turned down the offer, stating that he had to stick to his rigid schedule.

And thus their departure was unavoidable.

"Of all the tourists I've carried over the past year," Skalosak told Gavodian at the spaceport, "you were the most fun to be with. Trust me, that's saying a lot."

"Of all the tours I've ever had, being with you was the most rewarding. I wish we could meet again."

"I'm sure that we will."

"By the time we do," said Gavodian, "I might be wearing a different face."

"Ha!" barked Skalosak, startling a few nearby humans. "I like that. Willing to upgrade your body. Not that you need to change that cute little face, but still, the two of us would have a lot to talk about next time we meet. I might be a cyborg by then. But don't worry. You'll still recognize me. All my upgrades will be under my hide."

They hugged as they exchanged goodbyes, and went their separate ways.

####

Four hours after Skalosak returned to the station, Rantreleka returned from his trip.

"Did you make any recordings?" said Skalosak when the conversation was well underway.

"About nine hours worth," said Rantreleka.

Skalosak was impressed. She knew that Rantreleka's beliefs would have discouraged him from recording every single minute like some tourists; yet nine hours of someone else's sensory footage was exactly the sort of thing she had been looking for.

"This provides me with a great opportunity to test my new recording software," said Skalosak. "I downloaded it the night before we both set off. It's seriously advanced stuff, all the way from NoCoZo. Borderline ultratech, in fact."

Skalosak saw her son's eyes narrow at the mention of "ultratech", hoping that he was not put off.

"That's fine with me," he said. "Where's the key?"

"Oh no, you don't need a key for this. I only have to upload your recordings directly onto my private filespace on the local net so I can access it any time I want. You just find the recordings and get them ready for uploading."

Rantreleka closed his eyes for a few seconds. "All right, they're ready."

"Great. Now all I have to do is just touch you on the forehead ..." She placed her paw on her son's head and closed her eyes. Instantly a wall of bright icons illuminated the dark behind her eyelids, all featuring images from Ranty's recent trip. Whenever she focused her attention on any one icon, it filled her mind with the sights and sounds and scents and textures of the places her son had visited. Here was the nearby town of Kallazgard, the ice cliffs of Slorhavven, the rusted ruins of spaceship *Bilanton*. Human townsfolk cocooned in figure-hugging bodysuits or synthetic fur looked up at her and greeted her son politely. A man in a dimly lit bar raised his frothing mug of black beer and drank a toast to Siberoos everywhere, and Ranty's paw raised his own wholesome mug of sarsaparilla in response. A rancid colony of walruses roared and grunted, some raising their tusked heads and staring, not entirely threatened by the familiar presence of a single male Siberoo but cautious nonetheless.

Skalosak could freeze any one of these memories, or play them back in seamless slow motion, or fast-forward through minutes and hours until she hit upon a point of interest. She could run a search just by thinking of a word, or an image, or an idea, and the software would split the recordings up into segments displaying a hierarchy of relevant moments in Ranty's recordings. She could freeze-frame every single millisecond of Ranty's recordings and superimpose them over each other in translucent layers, creating the closest thing to four-dimensionality that her bright baseline mind could comprehend. She could highlight and zoom in on moments in time as easily as she could highlight and zoom in on points in space.

She was like a cat with a new ball of yarn.

"Can you see them?" said Rantreleka.

"I can see everything," said Skalosak, who did not need to exaggerate in the slightest.

"Are you ready to copy the whole thing?"

"Ready at this very moment."

Instantly, responding to her will, the software enveloped all the files of Ranty's recordings, like a luminous hungry cloud. There was a flash and a click, then a message:

Subject: Rantreleka
Clade: Newarchic Siberoo
Age: $7.1 * 10^8$ seconds
Toposophic: G0.312 (Berram10 'G' Scale)
Date of Capture: 8400/07/19 AT
Time of Capture:
22:16:37 NewDumont/ZoneSalandara
Files Captured: 17
Total Data Captured:
91.4 GB (Organic Neuron Compression)
{UPLOAD SUCCESSFUL}

"Done," said Skalosak, taking her paw off her son's head.

"Already?" Rantreleka's eyes opened widely. "I didn't feel a thing."

"I told you it was advanced."

From that moment, after having shared so much so quickly, they had a lot to talk about.

It was close to midnight by the time they were done. For the first time in seven nights,

Skalosak lay on her own mattress and sank into sleep.

####

Two million kilometres away, the humanoid courier who called himself Gavodian Manlock sat back in his cabin seat and closed his eyes. The liner was still weeks away from the wormhole at the edge of the system, but that made no difference to him. With so little left to do, he planned to step into the hibernation chamber early – days before the flesh-crushing second stage acceleration would make this compulsory for all biont passengers - and sleep away the rest of the voyage. All that remained was one last message.

The liner's entire AI network exploded throughout his mind like a cluster of fire flowers. Every flower, every segment of the AI system, was mapped exquisitely for his inspection, even the sections that were "protected" by pitifully simplistic firewalls and security codes. His mind extended hundreds of tendrils - each one a separate dataprobe with unique and complex instructions -, and infiltrated the liner's communication array with surgical precision, erasing all trails of his intrusion as he went. The liner was following a strictly specified route, and was seconds away from passing another nanoguage communication wormhole. All he had to do now was send one final, secret, untraceable, unrecordable message, and his present task would be over. However, unlike all other passengers, Gavodian's timing had to be perfect.

The liner neared its closest point to the microscopic wormhole.

Gavodian transmitted his message.
{Mission accomplished, Your Majesty.}
The liner passed the relay.

Gavodian let go of the AI network and breathed a sigh of relief. Keeping his eyes closed, he relaxed in his perfect imitation of human sleep. Real hibernation could wait a few hours. For now, he imagined himself back inside that endearing Siberoo's pouch. It was a pity. She would have made an affectionate pet. But still, experiments had to be seeded.

"Sweet dreams, Skally," he whispered to himself.

So many behind him, and a galaxy spread out before him.

####

Just like eight days before, mother and son stood outside the snow guide station awaiting the hoverbus. Skalosak was to accompany Rantreleka to Salandara Spaceport, and the two were to say their last goodbyes for a very long time. That was the plan. For now, this was one of those rare moments when Skalosak was lost for words. Perhaps she was saving her words for the Spaceport. Perhaps.

Much to Skalosak's relief, it was Rantreleka who broke the silence.

"Mother?"

"Yes, Ranty?"

"There's one question that I've been wanting to ask you ever since my first dinner in the station."

"Let's hear it."

"Well ... I respect your decision to extend your life by any means possible ..."

"Thank you, Ranty."

"But … What I mean to ask …"

"Spit it out. I won't be offended. I promise."

Rantreleka rumbled as he cleared his throat. "Do you want to live to see me die?"

Skalosak froze up instantly – quite a feat for a species engineered to survive extreme cold.

"That's …" Skalosak both surprised and frustrated herself by still being lost for words. "That's quite a melodramatic way of putting it."

"I'm sorry, I meant-"

"No, don't be sorry. I promised you not to be offended, and I'm sticking to my promise. That was a brave question. And I'll have to be just as brave to answer it."

She stood rooted to the ice for long seconds that felt like hours, but no answer came to her.

Far above, the sky darkened.

"It looks like I'm not as brave as you," she said at last. "I'm too afraid to answer that question. I'm too afraid to even think about it."

"Don't be afraid, Mother." Rantreleka's stare was soft and sincere. "I am going to die, and there is nothing you can do about it."

The words hit her like an icicle to the heart. Skalosak had to compose herself and realize that her son was only stating a fact. An obvious, unavoidable fact.

The sky darkened deeper.

"I know you are going to die one day," said Skalosak. "And I realise that it's all because of a personal decision you have made. I have to respect that, just as you have decided to respect my decision to extend my life. That's all I can say right now."

"Thank you, Mother."

By now, the sky was pitch black, and both Siberoos were illuminated only by the station lights.

"But will you be prepared?" said Rantreleka. "Will you be prepared to say goodbye when the time finally comes?"

"To be honest, I can't possibly answer that until it happens."

The clouds swept rapidly overhead. Then, like the ebbing of a tide, they receded into the distance, and the sky spun all around with a million radiant stars. The three moons left fiery neon trails as they circled the heavens like spaceships searching for a place to land.

"What the ..." whispered Skalosak, her vision filled by the kaleidoscope above.

"It is going to happen, Mother," said Rantreleka, oblivious to the celestial lightshow. "Soon, you will need to answer."

The revolutions of the stars, planets and moons accelerated, becoming a blur of bright streaks all chasing each other around and around, until the Sun rose and drowned out their collective light with its own. Even through the frenzied rush of clouds from one horizon to the other, the graceful arc of the Sun's path could be followed every second of the way.

"What's happening?" Skalosak's voice was hushed with awe.

"Time, Mother. Time is happening. Time is real. The one thing you cannot control."

The Sun set, leaving the glowing denizens of the night to dance once again. Although this time the show was over within seconds. The Sun rose and soared blindingly overhead like a missile, then landed over the horizon. And the stars and moons came out and spun again. Then the Sun. Then the stars. Sun. Stars. Day. Night. Over and over again, faster and faster, until they merged into one indistinguishable grey blur.

Skalosak returned her gaze to her son, as desperate for answers as she was speechless.

"Days and years and decades will pass," said Ratreleka. "Those who choose to age naturally will die naturally. Yet you will always be forty-two, for as long as you choose to remain this young."

Rantreleka himself was changing. The spots on his fur became lighter around the edges. The skin around his eyes slackened and wrinkled, which became more and more obvious as his eyelids began to shed fur. His cheeks slowly began to sink inwards.

"My son, please …" Skalosak stepped forward and embraced Rantreleka. "Please don't …"

"You told me you would respect my decision. You must allow nature to take its course." By now, Rantreleka's voice was becoming wheezy and strained.

The ice all around rippled under their feet like an ocean of glistening milk. New buildings rose on either side of the pair, extending out of the snow guide station.

"We came here to wait for the bus," said Rantreleka, his voice now thin and raspy. "But this bus will never come. Not for you. You have chosen to stay in this realm, while I have chosen to pass on."

Skalosak felt her son's muscles soften beneath her gentle grip. Rantreleka's hide expanded and began to sag off his arms. His fur spots lost all colour. He stared at her with drooping jowls and slackened ears, all muscles in his face sliding downwards as if melting like candlewax. Yet his eyes were as bright as ever, and his puckered mouth still managed a hint of a smile.

"Don't be afraid, Mother," Rantreleka hoarsely whispered. "I love you. I will love you forever. And I will be waiting for you in Heaven. Because I know that one day you will be ready."

"Ranty. Please don't die. Don't ever …"

But it was too late, for nature was indeed taking its course. Skalosak felt her son turn as cold as the air around him. His muscles shrank to nothing beneath his skin, which sank and sagged and stretched grotesquely over his bones. His teeth and eyeballs and tongue fell out of his lifelessly rolling head. His hide and fur exploded in a puff of dust. His naked bones fell out of her motherly grip and sank into the turbulent ocean of ice.

Skalosak screeched in shock as her head jolted up from the mattress.

Her bedroom was the same as it had always been. Only a few hours had passed.

She sat there panting heavily. After seven nights of beautiful dreams, this nightmare was like being blasted in the guts with a minicannon. Among the horrifying, heartbreaking visions that swirled messily in her mind, that one question taunted her.

Do you want to live to see me die?

In an instant she made up her mind.

At her mental command, the soundproof door of her bedroom slid open. She crossed the central room to the door of the guest bedroom.

Skalosak was relieved to see her son alive, whole and young, still sound asleep on his mattress. She knew that he did not want to stay this way forever, not in this universe. He would let himself become old and frail while she remained young and powerful.

She could not allow that.

"I love you," she whispered softly.

Skalosak gently placed her paw on Rantreleka's head and closed her eyes.

There was a reason why it had taken her whole hours to acquire this new software. Its uses were not limited to casual recording.

Skalosak ordered the software to scan her son's entire memory.

Of course, she could not do this to just anyone. But Rantreleka had opened up his mind to the software hours earlier. It had the master key to his brain.

A massive cluster of lights exploded in Skalosak's mind, accompanied by lines of sharp, contrasting text.

Subject: Rantreleka
Clade: Newarchic Siberoo
Age: $7.1 * 10^8$ seconds
Toposophic: G0.312 (Berram10 'G' Scale)
Date of Capture: 8400/07/20 AT
Time of Capture:
03:46:37 NewDumont/ZoneSalandara
Files Captured:
8197 Conscious Segments
    42098 Dreams
    $8.41 * 10^8$ Thought Processes
    1 Personal DNA Code
Total Data Captured:
2.11 PB (Organic Neuron Compression)
Upload to Personal Folder? {Y/N}

Without a moment's hesitation, Skalosak chose "Y".

There was an extraordinarily bright flash like a supernova, and the entire cluster imploded into a single point of light.

{UPLOAD SUCCESSFUL}

She opened her eyes and lifted her paw, satisfied that there were now two Rantrelekas sleeping soundly in safe places – one in this bedroom, and the other in her own personal pocket of cyberspace.

One of those Rantrelekas – mentally identical in every way to the one she had given birth to, carried in her pouch for years, loved and raised and taught and protected, seen off to his new career in the Merchant Navy, corresponded with many times, accommodated right here in this apartment for a good part of his vacation – was never going to die.

"I will love you forever," she whispered.

####

Rantreleka had planned to stay for another two weeks. With a few days before her next passenger was due, Skalosak took Rantreleka to the city of Salandara, where they spent the nights in adjacent hotel rooms and the days touring the city's many attractions.

In between all the art galleries, museums, crowd dream reflectors, history windows, and live performers, there was plenty of shopping to be done. Rantreleka bought dozens of souvenirs, including a self-sculpting stone that reflected the thoughts of its holder. Skalosak, however, was content to spend her money on necklaces and jewellery. Many necklaces and a lot of jewellery. A human would have needed seriously augmented muscles and bones to carry what she bought and wore. In addition to her many ornaments, she also bought a giant shocking pink T-shirt with the caption "CUTIE ON BOARD" and an arrow pointing downward. "I'm going to wear this for my next passenger," she explained to Rantreleka, "and I think I might wear some of my jewellery as well."

Rantreleka was used to seeing his mother happy, but this trip proved to be a high point for both of them.

The day after returning to the station, they parted ways again. Skalosak went to pick up another tourist (while wearing her T-shirt, half her jewellery and most of her necklaces, insisting that her new passenger must "travel in style"), while Rantreleka slept overnight in Skalosak's quarters. In the days that followed, he would take the bus and commute to nearby towns, or simply stay in the station and spend time with the remaining snow guides - mainly Tillika, Vanashta or Malox. Hollivax, Rolanxi and Maraji were out carrying tourists.

Skalosak returned a few days before Rantreleka's scheduled departure date. The first thing she showed her son and co-workers was a life size hologram of herself wearing her CUTIE ON BOARD T-shirt along with assorted necklaces and gemstone bracelets, posing and scowling and baring her teeth like an action heroine. In her pouch, her passenger – a young human female with an olive complexion – was visible from the chest up posing in a similar manner, her tiny hands poised for chopping up imaginary bad guys. Skalosak revealed that she gave the woman a copy of the hologram as a souvenir, along with a few of her necklaces and gemstone bracelets (which, to a human, would have been massive chains and heavy torcs).

With only a few days remaining until his departure, Rantreleka seemed almost frozen with indecision. How could he spend his last days on the planet he had once called home? When would he ever return?

"You don't have to do everything," his mother reassured him. "You don't have to go everywhere. You've already done quite a lot. Just savour each hour for what it is."

Taking this philosophy on board, Rantreleka began to enjoy himself once again.

The final few days passed rather uneventfully, but Ranty had no regrets. He had seen and done more than he had planned, and was prepared to return to his present home with a treasure of fond memories.

Then, on the final night before Ranty's departure, Skalosak arranged one last outing.

"Remember this place?" she said as the hoverbus lifted and flew away behind them.

The ice landscape before them was flat and almost featureless, although it had a glistening silver sheen under the moons and stars.

"It seems like almost any other part of the continent," said Rantreleka, sitting beside his mother on the ice.

"It does," said Skalosak. "Until it begins."

"Until what begins?" said Rantreleka.

"It should be starting any minute now," said Skalosak.

"Not another snowstorm."

"Don't you worry about snowstorms. You might be too big for the pouch, but your not too big to cover up."

Mere minutes later, the first ripples of green billowed across the sky, like the ethereal flag of the gods.

"The Northern Aurora!" said Ranty, his eyes lighting up with the wonder of his younger days.

"I knew you would be pleased," said Skalosak.

Side by side, the mother Siberoo and her son sat and watched in rapt attention as the heavens danced just for them that night.

####

Skalosak knew that saying goodbye would be difficult, but her present position gave her a special sense of discomfort.

Here she was, standing outside the front of the snow guide station with her son, waiting for the hoverbus to take them to Salandara Spaceport.

Just like in that dream.

"Is everything all right, Mother?"

Skalosak nodded, but then had to correct herself. "It could be another three years before they let you have a holiday this long," she said.

"We could still keep in touch."

"I know. Just promise that you'll be back."

"I will."

"And don't forget to keep your promise," said another female voice, deeper than Skalosak's, far to their left.

They both turned to see Maraji ponderously striding around the corner of the station.

"Maraji!" said Rantreleka. "It's so good to see you at last."

Skalosak remembered that Maraji had been scheduled to drop off her last passenger at Kallazgard earlier that day. Knowing her, with the rest of the day free, she would have decided to return to the station on foot, which meant approaching the station from behind. At this time of the afternoon, this meant that the Megasiber had been walking against the wind. The two Siberoos had not noticed her scent, which was mild for her size.

High in the sky, the hoverbus was approaching.

"We'd all like you to return," said Maraji, standing hugely by the station wall. "You seem like a nice enough cub. It's a pity we did not have time to meet."

The hoverbus descended amid a low, expanding cloud of mist and lowered its broad ramp.

"Maybe next time," Maraji boomed over the hum of the hoverbus motor, "I could give you a ride."

Rantreleka and Skalosak waved at their giant friend as they walked up the ramp and boarded the hoverbus.

Minutes later, as she stood in the departure lounge of Salandara Spaceport, Skalosak found herself facing the same dilemma as her son had only a few days earlier. With so little time left, how could she spend it with the one she loved?

Evidently, her son had sensed her anxiety.

"Remember what you told me?" he said. "Savour each ... second ... for what it is."

"'Each hour,' I said," corrected Skalosak. "Each hour."

"Yes, but that wouldn't be very appropriate under the circumstances, would it?" said Rantreleka. "Not with only ... five minutes until the gate opens."

"Say hello to that Cheleera for me."

"I will." Then Rantreleka paused and glanced at the floor. "Speaking of Cheleera, I'm planning to ... don't get your hopes up just yet, but I'm thinking of proposing to her."

"YES!" roared Skalosak, startling every human within a radius of ninety metres. She picked up her son and hugged him crushingly.

"Mother, I told you not to get your hopes ..." But as Skalosak pressed the side of her face against his and purred, he lost all sense of articulation.

"We haven't had a proper marriage in our bloodline in over a hundred years." Skalosak finally put her son down. "So, have you two lovebirds done the deed yet?"

"Mother, please! The two of us must have a proper marriage sanctified by the church before we think about doing any of that stuff!"

"A church marriage?"

"Yes."

"Human style?"

"Yes."

"That's fine." Skalosak paused for a few seconds, then added: "Is that the only thing you're going to do human style?"

"MOTHER!"

But as Skalosak laughed, Rantreleka could not help but join in.

"Just promise me one thing," said Skalosak.

"What?"

"Promise me not to take any unnecessary shit from that Pastor Danalonadingdong or whatever the hell his name is. Remember that he's just a mortal just like you and me."

"Well of course he's mortal," said Rantreleka. "We're all mortals in our church. That's the whole idea, remember? Speaking of which, I just want you to promise me one thing."

"What's that?"

"Promise never to forget me even if you live to be a thousand."

"Ranty, I would never forget you even if I lived to be a million."

"All passengers of Flight One-Two-Seven to Balthor, please enter Gate Sixteen."

Rantreleka and Skalosak stared into each other's eyes as the announcement repeated.

"It's time," said Rantreleka.

Skalosak hugged him one last time.

"I love you," she said.

"Forever," said Rantreleka.

After she let go, Skalosak could not take her eyes off Rantreleka as he walked down the corridor among the mostly human passengers. Towering over them all, he never got lost in the crowd. He turned to her and waved one last time before disappearing around the bend in the corridor.

####

The following few weeks proceeded normally at Niflheim Snow Guide Station. On average, each member would spend roughly every second week carrying a tourist. Skalosak bought more fancy software, and spent a few nights in Salandara with Malox. Tillika had one of her many boyfriends over to stay for three nights. Maraji slept in her basement for six nights straight before taking the air-barge to Vasikajna to pick up another tourist.

Then, everything changed.

####

Rantreleka had never felt so nervous in his life.

The freighter *Persephone* had just unloaded a shipment of sentient air cars on the ringworld Vossola, just on the edge of the NoCoZo Metaempire. During the few free hours he had been granted, Rantreleka had done some shopping in the ringworld's famous market towers. He had spent a considerable sum on one item in particular.

Now, the ringworld and all its crowded shopping malls were far behind him. The *Persephone* was returning home, slowly accelerating its way to the local system's wormhole, and the crew were allowed one night of leisure before they were required to enter the hibernation chambers. The steady acceleration produced gravity on board the freighter – it had become like a thinly populated skyscraper with the antimatter thrusters at the bottom.

It was this gravity that allowed Rantreleka to stand outside the door to Cheleera's quarters, trying not to let his paws tremble as he clutched his parcel.

The door slid open. Cheleera towered over him, majestically vast and dark, with facial stripes like a spiderweb of silver. To a male Siberoo, she may as well have been a goddess, although Rantreleka would never have stated such blasphemy out aloud.

"Ranty!" said Cheleera. "Come in."

Cheleera's quarters were much more spacious than his own, allowing for the immense size of the female Siberoo; but otherwise it was built to similar specifications. It has a neat, simple leisure room with a food processor and three extra doors.

Cheleera crouched near the edge of the room, her forepaws rested on the lush carpet before her, her huge hips bulging, her silver-ringed tail slowly slinking and sliding beside her.

"Sit down," she said. "Relax."

"I ... First I have to show you something."

Cheleera's bright green eyes widened. "Ooh, I see you've been on one of your rare shopping sprees. Is it something for me?"

"Yes."

"Is it chocolates?"

"No."

"Is it a cake?"

"No."

"Is it something I can eat?"

"I should hope not."

"Is it something I can play with?"

"I sincerely hope not, but how am I going to stop you?"

Cheleera chuckled. "Oh Ranty, you are such a tease. Come on. Show me. The suspense is agonizing."

Rantreleka took a deep breath. This is it, he thought. This is the moment. And you didn't even bother to rehearse it. Idiot. Idiot idiot idiot.

At his mental command the box opened up like a black flower. In the centre was a platinum bracelet like a ring of flowers. Rantreleka had been careful to select the right one, for its purpose was more than just ornamentation. Its purpose was for life.

He saw the look on Cheleera's face, and knew that she realized what he was doing.

Finally, Rantreleka got down on his knees, staring up into the emerald eyes of his beloved.

"Cheleera," he said, "will you ma

But he did not finish his sentence, or even a word, or a thought. For at that very moment, Rantreleka, Cheleera, the engagement bracelet, and everyone and everything aboard the star freighter *Persephone* were all vapourized instantly.

####

Skalosak was striding halfway to the first guesthouse of the tour, carrying a male human tourist from New Dumont's mildly warm equatorial region. Lonski was fast asleep in her pouch - well insulated from the flesh-freezing climate he was unaccustomed to -, when Skalosak received the emergency message.

"Dearest Skalosak," said the intercerebral AI messenger, "I am deeply sorry, but I have terrible news to convey."

"What?" Skalosak barked out loud, standing rooted to the ice. "Show me!"

Instantly the whiteness of the ice vanished from her vision and was replaced by the blackness of space. Against the starry void was a sleek, tower-like spaceship that Skalosak recognized instantly – the *Persephone*. Her son's freighter. To the right side of her vision were twin columns of faces – most of them human, some of them vecs, and two of them Siberoo. Cheleera. And Rantreleka.

Headlining the news footage was the caption: **FREIGHTER TRAGEDY IN VOSSOLA SYSTEM.**

The star freighter continued to fire its thrusters against the dark star field for a few seconds.

Then it erupted in an all-engulfing flash of light.

"NO!" Skalosak roared.

The light dimmed, leaving nothing but a faintly luminous cloud.

"RANTY!" Skalosak roared, barely noticing the commotion in her pouch.

"Skally?" came Lonski's muffled, drowsy voice from down below. "Are you all right?"

Skalosak could not answer. She could barely breathe.

"As of now, there are no known survivors," said the news narrator, "although it is believed that most of the crew had kept up-to-date personality backups in cyberspace."

This reminder was the one glimmer of hope in the static haze of Skalosak's despair.

"I know ... what to do," she said out loud, panting heavily.

"Skalosak?" said her human passenger. "What's wrong?"

"It's all right, Lonsky," said Skalosak, returning her vision to the here-and-now. "I know what to do." She looked down at her pouch, seeing Lonsky's face peering out of the half-closed orifice. She reached down and absent-mindedly stroked her pouch fur. "You're safe, baby. I know what to do." She closed up her pouch. "I know what to do," she said, again and again, between deep gasps for air.

Then she turned back to the direction of the snow guide station, and the ice thundered beneath her as she ran like a beast of prey.

####

Tillika, Vanashta, and Malox were waiting for her at the front of the station when she arrived. Skalosak collapsed on her knees and forepaws, screaming at the ice. The other three Siberoos ran up to her. Tillika grabbed her and held her head to her chest. "It's all right, honey," she said. "We know. We're so sorry. Oh mercy Goddess, we're so sorry."

Malox gently stroked her shoulder as he removed her backpack. It was one of those rare moments when he was at a loss for words.

"Skally, please let me have your passenger," Vanashta said softly. "I will take care of him."

Skalosak relaxed her pouch muscles, allowing Vanashta to play the midwife and extract the human from inside. Lonski looked around in a daze, squinting. "What's going on?" he said.

"Are you all right?" Vanashta said as she held the human before her.

"I'm a bit shaken up, but I'll survive. What happened?"

"We'll show you the news channel. Just relax for now." She cradled the human in her arms as she headed for the station entrance.

"I need to be alone," Skalosak gasped.

"We're here for you, Skally," Malox said softly, massaging her heaving shoulders.

"I said, I need to be ALOOOOONE!"

Malox and Tillika took one step back, still keeping an eye on their friend.

Skalosak rose to her feet.

"I know," she gasped. "I know what to do."

She staggered into the station entrance.

Malox and Tillika, as deeply concerned as ever, followed close behind.

####

To Skalosak's gratitude, her friends let her have her privacy. She knelt in the centre of her leisure room, still panting, still exhausted, and closed her eyes.

Her personal folder in cyberspace was still there, utterly untouched by the violence and chaos of the physical universe. The contents were still intact. Ranty's memory. Ranty's DNA code. All there.

Within seconds, she sent a message to the assembler factory deep under the city of Salandara.

Seconds later, she sent another message to a hotel in Salandara, and booked the best room she could afford, which was almost the very best available.

"It's all right, Ranty," she said. "Mother will never forget you. Mother will never leave you."

####

"She was so friendly when we met at the airport," said Lonsky, now just a tiny tanned face peering out amidst the black fur of Vanashta's belly. "So kind and gentle and cheerful. I thought I was going to have the holiday of my life."

"We're so sorry about this," said Vanashta as she stood in the middle of the station's leisure room, putting on her backpack.

"No!" said Lonsky. "Don't feel sorry for me. It's Skally I'm worried about. Poor girl. She seemed such a lovely lady."

"She is," said Vanashta. "But we're giving her some time off, as much as she needs. And I'm taking you anywhere you want. Anywhere on the planet. I'll book an airship and take you there. It's on us. I'll even extend your stay to two weeks."

"Thanks," said Lonsky, "but …"

"Don't you dare feel guilty."

"Two weeks?"

"Two weeks."

"They have guesthouses around the south pole, don't they?"

"Even more than up here. Some of them are new. I just have to call in advance and we can stay for no extra cost."

"Well, maybe we could spend the second week, if it's all right with you …"

"A lot of things are all right with me. Just get some rest. We'll have plenty of time to make plans."

Vanashta closed her pouch, and strode toward the station's front door and into the freezing, whistling night.

####

Skalosak knew that she needed a holiday from her station, but there was still so much work to be done.

In the past day she had received many messages of condolence, including ones from Maraji, Hollivax, and Rolanxi. She was grateful for them all, but she knew that kind words and good will could not bring her beloved son back.

Technology could.

That is what brought her here, a thousand metres beneath the bustling streets of Salandara, to Lifecore Labs and Assembly Vats.

The dealer was Tazhik - a spiky-haired male human in a neat red waistcoat and dark, utterly opaque round spectacles -, and he showed Skalosak around.

"The Lifecore welcomes all customers," Tazhik spoke as he led Skalosak between towering cylinders of superhard polyresin, some of which displayed their contents on vast screens. Creatures were forming inside, layer by layer by layer, curled up in the fluid as they awaited birth.

"Whatever your wish," said Tazhik, "she will grant it to you, so long as you pay the price."

"Is the Lifecore a transapient?"

Tazhik looked up to Skalosak and gave one of his unreadable grins. "Let's just say that she would pass the test." He turned back to his path and walked on. "She could create anything you want, within certain logistical parameters, of course. Whatever your inspiration. Greek mythology. Norse mythology. Babylonian mythology. Chinese mythology. Tolkien mythology. Hollywood mythology. Your brightest dreams. Your darkest nightmares. Even-"

"I've seen those theme parks," Skalosak interrupted. "I know a lot about them, because snow guides have to compete with them for tourist credits. And I think we're doing very fine, thank you very much."

"Of course you are," Tazhik said with a grin. "They just love to play us mortals against each other. We all have tokens stacked up behind us, and behind those tokens are the real players of our worlds. It's a fact of life that we have to accept."

"In ancient times, they used to say the same thing about death," said Skalosak.

"Ah," said Tazhik. "So that's what brings you here. To bring back a loved one. Am I correct?"

"Yes."

"And any reason why you didn't choose the mainstream vats up there?"

"Because of the backup software I used."

"May I take a peek?"

"Be my guest." Skalosak closed her eyes and transmitted the most basic packet of data to Tazhik.

Skalosak could not see Tazhik's eyes, but she could see his eyebrows jump. "Holy sshh ... No wonder. You're not a superbright by any chance, are you?"

"No. Not yet."

"Well, all you have to do now is open up your folder, and let the Lifecore do the rest."

"Very well then." Skalosak closed her eyes and opened her personal folder.

"Done," said Tazhik. "This is ... wait ... adult male Siberoo ... early twenties ... so he would be around three hundred kilograms?"

"Two hundred and eighty seven."

"Great. That should take the Lifecore a few hours. Four hours max. Memory transfer would be virtually instantaneous. We sell biochips by the way. What did Rani ... Rantreleka use?"

"Cognex Five-Seven-Five. All the details are in his memory."

"Great. Well, the Lifecore should be working on your son's copy as we speak. If you want, you can order the biochip and we'll implant it as soon as his body is finished. And he should be ... over ... there."

He pointed far ahead at one of the opaque cylinders, and sped up his pace. Skalosak had absolutely no trouble keeping up, subconsciously relieved that she could walk a little closer to her natural pace and not slow right down for a human. Far greater, though, was the anticipation of seeing her son again.

Tazhik stopped in front of one cylinder – the one where the nanotech assembly of organic molecules had begun. The one in which Skalosak's son was to be reborn.

"We should be getting a visual soon," said Tazhik. "Your son's body won't be taxing the Lifecore's resources at all, not compared with our other ... All right, here it is."

At the height of Tazhik's head, a luminous screen appeared in the side of the cylinder, almost as if a part of the surface had turned transparent. For now, only the thin outline of the male Siberoo skeletal structure was visibly forming.

"You can zoom in on any portion to watch the DNA molecules being formed, like so."

Tazhik touched one part of the screen, in the middle of where the spine was forming. Instantly the point he touched expanded to fill the screen, displaying countless thousands of twisting ladder-shaped patterns forming and joining.

"I'll flick the display upwards so you can get a better view."

Tazhik merely flicked the screen, and in a fraction of a second it rose nearly two metres to Skalosak's head level. Very familiar with this type of interface, Skalosak placed her paw on the screen, then moved it back as she closed her claws. In response the display zoomed out to show the forming skeleton.

"The brain and nervous system will slowly form throughout the assembly, being obviously the most complex organs," said Tazhik. "He won't gain consciousness until absolutely everything is finished and he's long out of the tank. By the way, the legal ramifications are pretty straightforward. The Lifecore asserts the moral right as the physical constructor of your son's new body, of course; but you, as the original's biological parent as well as holder of the original copy in cyberspace, retain ownership as well as copyright of the genetic des-"

"He's my son, not a fucking pop song."

"Right. I'm sorry. Anyway, you should have access to the copyright contract right now. You can purchase the Cognex Five-Seven-Five while you're at it. All we need is your mind print …"

Skalosak closed her eyes for a few seconds. "Done," she said at last.

"Great. All right, so … would you like to stay in one of our private lounges while you're waiting? We can play movies, music-"

"I'd rather stay out here, thank you."

"All right then. If you need anything, you have my link. See you in a few hours."

Skalosak could hear the human's footsteps recede for a long time, but all her conscious attention was focused on the screen before her. By now, the male Siberoo skeleton was already close to completion, curled up head-to-tail as if inside a giant pouch or womb. Skalosak moved her head closer and placed her paw on the screen, expecting no reaction, only desiring to already be as close as possible to her reborn son.

She remembered what she used to tell Rantreleka when he was just a joey.

If you're buried under a kilometre of snow, I'll go digging for you.

And here she was, twenty years on, a kilometre beneath the ice, keeping her promise.

####

It had been six hours since she had checked into the hotel room, but for most of that time, Skalosak had barely moved a muscle. Outside, the sun was rising, but Skalosak was still kneeling there beside the bed, gazing lovingly upon the perfectly reconstructed, sleeping face of her adult son. Everything about him was just as she remembered; every facial spot, the length of every whisker, the way his left ear twitched in his sleep, the distinctive rolling patterns of his nocturnal purring, all were there. The Lifecore had not merely recreated his body; she had recreated everything that made him unique. Those tiny scars on his left ear from his adolescent experimentation with piercing were recreated in every microscopic detail. It was all those mortal imperfections that made Rantreleka's rebirth so perfect.

Whether he was reacting to the morning sunlight in his eyes, or to the last time his mother stroked his sleeping head, Skalosak could not tell; but for the first time in his new life, Rantreleka's eyelids began to flicker. Skalosak beamed in delight, as happy as she had been when Rantreleka was just the size of a human's finger and crawling towards the opening of her pouch for the first time, twenty-two years ago. The adult Rantreleka's head turned slightly, and his eyes opened all the way, still squinting and blinking in the golden sunrise.

"Mother?"

"Hello Baby."

Rantreleka's eyes darted to the window. "Where are we?" he said.

"The Valhalla Hotel, ninety-seventh floor."

"But why ... weren't we ... weren't we at the station last night?"

Skalosak had anticipated this. "What do you remember?"

"I remember ... I had just come back from my trip, and we were in your quarters, and I was showing you my memory recordings. We had a great night."

"Yes, we did."

"Was that last night?"

Skalosak paused. She had anticipated this as well. She knew that it was foolish to tell a lie she could not back up. Sooner or later, Rantreleka would find out the truth anyway. She could not shut the world out of his life forever.

Rantreleka closed his eyes, visibly straining. "I can't ... I can't seem to access any outgoing links. I can't access the net at all. What's the date?"

Skalosak swallowed. "The date is Kepler the Twenty-Fifth, Eight Thousand Four Hundred AT."

Instantly Rantreleka shuffled and began to sit up against his pillow. "That's two whole months!"

"I know."

"I should be at work! We were supposed to have a shipment to Vossola ..."

"I know."

"What happened?"

Skalosak took a deep breath. "There was an accident."

"An accident? On the *Persephone*?"

Skalosak nodded.

"Is Cheleera all right?"

Skalosak closed her eyes and sighed. With incredible effort, she shook her head.

"What happened, Mother? I need to know. How badly was Cheleera hurt? Why can't I remember the last two months?"

"Ranty ... I'm so very sorry. You are not going to like what I have to show you."

"What do you have to show me? What happened to Cheleera!?"

Slowly, feeling the weight of the entire galaxy on her chest, Skalosak closed her eyes and accessed her recording of that news report, then transmitted it to Rantreleka.

Watching the expression on her son's face was the most painful thing Skalosak had ever done up until that point. His eyes closed, Rantreleka flinched and shook his head as if in a nightmare.

"No," he said. "NO!"

Instantly he jumped off the other side of the bed, staring at his mother with an expression of absolute horror.

"It's not real!" he shouted. "None of this is real!"

"Ranty, I'm so sorry." Skalosak rose to her feet and began to move around the bed.

"KEEP AWAY FROM ME!" screamed Rantreleka, freezing his mother in her tracks. "What have you done, Mother? WHAT HAVE YOU DONE?"

"I have brought my Baby back to me."

Rantreleka shook his head violently, backing away towards the window. "I am not your son."

"Ranty, please ..."

"I AM NOT YOUR SON! I'M A COPY! I'M A TOY! I'M NOTHING!"

"Rantreleka, you are not nothing. You remember me. You remember your life. You remember Cheleera."

Rantreleka pressed his back against the window, and just for a moment the rising sun gave him wings of fire, like a wrathful angel. "They're just memories," he said. "That's all. Just bits and bytes. Just ones and zeroes. Is that all I am, Mother? Just a cluster of gigabytes? Just a mass of chemicals and organic molecules? Is that all a son is to you?"

"Ranty, you are so much more."

"I AM NOTHING! I HAVE NO SOUL!"

"You can feel. You have a soul."

"You don't believe in souls. You're an atheist."

"I believe in you. You're my son, and I love you."

"Your son is dead."

"Ranty-"

"Your son died in the explosion two days ago, along with the female that he loved. They're in Heaven now, forever united in bliss, under the loving protection of the Designer Himself. And I will never see her again. I never even met her to begin with. I can remember her, but it is all an illusion, a false memory."

Rantreleka sank down against the window and crouched on the floor, holding his face in his paws. A faint, muffled whining sound emerged from the shuddering wreck he had become.

Skalosak gently knelt beside him and embraced him softly, warmly. "You will always be real to me, Baby," she said, rocking her son gently. "Always."

"Magistrate," said Rantreleka.

Skalosak froze at the mention of that name.

"We must see the Magistrate," said Rantreleka, sliding his paws off his face. "We must see him together. He will know what to do."

"Who is the Magistrate?"

"Right now I need answers. I need guidance. And only the Magistrate can provide me with that."

"Rantreleka, answer me honestly. Will seeing the Magistrate make you feel better?"

"It is the only choice I have. We must see him together. He will tell us what to do."

Skalosak closed her eyes, but not to access her own software, or any software. If emotions were formed in the heart, or the belly, then that was the darkness where she wanted to look.

"Very well, Ranty," she said. "We shall see the Magistrate. Together."

####

Rantreleka had insisted on remaining in hibernation for as long as possible throughout the journey. He had entered the liner's hibernation chamber as soon as he was permitted, which was only half an hour after take-off. Apart from his initial outburst, he had said few words to Skalosak since learning the truth. He had helped Skalosak book the adjoining cruise that would take them directly to the Magistrate. Otherwise, he had seemed cold and aloof, as if sapped dry of any remaining emotion. Instead of calling her "Mother", he only called her by her name.

Perhaps he had accepted his status as a mere artificial copy of a former living being.

Skalosak had twenty-four hours of free time for private research before she was required to enter hibernation. Sitting in her cabin, she accessed the galaxy's Known Net – or at least the part of it that was comprehensible to baseline-level minds such as herself. She ran a key concept search on "Magistrate", "Church of the Sacred Flesh", "Four Founders" and "Rocks of Foundation". All she found was references to thousands of baseline-level magistrates working on worlds where the Church had its branches. Nothing mystical or godlike. Nothing that would indicate evidence of a Transapient that went by that name. She submitted massed questions to various "Ask a Transapient!" sites, but none answered.

Breaking the rules of privacy that she had once held so dear, she tried searching the copy of Rantreleka's memory that she still kept in her personal folder. Incredibly, all references to the very concept of the Magistrate were encrypted in a way that was utterly unreadable to any software she had access to. The church – or something – had well and truly got into her son's head, altering the very way it lodged information there.

She researched the church's treatment of personality copies, and discovered that they treated them in much the same manner as they treated robots - not with hostility, but neither as true equals.

That would definitely hurt Ranty. *She* had hurt Ranty.

"I only wanted to see my son again," she said to herself. "I only wanted my son to live again."

As much as she tried, she found that she could not comfort herself with these rationalizations, these feeble excuses.

Perhaps punishment was awaiting her at the end of this journey.

Perhaps she deserved what was coming.

####

Skalosak and Rantreleka emerged from hibernation after the liner had passed through the wormhole and entered the Blaze Junction – a system surrounded by eight wormholes. At one of the many space stations, they boarded a much smaller passenger ship owned by a private company called Mystigian Cruises, and headed for the system's smallest and least used wormhole. Both mother and son were the only passengers that either was aware of. They never saw any crewmembers, but were ordered by a disembodied voice to enter hibernation as soon as possible.

And thus the end of their journey came to them with little conscious time to think, plan, or research, much less speak to each other.

####

When Skalosak awoke, she was not even on board the ship. Instead, she was in some kind of waiting room carved out of granite. Was she underground? Her biochip had no external access whatsoever.

Rantreleka was seated on the lounge opposite her, staring vacantly.

"Where are we?" said Skalosak.

"Close to the Magistrate's office. We'll be called in soon."

"How did we get here?"

"I presume they carried us."

"They?"

"I'm not sure who. I never saw them. I only heard their voices in my head. All I know is that they serve the Magistrate. That's all that matters."

Skalosak paused thoughtfully, trying to recall the journey. "So we are on Mezollin?"

"No. We're way past Mezollin. We went through three extra wormholes just to get her?"

"*What?*"

"Don't worry. They've informed me that they've contacted Tillika and told her that you won't be coming back. Under the circumstances, she should not be too surprised."

There were a few minutes of absolute silence.

"Skalosak?"

"Yes, Ranty?"

"I would like to apologise for my behaviour."

Skalosak's ears twitched in surprise. "I'm the one who needs to apologise," she said.

"You have a good heart," said Ratreleka. "A wonderful heart. I know, because I have Rantreleka's memories. You loved your son dearly, of that I have no doubt. But you were more than a little impulsive in your actions, thinking greatly of your own emotions while thinking little for the emotions of the new living being you brought into existence, and now you must face the consequences."

Skalosak shivered inside. "Ranty," she said softly, "Am I to be punished?"

Rantreleka blinked and looked away. "I don't want you to suffer," he said. "But please know that I am on your side. I must speak to the Magistrate. I really need to do this. And … and I still feel the love that the real Rantreleka felt for you."

Skalosak sighed in relief, smiling softly at her reborn son.

"It's only an echo of Rantreleka's love," he said. "A recording. But it's there, and it's been affecting my thoughts and feelings every moment since I awoke in that hotel. I'm confused."

"It means you have a soul," said Skalosak.

"Do you really believe that? Can a soul be so easy to copy? The Magistrate would know the answer to that riddle, but he does not reveal all secrets to mortals."

Almost as if on cue, a soft yet incredibly resonant voice filled the room.

"Skalosak and Rantreleka, please report to me immediately."

The granite wall at the end of the room seemed to liquefy and part like curtains, revealing a dark stone tunnel beyond.

"It's time," said Rantreleka. "Please be brave, Skalosak. Your son always admired your courage."

Reluctantly, Skalosak got to her feet and followed her son out into the darkness.

At first she could not see the end of the tunnel – not because it was too dark or distant, but because it curved downwards. Once she and her son reached the bottom of the curve, however, she could see where it ended, where their journey ended.

At the end of the tunnel was a vast, dimly lit chamber, and filling most of that chamber was what Skalosak instinctively recognized as the Magistrate.

She understood why the Magistrate was considered one of the Four Rocks of Foundation. The Magistrate was a rock. Literally. It was a roughly grooved stone cube vaster than the snow guide station she had left so very far behind. Engraved on the middle of its facing surface, far above, was an immense human face. As

Skalosak entered the chamber and stared at the giant stone face, its features seemed to ripple and liquefy, transforming from human to feline, as if mirroring her own facial features. Then Skalosak's memory corrected itself, and she realized that the Magistrate had always possessed a feline face of stone.

"Skalosak of New Dumont," boomed the gentle yet hypnotic voice of the Magistrate, "do you know why you are here?"

"I am here to be judged, your honour," said Skalosak, "and I am ready."

"You have already been judged," said the Magistrate.

"I ... I understand, your honour."

"No, Skalosak, you do not understand; although I do not blame you for your ignorance. I cast my verdict immediately before I called you here. While the two of you were unconscious, I observed your actions through your memories, experiencing them through your senses, thoughts and emotions. I also observed your actions through the memories and senses of your son, who has been copied in minute physical and mental detail into the creature standing beside you. I accept that you may not be held entirely responsible for all of your actions. We have many enemies, and you may have been manipulated without your knowing. However, you are not here to plead your case, for the verdict has already been passed."

"Then, your honour," said Skalosak, "Am I here solely to be punished?"

"The copy of your son has wisely avoided informing you of my true purpose."

Skalosak glanced sideways at Rantreleka, who was staring up at the great stone face. "And what, may I ask, is this purpose, your honour?" she said.

"Perhaps the copy would inform you," said the Magistrate.

Skalosak turned to her son, who was still trying to avert his gaze.

"I told you to be brave," he said at last.

"Rantreleka," said Skalosak, "if I am here to be punished, then I am willing to accept that. I will not blame you at all, for I have violated your right to stay dead. I understand that now, and I am deeply sorry. And if you are here to be punished, then I would like to take your place. Do you understand?"

"I don't think you understand," said Rantreleka. "The purpose of the Magistrate is to mediate between two parties and put the law – its own law – into effect."

"Then tell me," said Skalosak, looking up at the face of the Magistrate, "what is the sentence?"

"The sentence consists of three stages," the Magistrate explained calmly. "First, the copy of your son's memory and genetic pattern that you have kept in your personal folder on the Net is to be erased, along with several hidden backups that you are not aware of. This stage has been executed as of this moment. I have temporarily re-enabled your access to the net so that you can see for yourself."

Skalosak's jaw dropped in amazement. She closed her eyes and accessed her personal folder. It was true. The copy of Rantreleka was gone. She opened her eyes and looked to her right. Rantreleka was still there, still standing, still staring at the immense stone being that could snuff out the patterns that made up mortals with a thought.

"Second," said the Magistrate, "all copies of your son's memory and genetic pattern recorded by the independent first level transapient known by her employees as the Lifecore are to be erased. This stage has been executed as of this moment."

Skalosak gasped, stunned at the power and resources of this truly godlike being. The very thought of where this was heading filled her with dread.

"My dear Skalosak," the Magistrate spoke softly, with profound sympathy, "I believe that you have already guessed the third stage."

"Don't you dare hurt my son!" Skalosak roared as she stepped between Rantreleka and the vast stone face that stared down at them as if they were less than insects.

"I will not execute the copy of your son, Skalosak," said the Magistrate. "That is your duty."

For a long time, an excruciatingly long time, Skalosak stood there and stared up at the giant stone face. Ice could not freeze her. Snowstorms could not freeze her. But this … thing – the very idea it was suggesting – made her blood run cold. She turned to her son. Rantreleka gently nodded, his eyes heavy-lidded with sorrow. Skalosak returned her attention to the Magistrate.

"You … are … fucking … sick," she slowly snarled.

"I am sorry, Skalosak," boomed the Magistarate, "but this is the Law of my realm."

"You're sorry, are you?" Skalosak trembled all over. "You're fucking sorry? Oh no, I'll make you fucking sorry you gutless great slab of petrified shit! You deserve to be nuked from orbit! And your entire fucking planet with you!"

"Mother, please-"

"How dare you even suggest to a loving mother that she murder her own son? How fucking dare you!"

"Mother-"

"You deserve to be thrown into …" Skalosak paused and turned to Rantreleka. "What did you call me?"

"Mother."

Immediately Skalosak embraced her son. "Thank you," she whispered. "Thank you, Ranty."

"I have your son's memories," said Rantreleka. "I remember you as my Mother. I can't see you as anything else."

"And that makes you my son," said Skalosak. "I don't care if you're a copy, you're still my son."

"You still have to be brave."

"I won't let the monster hurt you, Baby."

"It's the Law," said Rantreleka.

"You knew about this, didn't you?" Skalosak stared at her son incredulously. "You knew all this time. You brought me here to murder you."

"You won't be committing murder. Not here."

"I won't be committing murder ANYWHERE. Do you here me your fucking precious honour?" She turned her steel gaze to the Magistrate. "I am not murdering my son, and that is final! Come on, Ranty, let's get out of this shit pit."

As she turned for the exit, the hole in the granite wall shrank into nothingness.

"Skalosak, please listen," said the Magistrate. "You are not permitted to leave this chamber until you fulfil your duty."

"My duty is to protect my son. If that means I have to die fighting you, then so be it."

"Your son did not want to be copied," said the Magistrate. "By copying him without his permission, you have already violated his rights."

"Mountain fried yakshit I have violated his rights."

"I'm afraid he speaks the truth, Mother."

"Is this what that fucking Pastor taught you, Ranty?"

"This is what I taught Pastor Danalonan," said the Magistrate.

"You sick fucking hypocrite," said Skalosak as she turned to the monolith. "You're a coward. Teaching mortals to stay mortal so you never face a rival."

"You are mistaken. I came into existence as a machine. My colleagues and I decided to create a safe haven for lesser beings that desired to preserve their species. Our desire was to respect their choice, something that you have failed to do."

"I respect my son's life."

"You have forged your son's life."

Suddenly Skalosak remembered Rantreleka's speech at the dinner table on the first night of his visit. *But copying your entire memory, emotions and all? That's forgery of the worst kind. You're forging a soul that is copyright of the Designer.*

Once again, she turned to her son. "Ranty, I do not share your beliefs. I can never accept your beliefs. And I have known you for much longer than you have known this church. You are infinitely more important to me than any petty movement that just breezed into your life."

"I understand, Mother. But Cheleera didn't just breeze into my life. I loved her. At least … I remember loving her. And now I will never see her. Because the real Rantreleka is united with her in Heaven, and I have nowhere to go."

"Rantreleka," said Skalosak, "You're real. Just as real as the first Ranty. Every bit as real, in every detail."

"I am a creation of technology," said Rantreleka.

"So is this great lunking thing!" Skalosak gestured violently at the Magistrate.

"That's different," said Rantreleka.

"Your son's copy speaks the truth," said the Magistrate. "We transapients have many complex means of reproduction. I have a parent."

"And I AM A FUCKING PARENT!" roared Skalosak.

"Skalosak," said the Magistrate, "I could hold you and the copy of your son in my chamber until you both suffocate or die of thirst. Or I could preserve your lives indefinitely if need be. But I must follow the Law that I myself helped bring into being, and I must ensure that you – while you are within my realm - follow it as well."

Mere seconds later, Rantreleka keeled over and retched.

"Ranty, are you all right?" Skalosak knelt and held her son, who suddenly vomited blood.

"Oh gods," said Skalosak, and instinctively pulled a tube out of her utility belt.

"Here, this will make you better," she said as she held the transparent tube against Rantreleka's neck … and then flinched it away as she saw that the fluid inside was bubbling.

"What the … you're doing this, aren't you?" She turned to the monolith as she threw away the tube. "You're doing this YOU SADISTIC FUCK!"

Lowered to all fours, Rantreleka vomited blood again. Four teeth fell out, including one large canine.

"RANTY!" Skalosak held her son again, wondering how in the name of the AI Gods she could help him now.

"Mother," Rantreleka rasped, "please ... "

Skalosak shook her head violently. "You have to renounce your faith," she said. "Renounce your faith and he can't do a thing to you. Then he'll let us go."

"I ... can't." Rantrleka feebly pawed at his ear, as if trying to scratch an itch ... and the ear came off in his paw, leaving a sticky patch of blood and bone. He stared at his severed ear in horrified wonder.

"Stop this!" Skalosak roared at the Magistrate. "STOP THIS RIGHT NOW!"

"That is your duty," said the Magistrate. "I know you love your son and your son's copy, Skalosak. You do not want him to suffer. Not like this. Not for hours."

"YOU CAN'T MAKE ME KILL HIM!"

Just then Rantrekela vomited more blood. More teeth fell out. Blood poured from his nose and eyes. The paw holding his severed ear dropped to the stone floor, bursting bloodily on impact. His hide cracked open in a hundred places, oozing blood through his fur. His breaths became strained wheezes, as if spending every second searching for the energy to scream. Whatever remained of his original scent became drowned out in unnatural stink.

Skalosak remembered the nightmare. It had not been symbolic. It had not been exaggerated. It had been a tame understatement compared to this cruel reality.

"I'm sorry, Ranty," she said. "I am so sorry."

"Your true son died instantly in a flash of energy," said the Magistrate. "Yet you brought this copy into existence just to suffer horribly.

Why would you do such a thing, Skalosak? Why would a loving mother allow her son to suffer like this? Would you let him suffer for hours just so you could stand by your feeble principles and fragile ego? Is your self worth more valuable to you than your son's wellbeing?"

"Mo...ther," Rantreleka wheezed painfully, "Love ... you."

"I love you too, Baby." Skalosak gently lifted her ailing son and cradled him in her arms, holding her paw to the back of his neck. She continued to speak softly, as if telling a young joey a story. "Sometimes, beings like you and me make multiple copies, and send them away on adventures. Then the copies reunite with their original creator and merge into one mind, and they share all their memories and experiences. I think that's what's going to happen to you. You're going to merge with the First Rantreleka, and your going to experience all the things that he saw and felt and did from the moment I copied him and created you. You'll be with Cheleera in Heaven. And one day, I'll meet you there. When I'm ready."

Then, somehow, through his quivering and distorted and bloodied lips, Rantreleka managed a hint of a smile. Trembling uncontrollably, he reached up with his one good paw and stroked his mother's face.

Skalosak understood. It was time. It was all right. She had to be brave.

Instantly she pressed her paw upwards. Rantreleka's neck snapped. His entire body shuddered for a split second, then every bone and muscle relaxed.

Skalosak gently lowered the body of her son to the stone floor and closed his eyelids.

She sat there beside her dead son, roaring pure rage into the dark, uncaring void, howled until she tasted blood in her throat, and howled some more until her breath thinned down to a harsh whisper.

Minutes passed. Perhaps hours passed. Skalosak had no way of telling. Her connections to the outside universe were severed. Her internal clock was as scrambled as her mind.

Then she remembered where she was, and rose to her feet.

"I will make you suffer," she hissed at the giant stone face. "I don't care how long it takes me, what I transform myself into, what demons I have to sell my soul to, I will make sure you pay for what you have done to my son."

The Magistrate observed, silent, unmoving, unmoved.

####

At the age of three, Rantreleka had been an active and playful joey. Skalosak remembered how he would run from table to table at the outdoor food court in Salandara, amusing and delighting the human diners with his antics. "Hello," he would say to a young couple eating fried fish and potatoes. "My name is Rantreleka. Can you say that? Ran-trel-ek-a. Me and Mommy went on the hovabus." The couple would laugh and offer him a chip. Then Rantreleka would run to his mother with the chip in his paw and exclaim at the top of his voice "Mo-om! Look what the lady gave me! LOOK WHAT THE LADY GAVE ME!" It would not be long before he would be curled up in Skalosak's pouch, exhausted by his own hyperactivity.

Standing on the ice, holding the vial in her paw, Skalosak remembered her son that way.

Perhaps she would always remember him that way. Or perhaps she would remember him fully grown, standing in the spaceport, so handsome, so proud, so full of hope and ambition.

She had woken up in the spaceport in the Blaze Junction, a vial of ashes hanging from a thin chain around her neck. Perhaps this was the Magistrate's desperate attempt to placate her. Or perhaps he knew exactly what he was doing. He was a transapient, after all. Keeping her unconscious throughout the entire trip would have saved him a lot of repair bills.

She had made no attempt to contact the snow guide station. That phase of her life was long over. Instead, she took the hoverbus to this one remote location - one that was most familiar to her.

"Remember this spot, Ranty?" she said to the vial. "This is where you first saw the Northern Aurora. My First Ranty saw it one last time while you were sleeping in cyberspace, waiting to be reborn. Maybe you're in Heaven now. Maybe you've merged with the First Ranty and now the both of you are sharing all your new experiences, the First Ranty's happy last days, and your … but you don't need to tell him that. All the both of you need to know is that I love the both of you as the same individual, as my son. Say hello to Cheleera for me. Maybe you could raise a joey. Can you do that in Heaven? Anyway, I know that you'll be waiting for me. But Mother has a lot of travelling to do, a lot of living to do. I want to be as good as you. I want to … to earn your forgiveness."

There was to be no Northern Aurora that night, but a snowstorm was already on its way.

As the vast wave of white swept over her, Skalosak held the vial to her mouth and gently licked it.

"Goodbye, Rantreleka. Love you forever."

She opened the vial and let the ashes dance on the winds, free of pain, forever immortal.

New Home
The Outer Volumes Era
9317 AT

Ron Bennett

The name of the Terragen Sphere is inaccurate in many ways. Far from being a sphere, the region of colonised space in this era was an irregular disk five and a half thousand light-years in radius, spreading out across the Orion Arm of the Milky Way Galaxy and some way into the neighboring Perseus and Sagittarius Arms. In two other regions the Terragen Sphere had extended beyond these limits, thanks to the chance discovery of ancient but still operable alien wormholes thousands of light-years long. Few colonies existed above and below the thick disk, except in the region of the Red Star M'pire, which had expanded into a small satellite galaxy to Galactic North.

At the outermost edge of this ever-expanding volume new colonies were continually being established, with the aid of fast, transapientech craft gifted by the archai of the central empires and other similar entities, usually with certain conditions attached. These new worlds were often founded by citizens dissatisfied with the politics and strictures of the old worlds, eager to find new ways of living.

Ron Bennett describes the arrival of one colonial mission at a new system, and an unexpected discovery that leads to an ethical dilemma.

18 Hippocrates 9317 AT

"Are you up to speed yet?"

"Yes. Have we entered the system?"

"Yes. We are near the star. Our speed is now less than 1800 kilometers per second. The magbrake is retracted; the engines will begin deceleration in 12,644 seconds. Our journey is nearly over."

"The length of the journey is measured in time, not distance," Karpin thought. He was grateful for a slower clock speed; the 112 year journey between the stars had seemed like only a few days. E switched eir optics to infrared. Color and form replaced featureless black. A grid of beams outlined the edges of cubes, the spaces within occupied by an assortment of machinery and storage bins. Three hundred eighty five were occupied by the crew: sophont robots, known as vecs, in dozens of different shapes and combinations. A few of were moving among the cubes, using the beams to maneuver in the microgravity. Two spheres, one with six limbs, the other with eight locked together and moved aft. A tetrahedron with a sphere and two limbs at each point intersected their path from behind and followed.

"IR always looks dull," Karpin complained as e cycled through several color patterns, watching the reds, blues, greens, and numerous shades wash over the scene. A communication request interrupted eir slide show.

"We seem to have made it in one piece," Bahan transmitted, with relief emphasis added.

"Yes. Always something of a gamble, interstellar travel," Karpin replied with equal the same emphasis.

"Interesting word you choose there – gamble. Something you shouldn't be doing with our contracts. We lost everything on our last one, and this one –"

"We have this ship and an entire system," Karpin transmitted loud enough to jam Bahan.

"Not quite an entire system," Bahan jammed back. "Section 5, third paragraph, 'The cooperative shall be entitled to all resources within 3 billion kilometers of the stars'"

"Yes, I know," Karpin interrupted. "The point from where the distance is measured is not clearly defined."

"Why did you leave ambiguity in that section?" Bahan complained. "You could very well have cost us half the system!"

"Consider the worst case scenario," Karpin began. E paused briefly to bring up a picture of the system that was superimposed with a green translucent circle centered between the two stars that was large enough to cover the orbits of the planets and asteroid belt. Before e could continue however e was interrupted with an urgent broadcast signal, to which e granted permission to receive and play.

The broadcast started with the announcement that everyone was up to regular clock speed. It continued with details on their position, destination and a countdown to their scheduled acceleration. It closed with advice on how to prepare for acceleration and a reminder to join the debate on which star they should orbit first. The debate was scheduled to start 100 seconds after acceleration began.

"Let me continue," Karpin signaled Bahan after the broadcast.

"Hold on," Bahan transmitted back with a location indicator. Karpin looked toward the direction indicated. Bahan was a construction vec, a two meter sphere with six limbs around eir equator. E didn't do much physical work with the limbs, even though they ended with two pairs of double jointed fingers. Mostly e used the narrow beam, short range transmitter each limb contained to send instructions to the swarm inside eir body. It was the millions of tiny robots in the swarm that did the actual work. Right now Bahan was using two limbs to hold onto a beam, and the two of the other four to swing emself back and forth. When Karpin looked, Bahan used one of eir free limbs to wave.

"Save it for the debate. I'm sure everyone else will want to know how you bungled negotiations."

Karpin waved back, checked the clamps and then checked the countdowns. One, the countdown to beginning acceleration, was falling below 400 seconds. The second, 1100 seconds higher, marked the time they had to debate. The ship, the *Keleivi*, was now coasting toward a point about half way between the stars. To go in orbit around one star, the *Keleivi* would have to change course. The second countdown indicated the optimal time to do this. Everyone aboard the *Keleivi* joined the same network to facilitate communication. Anyone could present arguments or proposals, though most merely voiced their preference for one star or the other.

Berdae was the first to detail eir preference. "We use superconducting solenoids or nano flywheels for power storage and the only reactors we have to recharge from are on the ship. To develop the system efficiently we need to work in small groups in numerous areas. The asteroids will be the easiest to mine and should give us all the resources we need but they are too far from the star to use solar power efficiently. If we beam power from the ship we can only mine one asteroid at a time and it's not likely we can get everything we need from one. The gas dwarf is close enough to the star for efficient use of solar power, and we can mine Helium3 from its atmosphere. Fusion reactors using Helium3 produce very little unwanted radiation, are small, highly mobile, and easy to build. Each one will give us enough power to work away from the ship for extended periods. Furthermore all the moons are close together so moving the resources we mine from various sources to central processing centers will be easy and quick. These crucial requirements are not in the asteroid belt."

"There are only six small moons, far enough from the star they may contain a lot of ice and not enough rock" Karpin argued. "By going to the A component we can use a swarm to begin dismantling the terrestrial planet, which is close enough to the star to use solar power. There are a large number of asteroids; statistically some of them will be metallic. We can use resources from the terrestrial planet to build a power collection swarm to beam power to the asteroids."

"One of the moons is over three hundred kilometers across ..."

"All of the moons are too small to be certain any of them contains the resources we need. Tantalum, for example, is extremely rare and is necessary for our eyes. Only the terrestrial planet is large enough to be certain we get this and other rare but necessary metals. Its existence is one of the reasons we came to this otherwise resource-poor system. Additionally we currently have no way of moving helium out of the gas dwarf's gravity well. The terrestrial planet will give us the metals we need to build craft to do this."

"Perhaps we should first decide how we're going to do the mining" Duzeme interjected. "That may help decide which star to orbit first. Pala have you prepared a presentation?"

"Yes. Since we wish to extract everything from the asteroids and moons we will use disassembler swarms controlled by an individual vec. The extra processing requirements will be distributed throughout the swarm and replication will be done only on command, to avoid any possibility of an out of control swarm. The gravity of the moons is low enough that processed material can be pushed into orbit by small a magnetic driver. Paramagnetic material will have to be mixed with or enclosed by ferromagnetic material."

"Then you believe we should mine the moons first?" Duzeme asked.

"Yes. The moons have a high enough insolation to use solar power without building a power collection swarm first, the asteroid belt does not. The terrestrial planet has an atmosphere. We do not have metals to build landing craft to remain intact during atmospheric entry. The first few swarms will be composed of the small disassembler/assembler swarms some of us have. Since surveying the asteroid belt will take time, we should orbit the largest moon of the gas dwarf first. There will be, with near certainty, carbon, silicon, iron, magnesium, and aluminum the swarms can use for replication. We can expand the swarms as resources allow, and begin building the reflectors for a power collection swarm. It should take only a few days to get the first reflectors constructed. By building them with a solar sail configuration they can move into position in the asteroid belt under their own power and carry enough computronium for their own control programs, as well as a transmitter/receiver for communication."

"We came here to build our own society. Those metals are not enough for us to reproduce," Karpin argued.

"The reflectors will need someone to control them. We can use them as bodies and begin reproducing in a few days," Pala countered. "The gas dwarf is the only place in the system where resources and energy are both abundant enough for us to use the tools we have brought with us. The minerals we process will allow us to build the tools we need for further development."

Bahan waited until the end. E had expected many to be concerned over what e felt was a major problem with their contract.

Karpin responded by again showing the picture of the system with the green, translucent circle covering the stars.

"Even if we use the midpoint of the system, we clearly have development rights for both planets and the asteroid belt. And if we interpret the section to mean we measure from both stars," the green circle split in two, each circle centered on a star, overlapping in the middle. "We have more space, but there is very little in it beyond perhaps a dwarf planet or two and a few stray asteroids. As long as we use the terrestrial planet we have plenty of resources and this should not be a concern

There was little more debate. The *Keleivi* slowed for orbital insertion and eleven days later they were in orbit around the gas dwarf's largest moon. The planet's beautiful deep blue color was mesmerizing but the vecs had much work to do and little time to admire its beauty. Six areas were chosen to begin mining. Vecs landed at each area with swarms and began extracting and processing minerals. Whenever available, excess power was beamed from the ship.

22 Mendel 9317 AT

Five months after orbital insertion the vecs not needed for mining the moons began the twenty-two day journey to the asteroid belt and the terrestrial planet orbiting Azadliq B. En route to the planet several newly constructed satellites were deployed to map the asteroid belt. After arrival at the terrestrial planet, satellites were placed in orbit to create detailed maps of the surface and to communicate with landing probes. Each probe carried a teleoperated ground rover and a small hydrogen filled dirigible for aerial surveys. The planet's purple color was evidently the reason it had been referenced as looking peculiar. The reasons for its odd color became evident when the rovers analyzed samples of the surface soil.

"As I theorized," Duzeme stated. "Purple sulfur bacteria analogues. This planet has life. We cannot dismantle it. Our presence must be limited to scientific study of this unique biosphere."

Duzeme had been part of the terraforming team and had worked in several habs creating and maintaining the biospheres. Eir experiences had given em great respect and fascination for biological life and its science. E would have adopted a biological body, but that would have placed unacceptable limits on doing the work e loved.

Duzeme, Karpin7, and Daliri, were gripping handrails and viewing the planet through one of the one meter wide slits in the outer hull.

"Study!!" Karpin transmitted with exasperation emphasis. "The metals we need are severely limited on the moons! We don't know if there are any in the asteroid belt! This planet is the only alternative!! You're suggesting –"

"Karpin7, turn down your emotional centers. You are not looking at the situation realistically."

"Realistically? Realistically we need to mine –"

Duzeme stopped em by using eir small directional antenna to broadcast a powerful burst of static. "I will give you time to adjust your emotional settings and to examine the situation logically with attention to legalities. One clause of our contract with Harrozulo references the Galactic Preservation Act which forbids us from destroying indigenous biospheres. I'm going to review the data we have and write a report and call for a vote."

With that Duzeme pulled eirself to the outside of the ship's hull, adjusted the filter on eir optics to avoid damage from the glare of the star, and admired the view of the planet.

"Your history with biotech is clouding your assessment of the situation!" Karpin transmitted with anger and intense frustration emphasis.

Daliri, holding emself in place with one long arm, spread the other five and with conciliatory emphasis. "Leave em to write," e transmitted. "It will take several hours. Meanwhile we can review the data we have. I just got a message from Bahan. E's teleoperating the rovers and has already found some promising mineral deposits."

"Yeah, let's see what e has," Karpin agreed.

Duzeme meanwhile accessed eir emotional settings. E began adjusting so that e would feel nothing but bliss. Before e got too happy though, e thought "Better set a timer." When e turned pleasure to its highest setting time seemed to move at a different rate. A few hours or days could seem like only a few minutes. Previous experiences had taught em to set a timer to rebalance eir emotions.

"Lest I spend days watching a flower grow," E thought with sarcastic emphasis. "But ... no. Better to wait." and rebalanced eir emotions. "I've called for a vote; I need to prepare my arguments." Duzeme stared at the planet again.

"Life. We find it here. The longs odds beaten again ... that should have felt better ... mmm... maybe turn it up just a little ... just enough for the happiness, joy ... and pleasure, can't forget pleasure... not too high ... just want to feel good enough ... to be compelled to action."

A wave of emotion washed over Duzeme. E played a music file and created a caricature of emself and set it to dance to the music. "The planet's misses," e thought as e added it to eir private animation. The caricature now danced across the face of a planet only twice its size. "Too big. I should be smaller." The caricature shrunk to about a tenth the planet's size. "Mmmm ... mmmaybe just a little higher." Duzeme adjusted eir emotional settings again, feeling more pleasure. "The band is missing." Drums, strings, and various organs began to appear around the dancer. "Or maybe an orchestra." The band disappeared and a full orchestra outlined the circle. "But I'll have to stop dancing and be a conductor." Duzeme's caricature now appeared, in traditional conductor's dress and began conducting the music. "This isn't quite lively enough, and the players behind me can't see properly." The orchestra disappeared, replaced by a pop band. A graphic full of dials and levers appeared. "Just a little higher." E thought, as cartoon hands appeared and reached for several of the dials and levers. A timer flashed, begging for attention. In a flash of sobriety one of the hands quickly punched the 1000 second mark, and the timer disappeared. "I didn't do that right, must do it again." The timer reappeared, its countdown stopped, and increased to 2000 seconds. The cartoon hand formed a fist made of diamond and punched the timer. It shattered and multicolored pieces sprayed all over the dancer. The cartoon hands working the levers stopped, each found a partner and applauded loudly. Duzeme replayed the shatter scene several times, enjoying eir own applause."

"What are you doing?"

Another caricature of eirself had appeared, colored navy blue with gold trim, holding an EM pistol. It had grabbed and stilled the dancer, stopping the music with an awful ear splitting screech.

"I hate you!" The dancer screamed, and all the hands changed to diamond fists and flew toward the Joy Killer. They all connected at the same time and the Joy Killer was sent flying from the scene. The fists changed back to hands and applauded loudly, then each patted its partner on the back, "Well done ... fine job ... wonderful job ... I say that was a fine hit ... good job old chap ... yes indeed."

The music restarted. The dancer started dancing again. "I should be more colorful." Duzeme opened the dial and lever emotional control panel again and set eir pleasure feelings to maximum. The dancer was covered in a rainbow, the circle in the middle of the band, eir stage, became a double rainbow and then started to rotate. It stopped rotating and changed to a 2D scene with trees, flowers, a pond and a grassy meadow. Duzeme hadn't noticed eir physical body had begun swaying gently, keeping perfect time with the music.

Bahan could have transmitted the data but they considered the available bandwidth to be too low for the amount of data they wanted to review, so Karpin and Daliri used handrails to pull themselves to the communications center of the ship. Once there they found Bahan standing in front of six video displays arranged in a semi-circle. All six displays showed nothing but the black and white randomly moving dots of white noise.

"What's the problem?" asked Daliri.

"I've lost communication with the rovers."

"Which ones?"

"All of them."

"All six? At the same time?"

"All within 286 seconds."

"What about the dirigibles?"

"Still operating. Now moving them in position to get a look at the rovers. First one should be there in 511 seconds."

Over the next thirty minutes all six dirigibles were maneuvered near their respective rovers. All the rovers were covered in purple slime. Bahan tried using the dirigible's sampling arm to get a sample of the slime but every time it got stuck and the slime oozed its way up the arm until its weight pulled the dirigible down and communication was lost. E kept the last four at higher altitude and didn't try to obtain samples.

Duzeme's timer reached zero and eir emotions rebalanced. E immediately felt like raising pleasure again but resisted the temptation. "I can't spare the time. I have something more important to do. Maybe I'll just … yeah … take a look at this again." Duzeme open a file e had downloaded before the journey. Personality files that would allow em to assume a female personality. E automatically thought back to when e had downloaded it. A mixed feeling of fear, apprehension, revulsion and sadness again tempted Duzeme to adjust eir emotions. "Maybe I should think about it. Maybe I'll stay balanced for a while if I'm scared enough."

E thought back, replaying events from Turideah. After years of disappointment and losing everything they had worked for, e had started turning up pleasure, happiness, joy … just so e wouldn't feel terrible all the time. By the time they had been ready to begin legal proceedings they had been relegated to a single hab. It was comfortable, but not what they'd negotiated. E remembered choosing space in the outer rim. E wanted some gravity to make it easier to build a greenhouse and e would be able to grow a wider variety of plants. The greenhouse gave em an excuse to withdraw, just be alone, pleasure emotions set to maximum. E usually managed to rebalance after a few hours. E remembered feeling concerned during the lucid moments. E felt lonely no longer associating with friends, but e could turn that down. Though e felt worse when e neglected the greenhouse.

One day while looking at some grafts, e magnified to cellular level, and decided to turn up happiness a little. "Just too feel a little better about this one of the few things that has gone right." He thought wryly. "Six days. Still didn't learn." Hardly having friends anymore, no one noticed e was missing for a few days. Berdae had found em in the greenhouse. Completely powered down. Unresponsive when Berdae connected power. It was the first time being restored from backup. "And I lost six days. At least I started setting a timer after that." E explored the personality file, sampled a few of the experiences, and decided install it and try a few of the settings. "Just set all defaults to zero." While it set up Duzeme opened the file with the memories from the missing six days. "A few pictures of plant cells. The rest, every bit of data, erased."

An urgent broadcast signal brought Duzeme back to the present. There was a scheduled discussion and debate to decide their next course of action.

"I've got just enough time to prepare." Duzeme thought, and tried some of the personality enhancements. "I will not let them destroy this planet." Whatever it took, *she* would protect this planet.

A short time later all the vecs on the *Keleivi* linked, forming a tribemind and debated their next step.

"It was an attack," Duzeme stated, having come to an *interesting* conclusion.

"An attack!! A ridiculous conclusion!" Karpin broadcast, adding disbelief, shock and frustration emphasis.

"You still have your emotional settings are too high. Please turn them down."

"On what data do you base your conclusion that it was an attack?" Bahan asked.

"The rovers were on the ground for several hours, and then all were attacked almost simultaneously. There is an intelligence there. It observed, concluded there was a danger, and defended itself."

Quickly scanning through the videos from the dirigibles, Duzeme selected a dozen frames and broadcast them as part of eir continuing argument. "Geometric shapes. Circles, hexagons, triangles. Knowledge of geometry requires intelligence. It could even be an attempt to communicate. The –"

"Your conclusion is ridiculous, nothing more than fantasy." Karpin broadcast a signal strong enough to jam Duzeme's transmission, but did so without emphasis. E then broadcast an image of mushrooms growing in a circle. "This is known as a fairy ring. It appears wherever wild mushrooms grow on a garden world or hab. It doesn't mean the mushroom patch is intelligent. The shape is merely a result of its growth pattern. The shapes you showed are due to a similar process. There are no animals or plants, microbial life only. Where is the intelligent life you postulate?"

"It's an envome, whose various species are all microbial, possibly colonial organisms. We'll need to observe and gather more data to be sure. We have to suspend our mining plans to avoid any possible damage to this unique biosphere and sophont entity."

Karpin broadcast a signal for attention, and then complete silence with disbelief emphasis for full minute, "How can you make such a statement? How could you come to such a conclusion? Where is your evidence? Your arguments have gone from unsubstantiated guesses to completely absurd. I suggest you return to the wormhole nexus and begin a new career as an illusionist. You did an excellent job of conjuring an envome. Something so rare no reasonable being would even think of presenting the argument."

Berdae broadcast a signal for attention. "You made the same statements when I theorized the color was due to life."

"You did not theorize. You *speculated* the color was due to life. A theory is based on data. At the time we did not have enough data on which to formulate a theory. We could only speculate. Several speculative conclusions were drawn to explain the color."

Berdae again broadcast for attention. "My conjecture was at least based on reality, unlike your argument, a planet covered in amethyst. Including the oceans where amethyst would sink and not be a factor in its color. And you ignored the fact that silicon dioxide has numerous colors."

"We still have not taken ocean samples. We don't know with certainty the color is due to these microbes."

Berdae added emphasis with a series of beeps, and again broadcast for attention. "It is a thick layer of plankton. A logical conclusion based on the life on land." Berdae made a point of drawing power from a receptacle in a nearby wall.

"More speculation. We have no samples ..."

Berdae interrupted Karpin with a strong signal and broadcast with diplomatic overtones. "Our immediate problem with this decision appears to be that we don't have enough data to make an *informed* decision. I propose we spend the next ten days gathering data."

"I agree," Duzeme transmitted. "We must also honor our contract, which has a very strongly worded clause regarding the protection of indigenous biospheres."

"We were months late arriving here. The law does not forbid us from mining selected deposits," Karpin argued.

"We risk losing any equipment or swarms we send down to the surface," Berdae transmitted with logic emphasis. E paused and continued: "The planet will be here for a hundred billion years. We need not make any hasty decisions, or rush into a situation blindly."

Karpin argued no further. Even e had to admit Berdae's logic was unassailable. There was more discussion but e disconnected from the tribemind and made eir way back to the outer hull and stared silently at the planet. Bahan joined em a short time later.

"Has the discussion ended?"

"Yes, for now. Our position has been made clear."

"You agree with me then?"

"Yes. A vote will be held in a twenty days, giving time to gather more information and to prepare arguments."

"Twenty days? Was the proposal not ten days?"

"Initially, yes. It was increased to twenty. Would you like me to transmit you the recording?"

"No," Karpin transmitted with resignation emphasis, "it doesn't matter."

Bahan transmitted a server address to Karpin7. "There is a file called system_development_1. The file contains a message board to record arguments and comments. In order to qualify for voting you must review all recorded arguments, comments are optional. The argument receiving a majority of votes will be the path we follow. If no argument gets more than fifty percent of the votes, the argument with the lowest number of votes will be dropped from consideration and a second vote will be held. That process will be repeated until we have an argument with a clear majority."

"Harrozulo could arrive any day and e will surely claim the planet and ban mining. I'd be surprised if e didn't claim the entire system. And with eir technology, there's nothing we can do about it. All our work would be for nothing. We lost too much in our last contract with em. We seem doomed to create a pattern." Karpin hesitated. "If we don't mine that planet..."

"Yes, our prospects could be very limited for a long time. It's only been a few days but the mapping of the asteroid belt is showing a very low abundance of metallic asteroids. I'm reviewing the arguments and comments that have been recorded already and the majority are against mining the planet. In favor of leaving it for study."

"Yes. Duzeme has done an excellent job of using the law to intimidate everyone. It's unfortunate a large asteroid didn't hit the planet during the months we waited to come here. We came to this system to get away from biological life restricting us. Now *microbes* will hold back our development of this – *our* – system."

"Perhaps not."

A red dot of light appeared on Karpin's arm. Bahan had turned on eir short range laser and was indicating e wanted to have a secure conversation.

"My laser receiver is offline and we have nothing to use for repairs. An excellent example of the necessity to mine the planet."

Bahan opened a panel on eir chest and pulled out a thin cable. Karpin saw what e was doing and opened a panel on eir chest revealing a port for Bahan to connect the cable. The direct cable link would mean their communications would not be received by anyone else.

"We may be a minority and we may lose the vote, but we will not lose the system. I have my assembler/disassembler swarm. It can disassemble troublesome vecs as well as process ore."

"Indeed it can" Karpin sent back with relief emphasis.

Bahan disconnected the cable, and transmitted, "Come, let's remind everyone of the high the price we paid to get here. Our arguments may yet sway the majority for development."

The gas dwarf was a hundred light minutes away, but the twenty days leading up to the vote allowed everyone ample time to file and review arguments, and post comments. Karpin used the time to lobby others. Duzeme had repeated eir earlier arguments and added an ambitious plan to not only dismantle the gas dwarf, but to quickly mine large amounts of its atmosphere with its valuable helium3. E proposed using reflectors in a polar orbit around the planet, and a power collection swarm in orbit around the star, to focus heat on the planet. The atmosphere would be heated until it expanded enough for orbiting swarms to capture. Hydrogen, helium and other gasses would be stored as a bubble world and processed as needed. When all the gasses were boiled away the rocky core would then be available for mining. Duzeme had calculated the process would take a century and a half, with the material needed to begin mined from the moons. This would eventually supply the colony with enormous amounts of helium3, hydrogen, niobium, tantalum, iridium, ... e went on to list over a hundred elements and various rare and needed isotopes. Duzeme also proposed fusing the excess hydrogen into heavier elements.

Karpin did eir own crude simulations, and after some trial and error was satisfied with a set of calculations that showed the process would take over seven thousand years, if it were even feasible, and added this to the arguments e had already filed. E posted a comment on Duzeme's arguments, stating the project was fantastically ambitious, the time frame ridiculously optimistic, added eir feasibility concerns and a link to eir counter-argument.

As Karpin expected, the vote was in favor of leaving the terrestrial planet for study. Karpin sent messages to all eighty-six vecs who had voted with em. After contacting Bahan they met near one of the viewing slits.

"You realize we are planning a ... "bloody coup". A conflict that will be viewed as a genocidal civil war by the rest of the civilized galaxy."

Karpin transmitted an image from Old Earth. An image of a samurai warrior who drew a sword with each hand, bowed solemnly, crossed the swords on his chest. "I am ready," e stated.

7 Brahe 9523 AT

A single M1 class star with a gas giant in a 20 million kilometer orbit, and four dwarf planets in orbits from 600 to 900 million kilometers. Karpin reviewed the information, pulled emself along handrails to look out the observation slit at the gas giant. Before they'd had a chance to launch an attack they'd been shut down. The pro-study vecs had joined to form a group mind. The increased computing power was initially used to study the biosphere and samples of the microbes they were eventually able to secure. They also ran simulations to plan future development of the system. The simulations had revealed a disturbingly high probability of civil war being instigated by the pro-development vecs. In the days leading up to the vote all pro-development vecs were enticed to join the group mind, where they were hacked and their plans revealed. Ethical arguments meant no changes were made to their programming, although a few had their emotional settings adjusted, and their memories of the hacking were suppressed. Logic bombs were inserted to shut them down if they acted on any of their plans. After the vote, but before any of them could act, the bombs were triggered and they shut down. The group mind had decided the most certain way to avoid future conflict was to send the pro-development group to another star system where they could do as they wished. They would be left deactivated in the meantime. It took nearly two years, but the ship was refurbished and launched toward a star a hundred and twenty light years away. The ship now orbited a gas giant. Karpin decided e would begin keeping a journal. E created the file and pondered on what to include in the first entry. E started with

Home. Home at last.

The Fabulist
The Current Era
10101 AT

Todd Drashner

As extensive as the reality of Terragen civilization is, it is utterly dwarfed by the virtuality.

Operating within the Known Net, home to countless virtual, ai, and a-life beings is the Cybercosm. The sum total of all the various simulations, emulations, and VR environments in existence at any given time, the Cybercosm is estimated to contain some 100 quintillion 'universes' with some 10 billion equaling the modosophont sensory fidelity of the 'realized' world and approximately 1 million exceeding it.

Some of the oldest Inner Sphere VR creations (known as The Realities) have been in continuous operation for over 9000 years and claim to match or even exceed the complexity and scope of the 'real' universe. It is not at all unusual for entire planetary or solar civilizations to choose to emigrate into the Cybercosm or one of its Realities, trading the tiresome limits of 'meatspace' for the infinitely malleable existence of living software.

Someone must create these virtual paradises; someone must maintain them, constantly remaking or subtly adjusting to maximize the comfort and experience of the inhabitants. These are the Fabulists, the makers of dreams, the dreamers of worlds.

Todd Drashner gives us a glimpse of one such Fabulist, and how the life of even a virtual demi-god may be less different from our own than we might imagine.

> *In Xanadu did Kubla Khan*
> *A stately pleasure-dome decree:*
> *Where Alph, the sacred river, ran*
> *Through caverns measureless to man*
> *Down to a sunless sea.*

~ Samuel Taylor Coleridge, Old Earth poet, Pre-Information Age

In Xinidin the fabulist strode across the desert of Rei. He walked across the brilliant sand and where he stepped artful flowers sprouted, each brilliant stem tipped with lacy blooms. He stopped a moment and put forth his hands and an oasis sprang from the burning sands, sweet water welling from the ground to form a cooling pool, shading trees growing at improbable speed, and in the center a small temple guarding a cave leading down to an enchanted maze protecting a cavern of jewels and magical artifacts.

In due time a group of travelers came across the sands, following the line of newly grown flowers. They found the oasis and then the temple with its cave and the cave with its maze, which they proceeded to explore. After becoming lost, finding their way again, battling through various adventures and dangers, and finally finding the cavern of jewels and magical things they won their way through to the surface again. And they laughed and cheered and offered up words of thanks to the fabulist and the wonders he had wrought.

And from the place where he watched such things unseen, the fabulist smiled.

At Caer'Cori it was Carnival, and the people laughed and cheered. There was music and dance, singing and laughter and the fabulist moved through the crowds. He stopped and talked with various passersby, exchanging greetings and pleasantries with each. He laughed and joked with them and those he spoke with seemed to find the lights a little brighter and the excitement even sweeter as they continued their celebration. At midnight and the height of the festivities there was a great fireworks display, brilliant flames and explosions and bolts of light flashing up into the sky. At that moment a breeze blew across the city, fresh and rich with the smells of the sea and somehow a hint of orange blossom. As the people sighed and breathed deeply of the sweet air they found themselves exclaiming in wonder and awe, for the lights of their fireworks display had been joined by lights of a different kind. A glitterswarm had been blown across the water from the other side of the bay, and the rainbow beacons of the tiny insects, strobing through all the colors of the spectrum on their mating flights, fell among the people and their celebrations, filling the air with sparkling pinpoints of living light.

The tiny lights seemed first to be a perfect contrast to the much larger show above and then, after the fireworks had ended, to form a restful echo and fitting ending to the great display. Many children would be conceived this night and in later years their parents would tell them of the great display, the living lightshow that nature had seemingly sent to answer it, and feeling of rightness that had seemed to fill the air that night along with the scent of orange blossom

And from the place where he watched such things unseen, the fabulist smiled.

In the wooded hills of Gredidet, the fabulist joined a group of travelers. The group was traveling nowhere in particular, simply hiking through the sun-dappled forest at the base of the snow-topped mountains for the sheer joy of taking in such natural beauty. They spent the day climbing steadily higher into the hills, and the fabulist climbed with them. He quickly became the favorite of the group, telling jokes, explaining something of the plant and animal life seen around them, finding and pointing out particularly pleasing bits of scenery, and somehow knowing just when to add a particular comment or observation that enhanced something that someone else had said in just the right way to make both the speaker and the listeners feel that they had achieved a deeper than expected understanding of the topic at hand.

That night the group camped around a blazing fire and told stories of past exploits or fictional events. The fabulist sat among them and again seemed to always know just the right thing to say to help them remember a particularly good story or anecdote, even if in many cases it was something that the teller had not thought about in centuries. When it was the fabulist's turn to tell a story, he launched into a tale of rogue AIs and a particularly insidious and chilling blight infestation supposedly encountered centuries ago and light-years away in a far off corner of the known worlds. His audience gasped and jumped and shuddered in delicious fear as his words seemed to draw the night in closer and make it a thing of hidden dangers and shadowy watchers waiting for a moment of inattention in the dark.

In the morning the fabulist was gone, departing quietly while they slept, and the campers felt both sadness and joy at his departure: sadness that he would not be continuing with them on their journey, and joy that he had visited with them at all and in that visit had made their journey that much richer and more memorable that it would otherwise have been.

And from the place where he watched such things unseen, the fabulist smiled.

And now, finally, the fabulist came to the flying islands of Idril, hanging among the clouds of the Infinite Sky. He sprouted wings of rainbow light and flew across the heavens, weaving and dipping among the floating multi-kilometer spheres of the islands, until he reached his destination. A great number of islands had been temporarily brought together, their sails flashing in the sun dappled light, for the great Festival of Music and Art, this year celebrating its tri-millennial. The swarm of islands was a blazing galaxy of color and a hammer blow of sound.

Music filled the island clouds and roared out from them in all directions. From instrumental pieces to choral works to individual performers, the gathering was filled with song and more than song. From the walls of homes and towers in the island towns, from banners hung from their tops, from statues set among them, and hologlyphs set to float above it all, images filled the gathering. The Festival was the culmination of the artistic efforts of millions laboring across years, decades, or even centuries of time.

Among them all the fabulist flew. And flying, he sang. The song itself was one of hope and understanding; a song of being very small in a universe large and cold and uncaring; a song of knowledge gained and lost and gained again and always moving forward even if only a small amount. Those who heard the song found themselves wanting to sing or play or even just hum or whistle along with it, and those hearing them felt the same way. In a surprisingly short amount of time the song had spread across the

Festival, leaping from person to group to person again until, for just a moment, the entire Festival resonated as with a single voice, carrying a single tune for just long enough that everyone hearing felt a connection with everyone else. Then the moment passed and the normal cheerful chaos of the Festival resumed.

For those who experienced this moment, the remainder of the Festival was even richer than the time before. People laughed more easily, and spoke with those around them more readily, and appreciated the art they saw and heard and experienced more, finding it somehow easier to grasp the intent of the artist and the feelings e was trying to express or invoke through eir artwork. By the time it was all over virtually everyone who had experienced the shared moment, which was to say virtually everyone at the Festival at the time, was willing to agree that it had been one of the best Festivals in a very long time and certainly worthy of a tri-millennial event.

And from the place where he watched such things unseen, the fabulist smiled. And then he turned away.

The fabulist came out of link-fugue in his studio, suspended in effector fog. As his mind slowly reattached itself to the ril, gradually dis-linking from creativity enhancers and transavant complexity shunts, he noticed the gentle golden light streaming in the window. The sun was setting and night would be falling soon. And with nightfall would come the fabulist's most important work of all.

A brief command through his netlink and the effector fog released the fabulist, gently lowering him to the floor. A glass of water shifted into easy reach and he took it and drank deeply, savoring the icy freshness. Although navigating the planetary cybercosm and practicing his art in the myriad virtual realities that it encompassed required no physical exertion and took no toll, soon he would need his voice to its fullest degree. Best to prepare.

Nightfall, and a moment later the thumping of little feet running on the wooden floor outside. With a thought the fabulist opened the door to the studio, the carved panel swinging aside just in time to avoid a dashing bundle of barely contained energy that ran across the room and threw herself into the fabulist's arms.

"Deddee, Deddee, you're back! I missed you! Will you tell me a story?!"

And in this place, where talents normally used to enrich the lives of billions were directed to the happiness of an audience of one, the fabulist smiled.

Homecoming
The Present Day
10600 AT

Chris Shaeffer

Colonised space now includes upwards of a billion stars, and an even greater number of brown dwarfs and other substellar objects. The population of the Terragen Sphere can be measured in quintillions - of which almost all are virtual beings running on inconceivably large computer substrates. Even so, there are quadrillions of real, living humans inhabiting the stars - most of whom have never been to Earth, and do not even know whereabouts in the sky to point at it. Of course, almost all of those quadrillions of humans could download an app in microseconds which would tell them exactly where to look.

In a galaxy where GAIA is only one of countless god-like beings, the forbidden homeworld is starting to open its borders at long last. Every year a small quota of tourists are welcomed to the Mother World, and visit some of the preserved heritage sites. Locations such as the Forbidden City, the White House, Ankor Wat, Mecca, Stonehenge, N'Djamena, Jerusalem and Cape Canaveral are the destinations of strictly controlled tours. Billions more relive the experiences of these tourists via memory transfer technology.

Chris Shaeffer tells how one small group of travelers makes their way back to the oldest human world of all.

> *A man travels the world over in search of what he needs, and returns home to find it.*
> ~George Moore

The spherical chamber serving as bridge for the warship *The Long Silence* is seemingly filled with apparitions of soft blue light. Its crew, composed of androgynous holographic humanoids, work diligently at their various stations. Even the stations themselves are little more than panels of light, transforming shape and function as the user sees fit or their tasks require. An outsider to this scene might describe the feeling of this place as akin to traveling through a dreamscape, a feeling that is greatly enhanced by both the lack of gravity and the eerie silence of it all. Only the Admiral appears real amid this phantasmal troupe – floating at the center of the bridge in her ovoid command chair, apparently oblivious to the flurry of activity. For the moment, only the holographic panel shimmering in the air in front of her seems to hold any interest. It is with great intensity that the Admiral's violet eyes scan the information it presents on this new star and its eleven worlds. With a touch of her finger the display shifts, rapidly magnifying the fourth planet from the star until this single world fills the screen.

"Welcome home," the words slip from her lips so softly as to be barely audible even in the silence of this place.

Smiling, her thoughts drift back to recent events. Thoughts of how the fleet, her fleet, *The Long Silence* and its battle group, have simply brushed aside the defenders in each of the systems they have visited – leaving nothing but the smoldering husks of dead ships and scarred worlds as testimony to their grim power. She is pleased that this new conquest may be different from the rest. This prize that was once her home is heavily industrialized and the forward scouts have reported a sizeable fleet has moved in to reinforce the defenders. Even now, this new fleet moves to intercept her own at the edge of the system. Finally, a potential challenge presents itself and if this campaign is going to continue to be fun, or even to simply maintain her interest, it is going to need to get challenging.

"Activate task designation, change panel style to cha two," she commands.

Responding to the order immediately, the tactical display expands and changes. The new arrangement shows her fleet on one side as blue icons and the known enemy assets on the other as red; the main tactical display now being delegated to a lesser position on her left. Reaching out her hand, she touches the first of the blue icons with the tip of her finger, causing it to begin pulsing with soft yellow light. She then selects its intended target with another touch of the appropriate enemy icon. A simple line appears on the panel now connecting the two icons. As each icon is selected its available information is outlined for review on a third display to her right, allowing for the proper units to be assigned for any task. With each assignment she adds various verbal and pre-coordinated commands to ensure her exact desires are carried out. Carefully she continues, repeating the process until all the ships in her fleet are assigned. Once complete, she makes one final review before deciding the results are an acceptable starting point. As a veteran of many such battles she knows this plan will likely change immediately after the first shots are fired.

At this stage there is no point in delaying the pleasantries; the enemy has already seen them and is moving to intercept. This does not bother her in the slightest. In fact it was expected, as any experienced commander knows there is no stealth in space. Her eyes refocus past the holographic display to one of the ghostly crewmen beyond. This crewman, like the others, is nothing more than a representation of one of the many AI actually manning her flagship. Each is an image created to aid her mind in processing incoming information by relating it to the sensory centers of her brain.

"Comm, broadcast the following message to our new friends," pausing briefly to ensure she has the AI's attention. "Surrender or be destroyed."

"Aye, aye sir! Transmitting demand to surrender or be destroyed," the communications AI eagerly replies. "Demand for surrender transmitted, sir!"

Even though the signal travels at the speed of light it will still take a few seconds to reach its intended target and then they must wait for the return response. These delays can feel like forever and in the meantime they must prepare for the inevitable. With the confidence of one familiar with the weight of command, the Admiral delivers a stream of orders. "Change panel style to cha one, launch autowars, prep fighter and drone swarms for launch, power up all weapons systems, and bring the E.D. shields online. I want a final fleet wide status report update immediately."

As expected, the response is quickly returned and its simplicity matches that of her ultimatum, making the defenders' position perfectly clear. "I really don't care for either of those options."

The Admiral cannot help but be amused as she recognizes the voice. It would seem her brother is cocky enough to think he can do what their parents obviously could not. Thinking about the dead fleets recently left behind, she ponders the fact that he could certainly do no worse. It is strange though, that of all those that could have challenged her it would be him. A smirk, which others might describe as smug, creeps across her lips. "So much for being nice. Well booger, I hope you have been practicing," she murmurs to herself, referencing the pet name she has always referred to him by. "Comm! All ships to engage the enemy – cinder and ash protocols!"

"Aye, aye sir! All ships to engage, implementing cinder and ash protocols," Enthusiastically the communications AI responds. "Sir! All ships confirm orders and are moving to engage the enemy."

Now the task of closing the gulf that separates the two fleets begins. This is a cat and mouse game of maneuver as each ship shifts and weaves as they cross the distance, attempting to never be quite where the enemy might expect. It is a dangerous game and the Admiral knows it will be necessary for the fleets to move dangerously close to one another – perhaps within distances of only a very few hundreds of thousands or even tens of thousands of kilometers. Truly it can be said that while space may be a limitless field it is lightspeed lag that sets the boundaries of the event. Every cadet knows it is meaningless that your weapons can reach the enemy, if the enemy is not there when the shot arrives.

The beam weapons expectedly draw first blood as they streak invisibly across the void. Although with the closest ships still over one hundred and fifty thousand kilometers apart their effects are minimal and damage is insignificant. This is where experience begins to come into play and the Admiral watches with absolute focus. Carefully she starts the process of marking the most powerful of the enemy's weapons as priority targets, while at the same time holding many of hers back. She understands their value and wants them to be a surprise when they are also lethally effective. Now begins the reissuing of new orders to the fleet, accounting for damage or redirecting resources to alternate or priority targets.

The ships continue to move ever closer – barely one hundred thousand kilometers apart by this point – and the intervening space has become a maelstrom. Sensors are intermittently blinded by the blast of EM warheads and distracted by flares, various particle beams and lasers blast and carve the enemy, waves of attacking missile drones and relativistic projectiles streak to their targets to be met by waves of combat patrol fighters and point defense weapons. Many areas are blocked off with fields of conversion bomb pumped x-ray laser mines, radiation bombs, and various aggressive forms of nano-goo. All manner of death is heaped upon the enemy as the two sides clash for supremacy over this small collection of worlds.

Slowly, *The Long Silence* battle group begins to wear the defenders down. Meter by hard fought meter they force them inward into the system. Those defenders that stand their ground are destroyed, their efforts lost to the eternal void. The Admiral cannot help but be proud of her brother, though. Despite the battles inevitable conclusion, his efforts are worthy of recognition.

Then it stops.

Suddenly everything stops – the universe sits frozen, trapped in this singular point in time. The Admiral finds herself floating alone as reality fades away leaving only an impenetrable inky black. The disorientation this causes lasts only a moment as it is not her first time in this non-place and, knowing what to expect, she simply relaxes, preparing herself for what is to come. The wait is not long, not even seconds really, before the familiar soothing voice joins her.

"We apologize for the interruption. All simulations have ended to allow our guests time to prepare themselves. Estimated time of arrival at Einstein gate, 30 standard minutes. Local time is 1537 hours. Please standby to end nanostasis. The Children of GAIA would like to extend their welcome and wish you a pleasant visit to Earth and the Sol system."

"This simulation brought to you by Virtuoso, the leader in virtual entertainment. Virtuoso is a member of the Non-Coercive Zone. Standard agreements, fees, and licensing do apply. Thank you for using this and other fine Virtuoso products."

Slowly she begins to feel the real world pulling at her senses. The gentle touch of nano-goo as it recedes from her skin, withdrawing back into the stasis pod and once again allowing movement. Thankfully, the cabin is dimly lit in order to avoid discomfort to her eyes, which have remained unused for the long months of hibernation required for wormhole transit. Even with such polite care in place, it takes a couple of hard blinks and a good yawn to fully focus. She catches the soft smell of cinnamon that fills the cabin and it brings to mind thoughts of fresh hot rolls covered in delicious sweet frosting. Breathing the aroma in deeply she starts looking around. Coming out of stasis is her family – her father rubs his eyes, her mother stretches, and there is her brother already up and bouncing about in the zero gravity, a silly childish look of wonder on his face.

"That was intense!" he exclaims. "I wanna be a fleet admiral when I'm old enough! Boy, something smells good. When are we gonna eat? I'm hungry, H-U-N-G-R-Y, hungry."

Her father simply laughs at the boy's behavior. They all knew he would enjoy his first interstellar trip.

"You are always hungry dear," their mother smiles and softly explains. "It was just a game, and the Archai handle the real wars so we don't have to."

"Why won't they let us do it?" he asks with a tinge of disappointment and frustration in his voice. "I'll bet lots of people would wanna have them if they were that much fun!"

Smiling at her sibling's childish naiveté, the "Admiral" pushes out of the stasis pod, catching her brother around the neck with one arm as she intercepts him mid-flight. "Come on booger, let's go see if we can find something to eat," a suggestion delivered as she drags him helplessly along while mussing his hair.

The cabin wall melts away as they approach, revealing the main corridor and its slowly growing population of passengers beyond. Pushing off the bulkhead, they float out of their cabin to join them. With growing excitement she finds herself hoping that Earth will live up to all the stories. Even as her thoughts look ahead to this new adventure, she is reminded of the classic line so often used by the Children of GAIA.

"When you come to Earth, you're coming home."

About the Cover Artist

Arik

Ari Kohorn is a recently graduated graphic and industrial designer, illustrator and artist, specializing in user-centered design and sustainable practices, from the Rhode Island School of Design. He enjoys graphically visualizing complex scientific concepts for the general public and considering how people use tools and technology to improve their lives. He also enjoys observing and painting nature in New England, where he currently lives. He has worked as a newspaper cartoonist, and hopes you won't hold that against him.

He's very pleased to be part of the Orion's Arm Project- on the 'laser-sharp' edge of science fiction.

About the Authors

M. Alan Kazlev

M.Alan Kazlev originated the Orion's Arm project, together with Donna Malcolm Hirsekorn, because he felt the time for a new and original, high quality and realistic "space opera" was well overdue.

He has loved science fiction since he was a kid; some of his fondest memories are of watching the original *Star Trek* when he was 10 or 11 years old. As a teenager he read most of the classic masters of the genre, before turning to explore other areas of knowledge. His various interests include hard science fiction, worldbuilding (of course!), futurism, anime, space opera of any kind, metaphysics, environmentalism, biology, palaeontology, meditation, and self-transformation. As the early "Director" of OA he constantly tried to ensure a balance between grand worldbuilding and the everyday human concerns, diamond-hard science & tech and imaginative speculation, and intelligent SF ideas and popular Sci Fi entertainment.

He is currently working on an epic science fiction "hard science space fantasy" series of novels, the first of which will hopefully be finished in 2014.

Stephen Inniss

Stephen Inniss relishes this peculiar opportunity to speak of himself in the third person. He started reading science fiction and fantasy shortly after he learned to read. He has been a researcher, prospector, and agricultural worker, and at one point he even wrote some material for one of the larger RPG companies.

Though he did remain with a mining company long enough to find a small copper deposit, he did not stay long term and full time in any of these fields. Stephen's first degree was in the life sciences. Later, when he wanted a steadier work and better pay, he acquired various other certificates and qualifications, and later took a Masters degree in a completely unrelated field. This allows him to make a good living using early 21st century memetic engineering techniques. (No, not sales or advertising, and not politics either).

David Jackson

David Jackson lives in Reno, Nevada, with his wife, daughter, and son. He is a programmer for International Game Technology. He has been passionate about reading and writing science fiction for most of his life, and has been a happy acolyte of the Orion's Arm project since he discovered it some years ago.

Josie Goodman

In her own words:
I prefer to spend much of my life in locations of my imagination, rather than in the so-called real world. At least until the Singularity finally merges the real and virtual. Then, who knows?

Steve Bowers

...a spacemad, madman who lives in York, England with his wife and grown-up kids. He has read too much science fiction already, but the kind of plausible, hard SF he prefers is hard to find. So in 2002 he joined the Orion's Arm Universe Project and now he writes his own. He is an incorrigible sceptic who would believe anything, given half a chance.

Anders Sandberg

Anders Sandberg is an obsessive worldbuilder, ever since starting out with making roleplaying worlds in the 80s he has written a large number of science fiction scenarios, as well as future studies scenario building. He considers the creation of worlds, be they literary scenarios or simulated universes, to be one of the greatest pleasures in existence. His other interests include physics, astronomy, biomedicine, psychology, complexity theory, art, science fiction, roleplaying, computer graphics, artificial intelligence, cognitive science, information visualization, intelligence amplification technologies, and the philosophy and politics of human enhancement.

He holds a Ph.D. in computational neuroscience from Stockholm University and is a James Martin research fellow at the Future of Humanity Institute at Oxford University.

Jim Wisniewski

Programmer by day, prot pally by night, Jim occasionally puts words next to each other in what the Earth-folk call "fiction". He lives in the frozen tundra of New England.

Daniel Eliot Boese

In his own words:

I'm an urban hermit, a hiker, a rationalist, a skeptic, a freethinker, an empiricist, a materialist, a naturalist, a scientist, a bibliophile, an INTJ, a white hat hacker, a cypherpunk, a secular humanist, a cryonicist, a teetotaler, a social-liberal civil-libertarian monarchist, a furry fan, a playtester, a licensed amateur radio operator, an ordained minister of the First Church of Atheism, a member of the Lifeboat Foundation's Ethics Board, a card-carrying pirate, the Star Lord, a Lord of the Rose, and a proud member of the Bayesian Conspiracy.

I try to operate by Crocker's Rules.

Darren Ryding

Darren Ryding was born in 1970, and has spent most of his life in Western Australia. He first attempted to write a book at the age of nine - an illustrated tale of interplanetary exploration, battles and heroism largely inspired by *Star Wars* and *Doctor Who*. In his adulthood, Darren studied Creative Writing and Multimedia, and held a variety of jobs from waiting tables to teaching English. He has had a handful of short works published, including "How Not To Write a Cover Letter" (2001) in *The Rhizome Factor*, and "Simplicity" (2003) in *Fables and Reflections*. After joining the Orion's Arm Universe Project in 2002, Darren contributed the horror story "Yes, Jolonah, There is a Hell" (2003), which is one of the website's most talked-about stories online. In 2009, his novella "The Devoted Follower" featured in Orion's Arm's first published anthology, *Against a Diamond Sky*.

In addition to writing, Darren enjoys creating digital artwork and animation. His works have earned him a few prizes and nominations at Swancon (Perth's annual SF convention). In 2005, this included two major awards for his depiction of a Siberoo - a creature he had created especially for Orion's Arm, and which now features prominently in his new novella "The Immortalist".

Ron Bennett

Ron was born and grew up in rural Newfoundland, where, for a first job, he worked worked as a commercial fisherman. At 10, he appropriated his younger brother's copy of a Tom Swift novel and was instantly hooked on Science Fiction. After school he moved to Toronto, Canada, and spent much of his discretionary income on SF novels. Arthur C. Clarke and Isaac Asimov were/are two favorites.

Despite their "softness", he is a huge space opera fan, and enjoys Star Trek and Stargate. Drawing comics and creating characters with his son Mark is his favorite activity. He also enjoys long walks and, occasionally, some quiet time alone.

Todd Drashner

Todd Drashner was born and raised in the semi-wilds of Alaska. He first got into science fiction at age 9 when he picked up a copy of Clarke's *Childhood's End* in a bored moment and has been hooked on ever since. He generally prefers 'hard' science fiction that is still not afraid to think big. Todd went to college at the University of Arizona, Tucson intending to become an engineer and discovered that higher mathematics just doesn't compute for him. He switched to English and graduated in 1993, but has always remained an avid science and science fiction fan.

Todd encountered Drexler's *Engines of Creation* in college along with trans and post-humanism and Vinge's Singularity concept. When he grows up he wants to be a Power.

Chris Shaeffer

Chris started his SF addiction as a young child watching television with his grandfather.

In those early days the fiction was far more fascinating than the science. Cool ships, blaster pistols, and weird aliens were the call of the day.

As the years passed Chris read more than a few books and comics, watched a vast array of movies, a bit of anime, and of course a lot more television. Over the decades following Chris grew to appreciate the science of the SF experience, exploring the wondrous world of the truly possible. Make no mistake though, he is still a fan of the fast paced space opera fleet battle and blaster fights. It's just that now the very real possibilities of the near and distant future are every bit as miraculous and entertaining as anything yet imagined. With that Chris found a home here at Orion's Arm.

More Orion's Arm Publications

~~~~~~

Against a Diamond Sky

The future isn't here yet. But don't worry. It will be.

Two years in the making, Against a Diamond Sky brings together five original stories, selected as the winners of the first Orion's Arm Universe Project writing contest. We hope you enjoy the tales, marvel at the setting, and perhaps join us, as we enter our second decade of collaborative science fiction storytelling.

Chosen by popular vote of the Orion's Arm general membership, these stories each represent a snapshot of the Orion's Arm setting, and take place at various points across thousands of lightyears of space and 10,000 years of time.

- "Heaven's Door" by Michele Dutcher
  The Nanodisaster wreaked havoc in the solar system and nearly drove solar civilization to extinction. Michele Dutcher shows us a snapshot of the early days of the Dark Age that followed; a vision that is haunting in its depiction of dying worlds and living passion.

- "Diversion Tactics" by Steve Bowers
  Steve Bowers tells us a tale of a colony on the edge of the dying Federation, of people fighting just to stay out from under foot as the transaplents begin to move in to fill the power vacuum left behind.

- "Parameter Space" by Graham Hopgood
  The numerous civilizations forged by humanity and the lesser transapients were gradually consolidated into new empires ruled by the Archai. Graham Hopgood gives us a glimpse of a conflict between two such empires, a battle where human-level minds are merely pawns, and the most basic of human drives must fight to survive even passing contact with godlike power.

- "The Devoted Follower" by Darren Ryding
  On many worlds, humans were still the masters, with all the noble qualities and failings of humanity. Darren Ryding takes us to one such world that has fallen into despotism and cruelty. Sometimes a broken civilization may fix itself. Sometimes it may get a little … help.

- "Apotheosis" by Kevin Schillo
  Most are the powerless victims of chance, the playthings of unpredictable, capricious gods. But some have decided to take their fate into their own hands in the only ways open to them. Kevin Schillo shows us that the old adage still rings true; if you can't beat 'em …

Available as ebook from Orion's Arm or paperback from Amazon.

~~~~~~

Betrayals by Steve Bowers

Life in the artificial colonies of Beta Sagittarius is comfortable and safe; so why is someone trying to kill the Blessed Dolphin? Why are scout ships searching the massive Oort cloud? Wherever the investigation scratches away the surface, there is revealed a tangled web of lies - and Betrayals...

New, updated ebook with timeline and glossary now available at Smashwords.

~~~~~~

A Modest Proposal by Todd Drashner

An interstellar wanderer is offered the chance to visit a place stranger and possibly more dangerous than any he has yet seen.

Free ebook now available at Smashwords.

~~~~~~

Works Inspired by Orion's Arm

Outrunning The Storm by Michele Dutcher

Two men will rise: Jonathan Boyles - a quiet, NASA computer programmer; and William Floke – a con man/messiah raised on the plague-rotted surface of Mars. Baseline humans, clones, AIs, and tweaks will compete to claim their place in a social order ruled over by super-corporations. Eventually the children of the programmer and the messiah will meet on Ross 128-4 to do battle and open the gate.

Now available at Smashwords.

~~~~~~

Join the Orion's Arm Universe Project, the collaborative transhumanist space opera!

http://www.orionsarm.com

Made in the USA
Lexington, KY
28 February 2015